EMERGENCE

a novel

GARY L. STUART

Emergence

For information about this title or to order other books and/or electronic
media, contact the publisher:
Gleason & Wall Publishers
7000 N. 16th Street, Suite 120, PMB 470, Phoenix, AZ 85020
www.garylstuart.com
gary.stuart@garylstuart.com

ISBN: 978-0-9863441-8-3 (print)
978-0-9863441-9-0 (eBook)

Printed in the United States of America

Cover and Interior design: 1106 Design, Phoenix, AZ

Other Books by Gary L. Stuart

The Ethical Trial Lawyer

The Gallup 14

*Miranda—The Story of America's
Right to Remain Silent*

*Innocent Until Interrogated—The True Story of the
Buddhist Temple Massacre and the Tucson Four*

AIM for the Mayor—Echoes from Wounded Knee

Anatomy of a Confession—The Debra Milke Case

Ten Shoes Up

The Valles Caldera

The Last Stage to Bosque Redondo

*Call Him Mac—Ernest W. McFarland—
The Arizona Years*

Let's Disappear

TABLE OF CONTENTS

PROLOGUE

Vince Manchester spent a half-day riding around Baytown, Texas, in his 2011 Chevy. Most cars he saw were a lot like his: cheap, white, and dirty. His blended in with traffic on every street. He made two trips to Julia Santerra-Evans's single-story building on Third Avenue, once in the car, and once on foot from a parking lot five blocks away. He took still photos from all angles. After viewing the small strip mall from the street, he walked back up Third Avenue and around the block. When he came back down the opposite street, he could see the small parking lot on the west side of her building. There were spaces for six cars. Each was marked reserved and warned that violators would be towed away. He walked across the street to the Berkley Apartments; he'd parked on the street opposite from it the previous day and thought then that it might be a good place to stake out Julia Baby. It was a two-story frame building that looked like it was a good fifty years old. A small sign on the front porch advertised, *Studio Apartment for Rent—Furnished—$90 per week.*

The young dark-skinned woman sitting on the porch eyed him suspiciously until he spoke the magic words.

"I'm looking for a small apartment on account of I just got a job here. It's a three-week job, but they told me it could take an extra week to finish up the drywall. I'm a drywall hanger and I walk on stilts. Are you willing to negotiate a little on the rent? I got eighty dollars in cash on me, right now. Whadda ya think?"

The woman got up slowly. She had a knee brace with a silver hinge on both sides.

"I think my grandfather would go for that. You want to see it first?"

"Does it face the street or the back?"

"Faces the street. Fact is, it's right on top of this office. Same view as looking outside from here. Only you go up the stairs from the back. We only have eight apartments, one that me and my grandfather live in, and seven for rent. Number 5, the studio, is the only one available. But you got to put up a $50 security and cleaning deposit. Which ain't refundable. One month's rent is 480 dollars plus the security deposit of fifty dollars. That makes it $530 for four weeks. You got $530?"

"Not on me. But I could get it back at the motel I'm in now. They charge forty-nine bucks a day and don't clean all that much. Let me look at it, and I'll give you twenty to hold it for a day. I'll come back tomorrow morning with the rest. OK?"

"Yeah, OK."

Vince went up the back stairs to look at Unit 5. One room about the size of a cheap motel room, but with a bigger bathroom. It had a cast-iron bathtub, a hot water heater, and a clean sink; it smelled of Lysol. The room had two windows facing the street, directly across from Julia's three businesses in the ugly concrete block building. With his binoculars, he could see the names on all three businesses in the strip mall—Pac 'n Mail on the west corner, Law Offices of Withers & Associates in the middle, and Houston International Savings & Loan on the east corner, by the parking lot. He estimated the distance across the street to be no more than fifty feet. Perfect, he thought.

He went downstairs and told the lady in the knee brace he'd be back tomorrow. Then he drove up Third Avenue for a few blocks until he hit Texas 330, which took him back to Lynchburg and the trailer park where he'd left Jumbo II, the RV his dad bought in Yuma. He spent the night in the RV surfing the Internet for Texas rules and regulations covering savings and loan companies. The Texas Banking Department's website listed Houston International Savings & Loan as inactive but in good standing. There was no listing for Julia's Pac 'n Mail store, except under the online Yellow Pages, which listed the correct street address, but did not list a phone number, or an email address. There were no Facebook pages, Yelp reviews, or BBB references. Julia's law firm, Withers & Associates, was listed with a low rating on Avvo. She was licensed by the Texas State Bar, and listed as the only lawyer at Withers & Associates. She didn't belong to any bar sections, committees, or have a disciplinary record. Other than the low Avvo rating, no other Internet site referenced her. Maybe she's practicing ghost law, he thought.

Next day, he moved into Unit 5 at The Berkley Apartments. Their parking lot was in back, not visible from the street. He lugged two bags up the back stairs. One held clothes, the other his new camera, tripod, the spotting scope, and snacks. He set up the tripod, locked down the camera, and took a half dozen still shots and one short video of Julia's three businesses across the street. Perfect. He could see who parked in the lot, who went in the front doors, and who went in the side door at the back of the little parking lot. He set the camera to video, used the widest angle lens he had, and turned on auto-record. Then he went down the back stairs, got his car, and made the circle around the block to park in Julia's parking lot. Giving his camera across the street a discreet nod, he walked to the front concrete pad.

First, he went into Julia's Pac 'n Mail store and asked if he could make a phone call because his battery died and he had to call his grandmother. They said no. He went back out to the car and drove off. He changed his shirt and put on a floppy hat and sun glasses at a gas station two blocks away. Then he drove back to the same parking lot. This time he went into the savings and loan office.

The name, *Houston International Savings & Loan,* etched in gold on the front door, was impressive. Vince opened the door, stepped inside, and surprised two people. It was a twenty-by-twenty-foot room with four metal desks, a row of tan-colored filing cabinets lined up against the back, and four fluorescent light fixtures on the ceiling. There were no windows, no teller's cage, no reception area, and nothing that resembled a place to save money, or make a loan.

The large woman sitting behind a desk piled high with stacks of what looked like stapled batches of letter-sized documents, said, "Sorry, we're not open."

Looking at his watch, Vince said, "It's quarter to eleven and the door was open."

The man at the desk behind hers stood up.

"Well, yes sir, that's my bad. Shoulda locked it behind me. We are not a walk-in place; we only make appointments for new customers. You don't have one, do you?"

Vince noticed that his desk had almost nothing on it, except a blotter pad, a telephone, and what looked like a daily newspaper. The man was bulky and dressed like a tourist, with a Hawaiian shirt, untucked, and jeans.

"Sorry, I just came in because it's quarter to eleven in the morning and I'm looking to open a savings account. No appointment. Don't want one. Just a savings account."

"Well, we are sorry, young man," the woman said, not looking the least bit sorry. "We don't have savings accounts."

"The gold letter on your door says savings and loans. How come you don't have savings accounts?"

The man motioned the woman to sit down and walked up to face Vince.

"She just said we're sorry. I'll say it too. We're sorry, OK? Door shoulda been locked. We arrange savings as collateral for loans, but they are not the kind of savings account you're probably looking for. Our customers are corporate, not individual. There's a Bank of America, two blocks south on Third Avenue. Just turn left out of the parking lot."

The man stepped around Vince, opened the door, and waved his hand out to the parking lot. Vince turned around, stepped out onto the concrete pad, and then turned to face the Hawaiian shirt man.

"Ok, man, sorry to have bothered you. Tell Julia I said hello and that I'm sorry I missed her."

"What? Julia? Do you know her?"

"I know her, man. I know her. She owns the place. She probably owns you too."

He got in his car and started the engine. He could see the man pull a phone out of his back pocket, tap the screen, and hold it up to his ear. Vince moved slowly out of the small lot and turned right toward Third Avenue. In his rearview mirror, he could see the man had followed him to the street and was now writing something on his wrist. Good for you, man, now go check my license plate out, and see what it gets you. Motherfucker.

Vince made the full loop around the block to get back to the Berkley Apartments and parked the Chevy behind the building. Taking the stairs two steps at a time, he bounded up and hurried into Unit 5 to check his video. Turning the dials to view video on the two-by-three-inch viewing screen, he watched himself park his car and walk up onto the concrete pad. He saw himself give a little nod up toward the window where the tripod and camera still faced. He watched himself go into the Pac 'n Mail store, then through the fake savings and loan door, and finally his slow walk past the front door of Withers and Associates. Then he smiled at himself, on camera, as he got into his car and made that loop out of sight of the camera. He deleted the eleven minutes of video that showed the two other cars in the lot across the street and waited to see the results of the Hawaiian shirt man's phone call.

It took twenty-seven minutes, but it worked. A yellow Jeep Rubicon pulled up into the parking lot with a screech of brakes, and a short woman in jeans and a white T-shirt jumped out. She ran to the side door of the building, took out a ring of keys from the canvas briefcase hanging from her shoulder, and opened the side door. He got it all on camera. Fifteen minutes later, the fluorescent lights went out in the savings and loan and the Hawaiian shirt man and his lady came out the front door, got into their cars in the parking lot, and turned north on Third Avenue.

"OK, Julia Baby, you ready for me?" Vince said to himself, as he straightened his tie and buttoned the jacket on his blue suit coat. He made sure his video was on and recording before he went out the back door, down the steps, and around to the front. As he crossed the street, he turned his head and gave his camera another nod. When he got to the other side he knocked loudly on the front door of Withers & Associates. No one answered. He banged again on the wood door. Nothing. He just kept hitting the door with his knotted fist.

Finally, the door cracked open a few inches and a high-pitched voice said, "Hey buddy, we ain't open. Get away, or I'll call the cops."

"Call the cops, Julia. Go ahead. But first, you ought to hear what I know about you. About Chaco Hernandez. About Boise, Idaho."

The door opened about a foot. Vince jammed his shoulder into it, knocking the little woman in the white T-shirt to the floor. He pushed his way in, kicked her in the stomach, and pulled the big .44 Mag revolver from the waist band of his suit pants.

"Goddamn you to hell, Julia fuckin' Santerra-Evans!" he screamed.

Then he realized she'd been holding a black pistol in her other hand, but had dropped it when the door slammed back into her. He kicked her again in the hip as she held both hands over her stomach. Scooping her gun up in his free hand, he aimed it and his gun at her.

"You ready to die, bitch, for killing my father? To die for the dumbshit you killed in Boise? For all the money you stole from whoever 'n fuck those assholes in Panama really are? From your bosses across the bay at Plankton Resources? You ready, Julia? Open your mouth. I'll shoot you in the mouth so you can taste your own blood in the split second you got left on this earth!"

She shut her eyes and clamped her jaw shut.

He slammed the door shut and crossed the room to the reception desk. Julia, on her back on the floor, could see his chest heaving up and down as he leaned backward against the desk. Then, to her surprise, his locked jaw seemed to relax, and he shook his head at her.

"No, Julia, I don't think I'll shoot you in the mouth yet. I think I'll wait until you help me get even with Plankton Resources, your *only* fuckin' client. Then I'll shoot you in the eyeball, two times. Once with my gun and once with yours. And I'll leave you outside in that stupid yellow Jeep of yours to wait for the fuckin' F Bee Eye. They'll come get your body when I'm done with you. You ready for them?"

Julia pushed herself to a sitting position on the floor. "Them? Who's them? Who the fuck are you? Do you know what's gonna happen to you when my people get here?"

"Ah, Julia. You're flat on your skinny little ass on the floor. Your belly hurts, right? Your hip is killing you, right? You thought I was gonna kill you a minute ago, but now you're asking questions and threatening me? I'm the guy with the big gun. A .44 Mag. If I shot you in the knee cap from here, it'd blow your leg in half. That's who I am, bitch. I'm the man with the big gun. That's all you need to know 'bout me for now. So here's what we're gonna do. I can see this shitty little room is for your secretary, or whatever. Let's go in the back to your real office. Roll over. Get on your hands and knees, like the bitch you are. You're gonna crawl back to your office, bitch, crawl, goddamn you!"

She crawled. When she got to the office door, behind the reception desk, she pushed open the door with one hand and crawled in. Once inside, on a dark red shag carpet, she vomited before she reached her desk. He stepped around her, reached behind his back, and slid his red Washington Redskins backpack onto the desktop. Then he kicked her again. In the head. She fell over and closed her eyes, moaning, with spittle coming from her mouth. Loosening the zipper on the top of his backpack, he took out the Zoomer G9 recorder that Vivian had used to tape the FBI in their own conference room in Phoenix. He turned it on and set it on the desk. Then he dug out a two-foot length of one-eighth-inch diameter, seven-by-nineteen, galvanized cable. He looped one end around her left wrist and locked it down with a steel wire clip.

"Get up," he ordered.

"Why should I, you shit! You're gonna kill me anyway, right? Go ahead, I ain't afraid to die."

"Get up,' he repeated. "I might give you parole, maybe even ninety days. You tell me what I want to know, I might parole you."

Grabbing the end of her desk, she pulled herself upright. She was still weak from the blows and steadied herself with her left hand. Vince stepped behind her and pushed her big black executive chair into the back of her bony thighs. She fell backward into her chair and he quickly looped the other end of the galvanized cable around the adjustable stem below the seat. Then he pulled the cable taut and locked down the lower loop.

"OK, Julia, now you're a prisoner in your own big-girl chair. You can use your right hand, but not your left. Scoot your chair so your knees are under the desk and your right arm is on top of the desk. First things first. Open your safe. Right now."

She just sat there. Her belly still hurt, as did the left side of her head, but she was focused on survival now and tested him. Again.

"Why? Are you a thief, too? Is that what this is about? My money?"

"It's about your life. And your money. And your asshole bosses over at Plankton Resources. And their money too. You want parole? First step in that direction is your safe. If you refuse, then I'll kill you in your chair, and open your safe the hard way."

She stared at him. She had seen men about to die. She had seen some about to kill. He smelled like them. Death. Vince's forehead beaded sweat. His upper lip quivered, and the lower one was red, like he'd been biting it. His motionless eyes seemed inflamed and he blinked constantly. So, she took the easy way.

"My safe is inside my desk, here on the right side. I can't reach it with the stupid cable thing you've got around me."

He took three steps to her and pushed her and her chair back five feet. Opening the large door on the right side of her desk, he saw the twenty-four-inch stainless steel safe. It had both a digital combination and a key lock.

"Where's the key? What's the combination?"

"The key is in my wallet, which is in my rear pocket. I'm sitting on it. The combination is 94 dash 07688. Help your fucking self."

"Good girl, Julia, you're cooperating."

He moved to her chair, slapped her across the mouth, and said, "Use your right hand to get the wallet. Toss it on the desk."

He fished through the wallet, found a small slot behind the driver's license holder, and stuck the small bronze key in the safe. That caused a small light to come on over the digital keyboard. He entered the combination and the door swung open. He turned back to Julia's chair and wheeled her around to the opposite side of the desk. Then he reached into his backpack, took out a second cable, and used it to chain her swivel chair to the right table leg on her side of the desk.

The safe had a foot-high metal tray in the middle. He took it out and dumped the contents on the desk. It was cash, in dollars and euros.

"How much?" he asked pointing to the currency on her desk.

"Maybe six or seven hundred thousand. It's getaway money. You're welcome to it, as soon as I get my parole," she said.

"So, you're saying I can get away with six or seven hundred thousand getaway dollars? If I do and let you live, how will you get away?"

"It's just money. I can always get more."

"Yes, I know you can. Let's see what else you got in here."

He saw two steel drawers, each about two inches high. The first drawer had a stack of bearer bonds. The second had two notebooks, one with ledger paper, and the other with plastic sheet covers, holding what looked like a half-dozen typed letters with inked signatures.

"How much in bearer bonds?"

Smiling for the first time, she answered, "Exactly two million dollars, American. Do you know about bearer bonds? I mean, how to use them?"

Ignoring her question, he continued, "And what are these letters, with inked signatures? They all say 'To Whom It May Concern.'"

"They are letters of introduction, signed by six bankers in six different foreign countries. As you can see, they introduce the person who has the letter, not by name, but rather by the fact they have the letter."

"For what?" Vince asked.

"For protection. These letters are almost better than money. They can keep you alive and safe in a new country. Sometimes, in my business, safe harbor is much more valuable than a safe full of cash."

"OK," Vince said, "I know you're a killer. That's your business. Lawyering is your cover, but killing is your business."

"You know shit," she said even though talking made her head hurt.

Vince sat in silence for a couple of minutes, staring at her.

"I'm considering parole. You keep these letters. I'll take the cash and bearer bonds when I go. What's the notebook with the ledger entries?"

"Things you'd never understand, asshole. But if you did, what's in this notebook would kill you. It's my life insurance policy, and your death warrant."

Vince sat on the end of the desk and flipped through the ledgers. A quick glance is all it took.

"These are American companies and South American banks. The account numbers and monthly deposits are arrayed in double-entry accounting schedules. This is Plankton Resources' laundry list, reduced to numbers, right?"

"What would a dick like you know about double-entry accounting schedules?"

"My dad was an accountant, remember? And I know as much 'bout the names in this notebook as you do. I been studying them for several weeks."

"Studying them? What 'n fuck you mean by that?"

"Meaning, I know how the currency exchange business is used by Plankton to launder drug money. That's what I know. I'll keep it a secret when I go."

"When you go, where?" Julia asked.

"Actually, that's the wrong word, bitch. I won't go. I'll disappear. But there's one more condition to your parole. You have to execute some electronic transfers for me. Two of them. For two million USD, each, payable to an account I'll write down for you, in a bank you'll recognize, down in Panama City."

"No, I won't do that. If I execute a transfer of their money to you, they'll kill me. If I don't transfer the money, you'll kill me. Either way I die. So, just shoot me now, take the cash, and see how fast you can disappear, you little prick."

"Prick? I call you a bitch and you call me a prick? So, we're speaking the same language now; you and me. But the electronic transfers are not to me. And they won't ever be executed because each transfer is from one of Plankton Resources' subsidiaries to another of its subsidiaries. And they are delayed transfers, effective three days from now. Here's the deal. I know you got other getaway cash and a getaway plan. Killers with law degrees always have a plan A and a plan B, right? When Houston sees these transfers, they'll know they have three days to hunt you down. They'll know you might have more numbers than these two, so they will work hard to find you. But they won't find you, Julia. I know that for sure."

"For sure? You don't know shit for sure. I'm telling you those notebooks are your death warrant. Even touching them will execute that death warrant."

"Julia, you haven't taken a good look at me, even now. I'm wearing surgeon's latex gloves. No finger prints on whatever I touch today. My face is nowhere. Not in any database in the world. And you're the only person in Houston to actually see me, or talk to me. If I parole you, you'll jump in that banana yellow car of yours and execute your getaway plan. By dawn tomorrow, if you're still alive, you'll be a million miles away from here, right? And you won't be you, anymore, right?"

"You are stupid. Why should I run? My friends at Plankton trust me. My friends in Culiacán and Panama City trust me. It's you who will be on the run. You can kill me, but you'll never hide from my friends."

"Julia, here's why you're going to run. Because you're smarter than them. Right? You've never fully trusted them, right? You've always known they might turn on you. And you have a foolproof getaway plan, don't you? I myself am an expert on disappearing. But you're even better, I know that. Which is why I don't need to kill you to keep you quiet about stealing the cash, and the bearer bonds in your safe. You can't tell the fuckin' F Bee Eye, can you? They'd arrest you. You won't tell your bosses, either—they'd kill you. And you won't hunt me down, because that won't help you. The only thing that will help you is to disappear. Me too. But not together. Hopefully on different continents."

Vince wheeled Julia back around to the executive side of her desk, powered up her computer, and stood behind her as she logged on, opened a secure browser, logged on again, and executed the first electronic transfer of a million dollars. It took one minute, thirty-seven seconds.

The second transfer took three minutes, flat. Vince used his iPhone to video all of it—the screen shots, the modulated voice he used to tell her which accounts, and which banks to use. And everything he had said to her, once she agreed to cooperate, was recorded on the Zoomer G9 digital recorder.

"OK, asshole, now you should get the fuck out of here. I'll give you my money and a one-hour head start. Then I call and warn my friends that you stole my money, a little of theirs, and my notebook. They'll hunt you down. They always do."

"Julia, Julia, what about your parole? I promised, remember?"

"Yeah, and I earned it. I did the transfers. You should get the hell out of here right now."

"Sorry, Julia Baby. I lied."

Vince hit her on the back of her head with the butt of his .44 Magnum. She slumped forward onto the desk top. He pushed the chair as far into the keyhole as he could. He took the extra-large roll of red Gorilla duct tape from the Washington Redskins backpack and taped her entire right arm to the table top, with the strips running all the way across the forty-eight-inch desktop. Then he taped the executive chair to the desk with tape tightly wound around all four sides of the desk. He also ran the tape around her upper body several times and twice around her legs and the swivel chair. She, her chair, and her desk became unyielding objects, in bright red stripes.

He waited for her to come out of the stupor of her head bang; it took five minutes.

"You bastard, you rotten bastard! I did everything you asked. Now you tie me up? With red duct tape? Jesus, you are sick."

"No, Julia, we're not sick. We know you killed our dad and we got one more thing to do before you get parole. Confessed killers get parole after they serve their time. But killers who don't confess, die. So, now we're down to your choice. Confess or die? You confess right now, speak clearly into this audio recorder, and I'll cut you free; well, mostly free. You can work yourself out of the duct tape in an hour or so. By then we'll be gone. Or refuse to confess, and I'll hit you with blue fire and smoke out the barrel of my .44 Mag. Two bullets in your forehead. Painless but permanent. Oh, I almost forgot. I promised I'd shoot you at least once with your own gun. I'll shoot you in the left knee cap—they say that's one of the most painful places you can take a bullet."

Julia rolled her eyes to one side of her head and then the other. She gritted her teeth, and tried to spit on the desk top. And she visibly leaned forward into the cushion of three-inch wide red duct tape stripes across her chest. Her shoulders sloped, head down, and she started talking to her own desk.

"OK, I'll tell you. But I didn't kill your dad, or the dope in Boise, Idaho. I was only the driver and pay master for both hits. That's why I was there, but I didn't kill anyone. I'm a lawyer and I know about felony murder. So, my statement here, into your fuckin' zoom recorder, will get me life in prison. I know that. But that's not so bad for you. There's a lot more I could tell you, about other cases, about Plankton, about all of it. And somehow, I think that's what you really want. You want me alive, to be a snitch, to be an FBI informant. That's what you really want, asshole, ain't it? I'm going to take that bet. That's why I'm confessing to what I did in Boise, and in Washington, DC. I can bring down the whole thing; you know I can. So, you got my money, my electronic transfers, and my ability to shut down Plankton. That's why you taped me up instead of shooting me. Go on, asshole. Get out of here. I only ask one thing. Tell the FBI I'm here before Plankton's inside people figure this out."

Vince turned the recorder off, placed his iPhone on the desk, and took his backpack off. He took out four digital video cards he'd used to film the FBI stakeout. He left the Washington Redskins backpack on the table, facing Julia. She couldn't reach it, but he knew who would. In five minutes, he was back at the Beverly. Still wearing the latex gloves he'd worn every second he was in the Beverley Apartments, he boxed up his stuff, loaded it into the Chevy, and drove to the trailer park in Lynchburg. There, he transferred everything from the car to Jumbo II and drove north toward Beaumont, on I-10.

Ten minutes later, he pulled off I-10 onto a freeway off ramp with a big truck stop. He bought a Cricket phone without giving an ID. He used it to call the FBI field office in Phoenix.

"Phoenix office of the FBI, how can I help you?"

"Give Agent Lin a message. Tell her to go to Attorney Julia Santerra-Evans's office in Houston, Texas. Right now; I know she's there, but I don't know her number. Julia Baby is waiting, and anxious to confess that she killed Jason Bloomington and Stephan Manchester. Oh, and I left a tape recorder there on Julia's desk, along with a backpack she'll recognize. It still has the recording of her meeting in Phoenix with my sister, Vivian."

He'd been watching the second hand on his watch while he left the message. It took nineteen seconds. Using the lug wrench in the trunk, he destroyed the Cricket phone and dropped it into a dumpster. An hour later, he pulled into another truck stop near Lake Charles. He gassed up, bought a bag of junk food at the Circle K, and looked at his map. Then he drove another three hours to New Orleans. He found a cheap trailer park, paid for a three-day stay, and never left Jumbo II.

Three days later, just a little after five a.m., Vivian stepped down onto the concrete pad from Jumbo II, dressed in jeans and a hoodie. She had a new bright-yellow suitcase. The taxi cab she'd ordered from her new Cricket phone was waiting. The driver tipped his cowboy hat in her direction as he opened the trunk of his cab.

"I'm taking you to the airport, right Miss?" he asked, smothering a yawn with his elbow.

"Yes, please," Vivian said as she settled herself in the back seat.

"You must have an early flight, Miss. Which terminal you want?"

"American Airlines, please. And please don't play the radio; I hope to take a little nap before my flight to New York. It leaves at 8:05 a.m. We'll be there in plenty of time won't we?"

"Yes, Miss. Will you be paying by credit card?" the driver asked with a nervous tone.

"No. Cash."

When Vivian got to the airport she gave the driver a hundred-dollar bill against the $40.50 meter reading.

"Thank you for not playing the radio. I hope my sixty-dollar tip is not the best one you'll get today. My husband is wealthy and waiting for me in New York. He is a big tipper."

Once safely inside the terminal, she went to the American Airlines desk and bought a first-class ticket for San Diego.

CHAPTER 1

The US Attorney's Office, at 1000 Louisiana Street in Houston, Texas, commands four floors in a commercial building known as Wells Fargo Plaza. It's a glass skyscraper that looks like half a giant watermelon when the west-facing sun hits it in the late afternoon. Travis Danders, looking very much the Houston version of a criminal defense lawyer, took the elevator up to the twenty-third floor. Just before he reached the front door, he moistened his lips, and patted his black suit jacket pocket to make sure the handwritten note was safe. Once inside, he went through the metal detector and told the receptionist he had an appointment with Deputy US Attorney Nancy Lee Sustern.

"How you doing, Nancy Lee?" Travis asked, as she walked toward him in the reception area.

"Well, Travis, I guess I was doing pretty good till I got your voicemail at five a.m. on my cell phone. What in God's green world got you up that early on a Friday morning?"

"Like I said on the message, I need to report something to your boss, who won't take my calls. Once I show you what I'm here to show you, you'll understand why I was so cryptic on the phone early this morning."

"Come on back to our conference room—the small one since it's just us—two old classmates from Rice—talking about crime and weekends, right?"

Travis and Nancy Lee had been classmates, but not just classmates fifteen years ago. Nancy Lee was destined to prosecute and Travis made it clear he thought prosecutors were predators. They'd engaged in a half dozen cases, but had never taken one to trial. Once settled on opposite sides of the government-issue conference table, set for no more than eight people, with note pads, and six-ounce bottles of room-temperature water, Nancy Lee got down to business.

"You weren't just cryptic, Travis, you sounded befuddled. What kind of note are you talking about and does it involve a pending case in this office?"

"Here's the nub of it. I was retained yesterday afternoon by a new client, Vince Manchester. I'd never met him before, and know almost nothing about him now. He's not from here. He seems to think there might be a pending case in your office against him, but there's a whole lot I don't know. He gave me a copy of a handwritten note. He said to give it to whoever 'n hell is the big-ass prosecutor in this town—that's the way he put it."

"Well, that ain't me. If you call me that, I'll file a sexual harassment case against you. Now if your client means my boss, Mr. Wellington Strauss himself, well maybe the description fits. What's the note say?"

Travis retrieved the envelope from his breast collar pocket and slid it across the table to her.

"Before I touch it, Travis, I have to ask whether you believe this to be evidence of any kind, and if so whether I need to call a security officer in here to witness how I handle whatever's in your little secret envelope."

"Call whoever you want. I've read the note. My guess is it will eventually be evidence of something."

"Oh, hell, just open the envelope and lay it on the table in front of me. I don't want to be accused of spoliation of evidence. But I'm going to take a picture of it with my cell phone, and I'm going to punch the recorder app too. You're now being recorded, Travis."

Travis opened the plain envelope, turned the short handwritten note toward her, and listened as she read the note aloud.

> You do not know me, but your brother Vince called me "Julia Baby." I mean you no personal harm, but I intend to find and kill him. He has destroyed my life. I am a hunted woman by the law, and by my former employers in Mexico and Panama. If you do not help me find him, I will kill you.

After she read it aloud, she twisted the plastic top off her little water bottle. Travis started to say something, but she held her hand up.

"Travis, hold up. I'm going back to my office. It'll take maybe ten minutes. Would you mind waiting?"

"Can I use your Wi-Fi to make some calls? Just give me your logon and I'll be happy for ten minutes."

Fifteen minutes later, Nancy Lee came back with another assistant US Attorney in tow.

"Travis," she said sounding very official, "this is AUSA Colorado Rust. He's here to take notes. He's also an evidence technician and will perform that function with your mysterious note. I presume this copy is for our office, right? It's not the original, I can see that, but we're going to do this right. OK with you?"

"Exactly what I thought you'd do. By the book."

"You said your client's name is Vince Manchester?" she asked, looking down at her note pad. "Is he the Vince that's named in this handwritten note?"

"I don't know. But that's probably a safe assumption on your part."

"You don't know, or you can't say because of attorney-client privilege?"

"I don't know. But if I did, I couldn't tell without client permission. I said I don't know because I want to be straight with you and your office. My client's name is not privileged, but his whereabouts might be if you suspect him of a crime. I'll say this. If he is the same 'Vince' referred to in the note, then it sounds like he's the potential victim here, not the perpetrator."

"Who's Julia Baby?"

"Nancy Lee, I don't know that either. But as I read it, Julia baby is who you should be looking for."

"The note refers to a brother. I think it means Vince *is* the brother. Does he have a sister?"

"Don't know that either."

"You said your client didn't tell you who Julia Baby was. OK, I'll accept that for now. But I want to give you a name. Julia Santerra-Evans—does that name mean anything to you?"

"Attorney-client privilege. You know that. I will say I don't know who she is, or why the woman called Julia Baby in the note says she's going to find and kill quote Vince end quote. That's the part of the note that brings me here to your office. It's a threat to kill someone called Vince. Don't know whether the Vince in the note is the same Vince Manchester that came to my office yesterday afternoon. I'm here because he instructed me to deliver this note to you. Well, not you in person, just . . ."

"We don't need your quaint description of my boss's derriere again, do we, Travis? You're still being recorded here."

During the next five minutes, Travis explained that his client was physically present somewhere in Houston, at least as of yesterday. He won't waive his fifth amendment rights. He won't cooperate in any government investigation. He'd allowed Travis to keep that copy of the note, and Travis told Nancy Lee he had no idea where the original note might be.

"How long have we got to figure this out, Travis? Is your new client a resident here, or just visiting?"

"I've had one short meeting with him. He told me he'd stay here a week. He won't talk to you, or anyone 'in authority.' That's how he put it—'in authority.' I have a telephone number, but I don't know where he's staying. I'll cooperate with you, and your office, but this is as strange to me as it is to you. I am his lawyer of record, as of right now. Please do not approach him without informing me in advance."

"One short meeting? You just said he retained you. For what? Are you his lawyer of record, as of yesterday? You know the drill, Travis. We have a rather large file on your client. Should we list you as his lawyer of record?"

"I guess you could say I'm a limited-scope lawyer for Mr. Manchester. All he wants from me, as of yesterday, is to connect with this office, give someone here the note, and report back to him. Not that it's any of your business, but he retained me for two hours of my time. Flat, nonrefundable fee. Paid in advance. Yesterday. He's got an hour left."

"Travis, is your firm in that much trouble? You're taking two-hour clients now? Wait, don't bother asserting attorney-client privilege again. Let me ask you a non-privileged question. Does the name Plankton Resources, LLC, mean anything to you?"

"No, should it?"

"Perhaps. I'm only telling you this because, as Mr. Manchester's lawyer, you ought to know that there were several passengers killed in a bombing of a Learjet over the Gulf of Mexico two years ago. The plane was leased to Plankton Resources, LLC. Do you remember the press coverage about that?"

"Vaguely, but what's that got to do with my client Vince Manchester?"

"Maybe nothing. Maybe something. I don't honestly know. But our office investigated that bombing. We also investigated a separate crime involving Julia

Santerra-Evans; she was the victim in that crime. There is a pending federal indictment. It's a multi-party, multi-count financial crimes indictment. We filed it under seal. It's still under seal, pending locating and arresting several defendants. Two of those defendants were employed by Plankton Resources, LLC. Julia Santerra-Evans was counsel of record for Plankton. One defendant is named Vince Manchester. I don't know if that's your client. But if it is, we want you to surrender him immediately. I'll give you until tomorrow to find out."

Travis didn't answer. He'd forgotten how irritating his classmate could be. Probably just as well he wasn't counsel in the case itself. He was just a limited-scope lawyer for a man named Vince. He had the uneasy feeling this might be a legal train wreck.

"Nice talking to you, Nancy Lee. Tell your boss I didn't say hello. He's been the boss here for what, five months now? Never met the man. He doesn't go to the same bars I do."

"Tomorrow, Travis. We'll give you until tomorrow to get back to us and we can arrange a non-public arrest process, if your client is the Vince named in our sealed indictment."

"Well, Nancy Lee, that'd be a first, wouldn't it? You have a sealed indictment. You don't know whether the Vince Manchester I represent is the one in your case, and neither do I. If you had him sitting here right now in your sealed conference room, you couldn't arrest him just because his name was Vince Manchester. He's entitled to due process of law, right? So don't threaten a man you don't know is a defendant, just because I said his name was the same as a name in a goddamn sealed indictment. Where's your probable cause? He's not presumed guilty because he has the same name as one defendant in a goddamn sealed indictment, is he?"

They did not bid one another a fond goodbye.

CHAPTER 2

"Boss, you're not gonna believe what just happened," FBI Agent Sally Lin said to her boss, as he got out of the elevator on the sixth floor of their Phoenix Arizona office.

"Agent Lin, how thoughtful of you to greet me at the elevator door. And with news I'm not going to believe? What is it—has our new president decided to take the fifth on his tweet this morning about us planting a spy inside the locker room of his golf club?"

Sally swung to his left side and matched her stride to his, as they walked toward his office.

"No, much more surprising than the president's tweet about spies, lies, and witch hunts. I just got a text from the Houston field office, from the agent I worked with two years ago on the Stephan Manchester bombing—remember that? The girl and her father who disappeared from WITSEC, and the boy—who might have been her brother—named Vince—well, he just surfaced in Houston, of all places. And . . ."

"Hold on, Sally. Why are they calling you? And, wait, don't tell me yet. I need coffee and a place to dump this shoulder bag; it's killing me. My wife stuck two dozen lemons off our tree in here for my admin, and they weigh a ton."

SAIC Marcellus "Stan" Stanza did what he always did when hit with a dead-end case. They settled inside his office, not waiting to book one of the conference rooms down the hall. He offloaded the lemons onto his conference table and poured coffee from the Bunn machine on the credenza behind his desk.

"Give me the elevator version, from the ground floor up, but in three minutes."

"Right boss. This one stumped us, the Boise field office, and Houston. Not to mention FBI HQ in DC. It hit the wall when FBI Houston snagged an international money laundering cartel, and arrested a woman named Julia Santerra-Evans in Houston. Remember her, the hilarious hit-lady who was duct-taped to her office desk by a man whom no one, except her, ever saw—who claimed to be the son of Stephen Manchester, who was murdered . . ."

"Stop doing that, Sally. I said give it to me elevator style from the ground floor up to ours. I remember the names, and of course the absurdity of it—the red duct tape—the hidden tape recorder in the back pack. Who could forget that? Top it off for me—what do they want from us—that is, you?"

"Not sure, boss. The text asked me to take an incoming conference call at 11:00 this morning. They are going to conference us—that is, me—and whoever I want on the line, with the US Attorney's Office in Houston."

"Read the text to me, Sally."

"It says, quote, Vince Manchester, reference your office case file re his father, Stephan Manchester, is in Houston. Retained local criminal defense counsel. Physical location unknown. Counsel will not surrender his client or provide substantive information re pending indictment. Can you conference via SecureNet channel this afternoon at 1300 hours CST? Confirm by return text. End quote. That's it boss, that's all I know."

"Ok, you better call up the files from the third floor. Do you want Standusky on the call with you? I can't make it—I have to be downtown at the federal court house for another meeting with the US Marshal's Office. Damn, I hate those meetings. It's always about a runner, or a gunner they can't find, but want us to brief them on background."

"Don't worry, boss. I'll check with Standusky. I'd like him to sit with me—he's got a knack for ignoring the obvious and asking about the empty box under the desk."

"Empty box? What empty box?"

"It's one of his little witticisms. He uses it to explain how to interrogate an innocent suspect. He asks them about things that only remotely go to the case itself. You know, get a suspect to talk about his own box, and then soon enough he'll start telling things you can put in your box, and before long, you got a confession, hidden away in the box under the desk, or table, or lunch counter. I don't know. It's just Standusky. Know what I mean?"

"No, but don't tell me now. I'll be back here by four. Pop in and fill my box up."

CHAPTER 3

When he got back to his office, Travis Danders dialed the number Vince had given him the day before. All he got was a voice message in a high-pitched voice. "Sorry, I am not myself. Say something." Travis left his name and number. He'd called on his office line, but within seconds his cell phone rang. The screen read, "Unknown Caller." He hit talk and said hello.

"So, Lawyer Man, you did the thing? What'd the big-ass prosecutor tell you?" the muffled voice asked.

Travis took in a deep breath, not because he needed air, but so he could gather his thoughts.

"Vince, is this you?"

"Don't be a dick. Of course it's me. You called me a nanosec ago. Who else would be calling your cell right back? Just answer my questions. Don't need no lawyer speeches yet."

"Vince, yes, I met with the chief deputy in the US Attorney's Office yesterday, her name is Nancy Lee Sustern. We had a very short discussion and . . ."

"She go by Nancy Lee? Two names? I almost forgot, this is Texas. Crackers here like their two names, don't they? Shit. I only been here once before. Felt the manacles itching to clamp down on me the whole time. Feeling's comin' back, Lawyer Man. What'd she say when you said my name? She react, or just dumb-up right in front of you? And why didn't you meet with the real big-ass prosecutor himself? His name is Wellington Strauss, case you didn't know that."

"Mr. Manchester, it would be best if you came to my office. As I told you day before yesterday, I can only give you advice on a limited basis because I do not know your legal situation well enough to take you on as a regular client until . . ."

"Hey man, chill. Don't mean to get you all agitated. Agitate—that's a word I heard on the TV this morning waiting for you to call. I like it. So, you delivered my note and what happened then?"

"I delivered the note. I had told her I represented you on a limited-scope basis only. She told me there is a pending sealed indictment in federal court against a man named Vince Manchester. She asked me if you were the same Vince Manchester named in the sealed indictment. I declined to answer her and asserted your attorney-client privilege. But she said if I was representing the defendant in the federal case, she wanted me to surrender you to federal authorities immediately."

"You asking me if I'm the man in the case, Lawyer Man? What's the case? She tell you that?"

"No, she didn't. It's a sealed indictment."

"She's just working for the United States government, right? She don't speak for the state of Texas?"

"Yes, Vince, you're correct on jurisdiction. But remember, before we talk further, I'm only representing you on a limited basis—I just agreed to deliver the copy of the note to the US Attorney. I'm not your lawyer in a federal or a state criminal case."

"Right, dude. I remember that limited scope line you fed me. It's OK with me, for now. But can you find out for me whether there really is a federal case, and whether the state prosecutor dudes are also chasing after a guy with the same name as me? Jus add that onto your limited scope, whatever in hell that means."

Travis started to answer, but the line went dead.

CHAPTER 4

Agents Lin and Standusky were in the sixth floor conference room at the Phoenix field office when the promised telephone call came in from the federal prosecutor's office in Houston. US Attorney Nancy Lee Sustern began the call by introducing her boss, US Wellington Strauss. It was short. Wellington took over.

"Agents Lin and Standusky, thanks for setting this time aside for us on short notice. I know you'll find this development fascinating. It'll take me ten minutes to bring you back up to speed on the sealed indictment we secured two years ago that now seems ripe for unsealing and a possible arrest."

It took more than ten minutes because, as Lin and Standusky immediately discovered, Mr. Wellington Strauss was a recent political appointment who was more front office than he was an in-court prosecutor. His appointment was secured by measuring his commitment to the kind of criminal justice system the new president envisioned.

They scribbled notes as fast as they could, interrupted a few times, but were consistently held off by Strauss telling them Assistant US Attorney Sustern would fill them in on case file details once he'd given them the profile and what he called the "prosecutorial goal here."

In crisp sentences, which sounded like he was reading bullet points off an iPad, he parsed the case. "Two years earlier, Agent Lin had been sent to Houston to assist, temporarily, in an ongoing investigation into a large money-laundering operation out of Houston, through a company then known as Plankton Resources, LLC. A Texas lawyer named Julia Santerra-Evans did legal work for Plankton and, as they later discovered, was also an assassin connected to an infamous Mexican drug smuggler named Leopoldo de Santos, head of the Sinaloa Cartel. The lawyer was, for reasons not clear then, or now, targeted by a young man named Vince Manchester. The young man's father, named Stephan Manchester had been murdered in a Washington, DC, retirement home by someone either hired by or directed by Ms. Santerra-Evans. Vince Manchester assaulted, robbed, and threatened to kill her. But in a bizarre attack in her law office, Julia was duct-taped to her office chair and desk by the younger Manchester. He forced her to confess her role in two murders, and her role in creating and advancing the money laundering ring for Plankton Resources. Agent Lin will no doubt remember finding Julia duct-taped to her desk and discovering the evidence left behind by the mysterious Vince, who has been missing for two years, but is now somewhere in Houston. He has a lawyer."

Wellington Strauss said he had another important matter he had to attend to, but he was sure Ms. Sustern could "plug in the blanks."

Lin and Standusky could hear what sounded like a chair being pushed away from a table in an uncarpeted room. Then, a female voice said, "Right, Mr. Strauss, I'll try to fill in the blanks."

They heard nothing for a few moments, then came the sound of a door closing with a bang. Lin spoke up.

"Ms. Sustern, this is Sally Lin. Agent Standusky is here with me."

"Call me Nancy Lee, please. We could really use your help here. We know so little about the defendant, Vince Manchester. Could we start there? What do you know about him?"

Sally jumped in. "Well, Nancy Lee, you probably know more than we do. We didn't know he was indicted. Do I understand correctly that it's a sealed indictment, even now, two years later?"

"Yes. We had it sealed pending the arrests of the actors and conspirators named in the indictment handed up by the grand jury. Technically, Mr. Manchester is an unindicted *coconspirator* in the case. His exposure on the financial crimes is limited. He has great risk in a parallel state of Texas criminal case. He's the primary there—it's not a financial crimes conspiracy. The state investigators and police were after him within a half hour after he left Julia's office in Baytown. We were also part of that case, because he crossed state lines to get here and kidnap Ms. Julia Santerra-Evans. A full description, based on Julia's description, plus some video he intentionally left for us, was broadcast across Texas and our neighboring states. But even with a full description, still pics from the video, and a wide net, he was gone—literally disappeared. No trace of him that day, or any day since. Two years of radio silence. We've put out national and international catch-and-hold warrants. We've monitored Interpol and DNI data weekly. Nothing has remotely suggested he's even alive, not to mention anybody spotting him. Can you point us to anything that explains this?"

Standusky jumped at that.

"You told your wide net you were looking for a white male, in his teens, right? You didn't look for his sister, right?"

"Sister? What sister?"

Before he could reply, Sally waved him off by crossing her right hand back and forth across her neck.

"Nancy Lee, we can probably help you by having a longer conversation about the Manchester family and its history that we developed here in Arizona. But first, can I ask a few more questions?"

"Shoot."

"What did you indict him for?"

"There were two indictments—ours in federal court for money laundering, wire fraud, and racketeering. The state indictments were for assault, battery, burglary, theft, false imprisonment, and kidnapping. The state case, filed by the Harris County prosecutor, was voluntarily dismissed about two, maybe three weeks after the attack on Ms. Santerra-Evans. Ours was sealed, the state charges were not."

"Why did you seal your case?" Standusky asked.

"Because the suspect was at large. We filed to get national and international arrest warrants, given what we knew about the money and negotiable instruments. And also because we tagged in FinCEN, and the CIA, given the amount of money that was wired out of Plankton's offshore accounts. We felt at the time there would be international repercussions, and probably an international find-and-kill contract on Vince Manchester, and perhaps others."

"Others?"

"Yes, Agent Lin, but I wasn't here at the time the charges came down. I was on leave, maternity leave—twin girls. I have read some of the 302s, and of course the grand jury presentation, but I have to say the fact that others were under investigation, but not under indictment, was very confusing, then and now. By others, I mean unindicted coconspirators. There were vague references to a female suspect, who may have been related to the suspect—her name was Vivian, but her last name was different. Short or Shortfield, something like that."

Sally felt that odd sense of talking to a ghost she'd first experienced when she met Vivian at a Starbucks in Phoenix two years earlier. So she just hinted to the prosecutor what might be going on.

"Nancy Lee, I know you'll find this weird, but our investigation and the related investigations in Boise, Idaho, and Washington, DC, all involved a female named Vivian. There is a record of multiplicity here. Do you know anything about that?"

"Multiplicity? Do you mean multiple crimes?"

"No," Sally said, "I mean the kind of multiplicity that stems from dissociative identity disorders. Years ago they were defined in the psychiatric world as multiple personality disorder. Vince and Vivian may be the same person. A female who was, as a child, diagnosed with this disorder. It involves at least two distinct and relatively enduring personality states. One is the host personality. The other is called an alter—sometimes misheard—or mispronounced as 'an other.'"

"Wow, this is a new one on me. Are there medical reports, or expert consultations here? How did you find out about this, and what causes it?"

"We have some documentation, but it's very thin. I talked to an expert—a Georgetown Hospital pediatric psychiatrist. She was very helpful. I did a little follow-up research on my own. These states alternately show in a person's behavior. Associated conditions often include borderline personality disorder, post-traumatic stress disorder, depression, substance misuse disorder, self-harm, or anxiety. That may be the case here, but my gut tells me that Vivian was and is the host identity. She withdraws, not intentionally, but whenever she is threatened, or deeply frightened. Then, somehow, Vince, her alter, shows up and acts to protect her by taking action against others who may cause her harm. Or others who are as much of a threat to him as they are to her because Vince and Vivian are really one and the same person displaying different personality traits. Confusing, right?"

"Confusing? Get out! I've had cases with defendants and witnesses who were mental cases—some bipolar, some schizophrenic, a lot of PTSD vets, and of course garden-variety psychopaths and sociopaths. But never two in one. Multiplicity, is that a medical term, or a legal term?"

Standusky, never one to stay silent during a conversation, spoke up.

"Sally was the one who broke this news to me. But I did a little looking on my own, on account of I got a lot of people in my family that bug me. My sister, who's a psychiatric nurse practitioner, gave me the two-dollar shine on this. She said multiplicity was a really broad term, but you can think of it like this. It's an experience of more than 'self' in your mind or body. Yeah, that's how she put it to me. People have very different understandings of what it means to experience this 'more than one' reality. She thinks I have one or two loose screws myself."

"Oh Lordy Mosey," Nancy Lee said. "Sally, if the man we indicted as Vince Manchester is an alternate personality of a woman named Vivian Manchester, who do we arrest if we actually find him? Himself, or the other personality—the one you called the host personality—Vivian?"

"Funny you should ask, Nancy Lee. The doctor I consulted on this case, her name is Dr. Elaina Socorro, asked me the same thing two years ago. If the host commits a crime, is the alter guilty, too? It's a medical question, but from a legal perspective, they are only one person—maybe with split, or dissociative identities, but still just one person. So, I'd say if the defense lawyer in Houston produces his client and identifies him as Vince Manchester, then that's who you arrest. If we're right and Vivian is his host, she will show up eventually, I guess."

Standusky interrupted.

"The hell you say. If that defense lawyer in Houston produces his client, a man named Vince, and you arrest him, then you've also just arrested a woman named Vivian. I don't know about this showing up stuff, but if the docs are right, you arrest either the host or the alter, you got 'em both in the same cell. Now that's a hoot. Breaks all the segregated rules in jail or prison, right? Man and woman in the same cell?"

"Well, Sally, I'll take it on faith you're right. But you're FBI. I'm an Assistant US Attorney. I need probable cause to make an arrest—and that means scienter. Actual knowledge of the crime committed, or at least charged. Does the host have scienter of something the alter did? That's not a medical question, that's a legal conundrum."

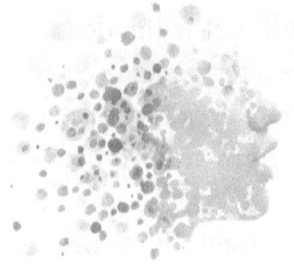

CHAPTER 5

Travis Danders sent Vince a text at 7:30 in the morning asking him to come to his office at one p.m. Then he spent an hour on the Internet reading media coverage about alleged money laundering by Plankton Resources two years earlier. It hinted at an assault on one of its lawyers, Julia Santerra-Evans. He'd never heard of her. The *Houston Chronicle* said she was with a Baytown firm, but gave few details. And it mentioned an ongoing investigation into unsolved murder cases that might be tangentially related. One was the bombing of a Learjet over the Gulf of Mexico, just after taking off from Houston. Another was a murky but bizarre murder in Boise, Idaho—the murder weapon was a garrote. A third bombing occurred in Washington, DC, according to unnamed confidential sources. One article referenced a Baltimore, Maryland, criminal case that connected a commodities broker there to Plankton Resources, LLC, in Houston.

All of it was unclear, but Nancy Lee Sustern seemed to link the newspaper coverage about money laundering to the sealed indictment of Vince Manchester. When they talked about the sealed indictment that "may" involve his client, she sounded confident that he really was the same Vince, referenced in the note, and the strange young man who'd come to his office yesterday. It was time to either withdraw from representation, or take on Vince as a regular, full-representation client. Vince showed up at 12:30.

"Hey Lawyer Man, sorry I'm early. Jus couldn't wait to hear the news. What's gonna happen? They got the goods on me, or what?"

"Mr. Manchester, I don't know enough to give you any legal advice at this point. Before we go any further I want to talk about the difference between limited-scope representation and a full lawyer-client relationship in a criminal case."

"Don't matter to me which way you want it, man. I just said OK when you said the thing was limited. But if there is a fuckin' indictment against me, I want you to be my full, no-holds-barred lawyer. I checked you out—you're the real fuckin' deal, man. So let's do the fee thing, or whatever it is you need to be my lawyer on all this shit."

"All right, but before I take you on as a full client, I need to know three things. First, are you the 'Vince' that's referenced in the note you gave me yesterday? Second, are you the Vince Manchester named in a federal indictment, and referenced in the state criminal case that was filed, but quickly dismissed two years ago? Third, is the 'Julia Baby' in the note the same Julia Santerra-Evans identified in the state case? She is listed as the victim of robbery, assault, and attempted murder, along with numerous other charges."

"Whoa, man. You got a lot of references there. I can answer, but before you ask more, I need some answers from you. First, hell yeah, I'm the Vince in the note. And that bitch Julia Baby got her name from me. She's Julia Baby to me, and me only. That's what I called her two years ago. Now, 'bout your third reference thing. Julia Baby's charges against me in the state courts. Have you read those charges, yourself?"

"Yes, I have. I can print a copy for you. The state charges are based on a state grand jury indictment, but were not filed under seal, like the federal charges were. They are likely different code violations, but based on the same factual details."

"OK, let's talk fees. I mean I already paid you one thousand dollars to be limited. What's it gonna take for you to go whole hog?"

"Mr. Manchester, going whole hog, as you call it, means a full representation in all pending criminal charges. It includes investigation, pre-trial services, trial and appeal representation, and advice concerning your state and federal constitutional rights in both jurisdictions. It would not include representing you in civil claims, such as torts, or defamation claims."

"OK, that's what I want, but you gotta tell me, does it include finding out exactly what they got on me, and telling me where Julia Baby is? I mean she has to be a witness, right? They can't convict me without her, right?"

"If I decide to take you on as a full client, it would include an exchange of inculpatory and exculpatory evidence the state and federal prosecutors have. They would tell me what evidence they have, who their witnesses are, and whether they have other evidence that might be in your favor—that's called exculpatory evidence. But it's often a time-consuming effort, so I won't know right away whether, as you put it, 'they have the goods on you.' As soon as possible I will assess the strength of the case against you in both jurisdictions and give you my views about possible plea offers and sentencing ranges if you are convicted."

"Ok, lawyer talk. I get that. I did my research too, before I called you. You graduated high up in law school and went right away into criminal cases. Defending always. You got your own law firm. There's five other lawyers working here, but your name's the only one on the door. You're the top dog. You won lots of cases and got some bad dudes off. You ain't never been debarred, or anything like that. Some prosecutors said, when you beat their ass in court, you were fair but very aggressive for your client. Shit man, you even got your picture on the front page of some bar association rag five years ago for criminal lawyer of the year. You're a big shit around here. Now, that means you get top dollar, but you do the job, right? If we cut a deal, and you become my full-ass lawyer, you will personally handle my case, right? Won't hand it off to one of them office lawyers you got here, right?"

"If I take your case, then yes, I will handle it personally. But I will engage other lawyers in the firm on specific assignments. If the case goes to trial, I will be the trial lawyer, whether in federal court or state court. But before we talk fees, there is one other thing we need to talk about. Who is Vivian and what does she have to do with your case?"

"First off, Lawyer Man, there ain't gonna be no trial. And second, I ain't involving Vivian."

"What do you mean no trial? And why won't you talk about Vivian?"

"None of your business. Don't be asking me about her."

"All right, we'll come back to that. What makes you think there won't be a trial?"

"Cause Julia Baby has disappeared herself. Cause without her, they don't have shit—you know that, Lawyer Man. It's hearsay, man, hearsay. I looked up hearsay evidence on law.com. They gotta put her ass in the witness chair—you know that better than me, right?"

"Vince, it's too early in the case to talk about evidence and the strength of the case against you. Let me explain how a retainer works in this law firm. We will sign a written fee agreement. You will deliver a cashier's check, not cash, to me today for $25,000. I will deposit the check in what's called a client's trust account. The first $10,000 is a non-refundable advance fee. The remainder, $15,000, will be billed to you on a monthly basis, at the rate of $500 per hour, for my time, and a lesser rate for other lawyers and legal assistants in the office. When and if the retainer in the account reaches a low of $5,000, you will have to deliver another cashier's check for $25,000. We will bill at our hourly rates against that. Are these financial terms agreeable to you?"

"I can do that, man. But this'll be in your trust account, right? And you're gonna stick with the Texas disciplinary rule, I think it's Texas Disciplinary Rule number 1.14, right?"

"Well, Mr. Manchester, I am impressed. You have indeed done your research. You're quite right about safekeeping client funds, and yes we have a client's trust account. That's where your retainer will be maintained. Any other questions about fees?"

"Jus one. The rule says it covers clients and third parties' money. What if the retainer money I give you is also a third party's money? That's OK, right?"

"I'm not sure what you mean. Is there a third party that will be financing your attorney's fees in the case?"

"I ain't gonna say yet. But here's the thing I wanna know. What if some of the money I give you is Vivian's money. That's OK, right?"

"Depends. Why is Vivian funding any part of your representation, and what is your relationship with her?"

"Already tole you that, Lawyer Man. Ain't going to talk about Vivian yet. Anyhow, the first 25K is all mine. I earned it. Let's just go with that for now."

"All right by me, Mr. Manchester. Can you get me a cashier's check for $25,000 today? We can sign a fee agreement in a few minutes. I'll have my secretary draw it up. Once you bring me the check, we can talk about the rest of the case, including Vivian. OK?"

"Sounds good, 'cept I don't do business by check. Jus give me your ABA Routing number and your law firm trust account number and I'll wire the $25K today. When you get it, call me. I won't answer. You know the drill, right?"

CHAPTER 6

Over the next thirty-six hours, the FBI offices in Phoenix, Washington, and Houston dug deeply into their collective files. The US Attorney's Office and the Harris County District Attorneys' offices conferred with one another regarding the status of the federal and state charges against Vince Manchester. Each office thought about consulting legal and medical experts on the unique challenges of arresting and charging suspects with known dissociative identity disorders. Rather than engage separately, they agreed to jointly consult a nationally regarded expert, Ahmad Estancia, MD, JD, PhD. Dr. Estancia was an academic psychiatrist on the Rice University faculty. He was also a practicing psychotherapist and a lawyer, with degrees in medicine from Rice, and a juris doctorate from Baylor. His mother was a devout Muslim from Pakistan; his father a devout Catholic from Mexico City. He told Nancy Lee Sustern he studied law, in part, to better advance his psychotherapy practice treating dissociative patients. He was an inactive member of the Texas bar, occasionally consulting with defense counsel retained by dissociative criminal suspects. What else could a Muslim-Catholic boy do in Texas, he'd asked Nancy Lee. All four offices agreed to hold a GoToMeeting video conference over the FBI's SecureNet servers.

After introducing eleven prosecutors and FBI agents, sitting in four secure conference rooms, Nancy Lee, as the self-appointed facilitator of the meeting, introduced Dr. Estancia to the video conferees. Microphones were tested and all participants were displayed on three large split-video monitors.

"Good afternoon, everyone. As you all know, our office retained Dr. Ahmed Estancia as a consulting psychotherapist on the federal case against Vince Manchester. We asked him to assume, for the purposes of this consultation, that he would only be a consulting expert, *not* a testifying expert. He has not reviewed or been briefed on the sealed indictment in federal court, and has not read the unsealed charges pending in the state court here in Houston. He does not know the facts in our case, the parties, or the legal theories. He won't be issuing a written report. We think this discussion is attorney work product under the discovery rules. And lastly, since this is only a one-time consultation, please ask your questions now. I have asked him to give us an overview of some of the challenges this case presents, assuming that the defendant, Vince Manchester, does suffer from a dissociative disorder. He does not know anything about Mr. Manchester's disorder; I've merely asked him to assume that the man has that kind of disorder. While all of us on this conference call are on the prosecution side of the case, I want everyone here to feel free to ask questions that might implicate the parties, witnesses, or related cases arising out of the multiple criminal cases in three states and the District of Columbia. As far as we know, this defendant is only implicated in the Texas cases, but there are other ongoing investigations. And some of us also have questions about both the perpetrator and the victim in this case—since the principal victim, Julia Santerra-Evans, may herself be a defendant in related cases. Dr. Estancia, will you give us an overview of the challenges in this case—the federal case against Mr. Manchester?"

"Of course. At the outset, I should say my knowledge of the criminal charges is miniscule. I haven't read the indictment in either federal or state court. I'm prepared to discuss the dissociative identity disorder from a theoretical perspective, not a legal one. Dissociation cases, sometimes called multiplicity cases, whether in a psychotherapy setting or in a courtroom, involve both multiplicity and criminality boundaries. They are vast wastelands of unknown, and unprovable states. As physicians and neuroscientists, we know a good deal about the medical, epidemiological, and etiology of dissociative disorders. But lawyers and legal scholars deal with much more concrete realities—criminal law and procedural statutes. The law is a lot less flexible than psychology's nuanced views of the dissociative disorders. All of you are presumably familiar with the DSM IV; it describes five such disorders. They involve a complex non-integration of psychological function, or dysfunction. The one that may be helpful to you in assessing criminal conduct of the defendant named Vince Manchester illustrates classic failure of the integration of basic notions of human identity."

The Harris District Attorney's representative, Grant Lumberson, a grey-headed man who, on the video screen looked pallid and unhealthy, interrupted.

"Excuse me, doctor, but we are all pressed for time. Maybe you could send all of us a medical study for background reading later, but for now I'm interested in criminal responsibility. Seems to me, we're hip deep in a legal-medical quagmire."

"You are, sir, you are. And your metaphor is excellent. A quagmire is a soft boggy area of land that gives way underfoot. Taking it one step further, or a step deeper in the bog, means you must understand the perpetrator's behavioral state at the time the crime was committed, rather than when the case against him reaches the charging level, or at trial. I'm going to take you through the different theories that blend behavioral states into criminal evidence."

Lin asked, "Doctor, what is a behavioral state? Are you talking about a state of mind?"

"Behavioral states are medically defined as essential components of consciousness. They involve configurations of psychological, physiological, and behavioral variables. They are ubiquitous. Psychiatrists see them as patterns of thinking, feeling, and acting, patterns that fluctuate like everything else in human beings. Normal people routinely experience a wide variety of emotional states with well-defined markers. But dissociative people live in states where intensity, lack of modulation, lack of generalization of information, and a sense of self are at odds with one another. The chief behavioral state circles around a sense of self that cannot be maintained between states."

"Can you give us an example?" the DC agent asked.

"Sure. Little babies. They're born with fluctuating behavioral states—respiratory rate—motor tone—activity level—vocalization—facial expression. They can move from being quiet, to asleep, waking and crying, anxious, and placid. As they grow, their states get more complex, they develop cognitive overlay, and they respond better and better over time. They develop pathways between existing states. But they have switches, or transitions between states. Babies don't understand or transfer information from one state to another. Young children also have difficulty transferring information learned in one state to another. As they mature, their capacity to generalize knowledge or awareness across states is very important for the development of a sense of self."

"Not sure what you mean, 'a sense of self,'" a male voice came across the video screens.

"Right, it's more a medical state than a legal environment. A sense of self is how humans feel about themselves. Disruption in the sense of self across states is a critical developmental problem. And that leads to the big difference between normal people and DID patients."

"Doctor," one of the two FBI agents from Boise, Idaho, asked, "are you saying that we go from childhood to adulthood always at risk of—what? —not being able to tell what state we're in, until our brains—what? —mature, settle in . . . or what?"

"No, almost all of us develop an early, childhood capacity to recognize behavioral states, be aware of who we are, and develop a healthy sense of self. What disrupts that healthy process is almost always a severe traumatic event. And almost always in childhood, before the teenage years. Mostly it's chronic child abuse. Great emotional stress, induced by the child abuse, is the instigator. Trauma, in a developing child, creates a state of intense fear, shame, helplessness, and anger. Those states can be internalized by the child. They are deep. Sometimes children fanaticize a way out of the pain, fear, and shame. For children, that's post-traumatic shock. We see it in military veterans—PTSD. Children can reconstitute themselves in the aftermath of trauma. If the trauma is deep enough, or the abuse too painful, sometimes the child is so off-balance mentally, they lose their sense of self. They dissociate themselves."

Sally Lin looked up from the pad of notes she'd been furiously taking, and waved her hand at the psychiatrist 1,500 miles away. Dr. Ahmed Estancia, the dark-skinned, silver-haired man smiled and waved back.

"I see a question from the Arizona monitor. Yes, young lady, what's your question?"

"Doctor, I talked to a pediatric psychiatrist two years ago about these issues, when we first discovered that a young woman, the daughter of a murder victim in 2017, may have been diagnosed as a young child as a DID patient. That doctor told me memory is the central component in DID patients and that very often the host identity has no memory of what an alter identity does. Do you share that view? And if you don't mind, doctor, can you help me understand how memory and awareness interact in DID patients?"

"Good questions. And thank you for connecting them. You cannot address one's sense of self—that is, awareness—without also addressing memory. The most distinctive feature about what we call 'pathological dissociation' is that there is often a total deficit of memory from one state to another. Just as there is a different, or total, lack of a sense of self between the host and the alter identity. But it's more complex than that. Let me read something to you. It's from a five-year-old study done in Great Britain. Quote, 'Alter personalities reflect the creation of a set of complex, enduring, identity-based, discrete dissociative states. They are created in childhood. They begin as trauma-induced states of consciousness. Over time they become increasingly differentiated.'"

Nancy Lee turned to Dr. Estancia, who was sitting next to her.

"Oh my God, doctor. Are you saying what I think you're saying? That these patients grow more and more mentally ill as they grow older? Do you mean more dangerous? Is that what you mean by 'increasingly differentiated'?"

"Not quite," Dr. Estancia said hesitatingly, looking down at what appeared to be notes on his iPad. "It may or may not be dangerous to others, but it's often dangerous to the patient. Let me explain it this way. For most of us, our mood at any given moment only minimally impacts how we perceive and represent ourselves. That's because our variable sense of self is sufficiently integrated. We maintain a sense of continuity of self across different states and contexts. That's the critical difference between the contextual self-image of normal people and the dissociated *selves* of DID patients. Does that help?"

Lin didn't respond, but Grant Lumberson, the sixty-year old prosecutor at the Harris District Attorney's Office, did.

"Dr. Estancia, I'm a Texas lawyer with almost no understanding of mental illness. I have to say I don't understand most of what you've told us here today. Hell, I ain't even sure I believe folks can be one person in the morning and a different person in the afternoon. That's what I take from your talk to us so far. But here's what I want to know. If we do have a defendant in the dock, is he criminally responsible for his conscious acts, no matter what he might remember the next day? That's the legal nut we got to crack here, seems to me."

"Well, sir, thanks for getting me down off my medical high horse. I'm a Texas lawyer, like you. And my interest is similar to yours—in so far as criminal responsibility is concerned. But this is not the kind of hornbook law you and I learned in law school. We both know what drives this discussion is guilt or innocence. I have to tell you that medical science and medical research is not of one mind on this subject. There are theories and arguments that go back decades on the issue. Here's the theory I think best fits the situation ya'll are in right now. A person afflicted with dissociative identity disorder, with a confirmed diagnosis, and left untreated, has to be understood, and dealt with legally, differently. It depends on whether the crime was perpetrated while in the host identity, or during a time when the alter identity was conscious and acting. I don't mean play acting, or acting like in a movie or play. I mean acting as in functioning as the existing state—as an alter identity—and not as the host identity. Now . . ."

Hands went up on two of the three monitors. Mr. Lumberson sat quietly, but noisily closed his note book and crossed his arms across his chest as though he'd heard all he need to hear. One hand went up from the DC monitor—an FBI agent with a beard and wearing a white turban. Dr. Estancia recognized him.

"You, sir, the man on the Washington, DC, monitor. You get the first question on what I sense is a highly controversial notion."

"My name is Sobhan Kumar Komala. Call me Sob for short. While I went to law school, and am licensed to practice here in DC, I am an FBI analyst—helping agents with forensics and interrogation issues. My question is whether your notion has ever been tested in court and used to draw a distinction between guilt and innocence?"

"Thank you, Sob. I actually did a quick search on Lexis.Nexis.Advance this morning to see if there was any case law on point. I found none. But there are law review articles by law school faculty addressing the larger issues arising out of prosecuting mentally ill defendants. I read one or two, but nothing on the narrow issue we're talking about now—the guilt or innocence of a DID patient. Let me go back to the theory I presented a few minutes ago— the importance of identifying whether the host identity or the alter identity was the actor committing the crime. It involves the legal question of intentionality, and the medical question of rationality. When you apply those elements to an alter personality slash identity, then the answer is the alter cannot justifiably be criminally punished."

"Hold on, doctor," Lumberson boomed, uncrossing his arms and raising both hands, palms up in the air. "As I understand you so far, the host and the alter are the same person, right? They are just in different moods, like mad as hell, or happy as a lark, right? How can being pissed off or calm as a clam make any difference in how the person is treated in court? I mean, Jesus Christ, it's all one person, right?"

"Another good question. The medical thesis is straight-forward. An alter can be both sane and guilty. But it is of course impossible to punish the alter without punishing the host identity. It is wrong to punish an innocent host, or even a different innocent alter, because other multiples, which the host identity is not responsible for, are the criminal actors—they are alters, *not* hosts. The host was neither aware, meaning acting intentionally, or otherwise of a guilty mind. There is no *mens rea* in the host. There is no scienter, either. The real key to understanding this, either from a medical or a legal perspective, is to remember that an alter personality is not a *person*. The host is a person, but he or she is not acting when the alter personality is. Every DID patient is a deeply divided person. The conscious act of an alter is an involuntary act of the host. The law, under this theory of multiplicity, should hold non-responsible someone who has aspects of him or herself that they are unaware of, and do not know. After all, in order to pronounce someone responsible for a given crime, the law demands that the actor knew he was performing the action."

Lin raised her hand when Dr. Estancia took a breath after that long dissertation.

"Ok, doctor, I think I'm understanding this now. It's not really a question of guilt or innocence, is it? It's a question of legal responsibility. But we charge suspects with crimes like involuntary manslaughter all the time. We hold some suspects responsible for involuntary acts, right?"

"We do. But those crimes are based on decisions made by the suspects, which support the crime. They have executive control over their acts. But with a DID patient, there is *no* executive control. More importantly, there is no executive. There is just a split-off consciousness, performing its own acts clearly separated from the wishes, likes, dislikes, and awareness of the host."

Perhaps sensing mutiny, Nancy Sustern took the mike in her conference room.

"I know I don't speak for all jurisdictions or even for our office here in Houston, but I think we should take a breath. We have a good deal of evidence about the specific event, a crime Mr. Manchester is charged with in the state indictment. He's an unindicted defendant in the conspiracy case that's under seal in the federal case. Our evidence comes from crime-scene forensics, some video footage intentionally left behind by Mr. Manchester, and a version of what happened given to us by the victim, Julia Santerra-Evans. But Julia is no longer a cooperating witness; she's a potential defendant herself. She has evaded the WHITSEC people, and she could be herself a target, again, of Mr. Manchester. Importantly, we know almost nothing about Manchester's emotional state, whether he suffers from a mental illness,

whether he is an alter, or a host, or just your garden-variety
thief, and . . ."

Sally Lin interrupted.

"'Garden variety' he is not. He lives. We know that
because a police detective in DC talked to him. Twice. He
was obsessed with his father's murder. Vivian also lives.
I know because I talked to her twice; one of those times
was a full interview. Most of you have read my 302 on that
session. Many of us have had cases where the suspect committed a crime in an enraged state—one associated with
psychopathology, psychotic acts, mania, borderline personality disorder, bipolar disorder, and many other serious mental
illness diagnoses. In those cases, there was always an assessment about how and whether the defendant appreciated the
consequences of his act, or was able to control his behavior
at the time of the crime. Those essential consequences were
often assessed by court-appointed psychiatrists. Why can't
this case be handled like those?"

Someone who didn't raise his hand snorted and said,
"Yeah what about the red duct tape? The guy knew enough
to pick a weird color to wrap the vic to her desk. Sounds
borderline crazy to me."

Dr. Estancia brought the discussion to an end.

"This case will continue to challenge the prosecution.
But it will also challenge the defense. That lawyer will have
to engage his client at a very different level. My guess is
long before any court tries Mr. Manchester, many doctors
and other experts will chime in. They will collectively or
individually seek answers to the fundamental pretrial issue.
Who has been arrested, if anyone? Is it the man called Vince

Manchester? Is he in the jurisdiction? Or is it a woman named Vivian, whose whereabouts are unknown? And of course, if Vince is an alter of Vivian, the host, who will the doctors examine? Who will the interrogators question? Who will the court try, with or without a jury? Actually, I think those questions are surface issues. The controlling issue will be whether there is anything intrinsic to the psychopathology of dissociative disorders that might diminish criminal responsibility. And as far as I can tell, no neuroscientist, or judge, has tackled the challenge at that level."

And with that, the conference ended with no clear understanding of the question, let alone an answer to it.

CHAPTER 7

On Wednesday morning, the $25,000 wire transfer from Vince cleared the Wells Fargo Bank trust account for the law firm of Danders & Associates an hour after the GoToMeeting went offline. Once Travis logged on and saw the clearance, he called Vince. Like before, the call was answered and immediately went to dial tone. A minute later, Vince called back.

"Yo, lawyer dude. Just saw you got the money. Now we can talk and you got to keep it all secret, right?"

"Good morning, Mr. Manchester. Yes, that's why I called you—the money cleared in our trust account a few minutes ago and . . ."

"A few minutes? Nah, that ain't right. It cleared in your account at oh seven ten this morning. That's two hours ago. You must not of got in that early. You just checked a few secs before you called me. Don't matter, I checked it for you. The money's there."

"I'm sorry, did you just say you accessed my bank account? Did I hear you right?"

"Ain't no big thing, man. But you ever want that kind of data search, you let me know. I'll give you a discount on account of our professional relationship. Be good for both of us. But, man, I got questions to ask now we're under fee contract. So my first question is . . ."

Travis interrupted, "Wait a second. I think we need to do this in person. I can clear my afternoon calendar for you. Will that work for you?"

"No it won't. Lemme tell you why. Did you tell the prosecutor over at the Wells Fargo Bank Plaza building that you were representing me? I mean it's alright, that's what I wanted you to do. But confirm it for me—you told them we were lawyer and client, right?"

"Yes, of course."

"So, that's the question. They can arrest me if they find me, right?"

"Yes. The file is under seal, so I cannot tell you whether there were any limits on the arrest warrant they must have secured, but you are subject to arrest."

"And they want you to surrender my ass to the feds first, right? You already told me that day before yesterday. So that's why I'm asking now. If I'm subject to arrest, I don't want it to be when you ain't present, by my side when they take me to the booking line. Know what I'm saying? Shit man, they're probably watching your office door right now, waiting for me to show so they can clap those shiny bracelets on my skinny wrists."

"No, Vince. I don't think they'd do that. But they want me to surrender you. That's normal."

"Well, I ain't doing that."

"Vince, you must understand that there is most likely an arrest warrant out for you."

"Don't matter. I don't give a shit about the federal case—it's just about money, right? The state case is about robbing, whacking Julia Baby, kidnapping her, duct taping her skinny ass to her desk. Shit, they probably added on more counts just because I used red duct tape and scared the shit out of her. Anyhow, the state cannot make that case against me without her testimony, right? She has to be there in court testifying against me, or I win, right?"

"Vince, I have not seen the federal indictment—it's under seal. So I could not begin to advise you on your chances in federal court. I have read the Harris County charges, but that case was dismissed. They would file a new one on you, if they arrest you. Or if the federal authorities do. Same thing for state court—no advice till I see the actual charges."

"Hey, Mr. Danders. I know you. I know your record. I know you are a courtroom warrior. Don't be a dick. I ain't your regular don't-know-shit client. I know what they got. I know what they don't have. The feds might make their case without Julia, but I promise you, the state case goes in the shitter if Julia Baby does not testify. And she ain't going to."

"How could you know that? Have you talked to her?"

"Not lately. But that don't matter. She's got the US Marshals protecting her in the federal case. But all she's got in the state case is the corrupt-as-hell Sheriff's Office. Those boys from the Sinaloa Cartel will blow out the sheriff's candle if she shows up in a state court for any reason. They got her lined out, man. Don't you know that?"

"Vince, this conversation is not helpful. I need to meet with you in person."

"One more question, and then I got an idea about meeting you—not at your office, though. The question is, how do we protect Vivian? She didn't do nothing to Julia personally. There is no state case against her."

Travis had no answers for Vince. He agreed to meet with him, but not in his law office. Vince told him he'd make arrangements. The next morning, a Lyft driver delivered a stiff envelope to his office. It held a round-trip airplane ticket on Friday from Houston to San Antonio. It was a one-hour trip. A handwritten note said, "See you once you get through security at the San Antone airport. Wear a white baseball hat, backwards. And sunglasses. You'll be back in Houston by lunch. Vince." He noticed the return trip from San Antonio back to Houston was set for two hours and fifty minutes after he arrived. Not much time to meet a new client with state *and* federal charges against him, he thought.

CHAPTER 8

Julia Santerra-Evans kept a close watch on everything that happened in Houston regarding her former client, Plankton Resources, and its international money laundering operation. She'd spent seven long months in Houston under the watchful eyes of the US Marshal's witness protection agents in Houston while the FBI drained her of everything she knew about Plankton and its connections to the Sinaloa Cartel. For a short two weeks, they loaned her to the Texas prosecutors probing her kidnapping and assault by Vince. During every free second, in the halfway facility in Bellaire, a suburb of Houston, she ground her teeth and pressed down on her stomach to keep the bile from coming up. Every time she thought about what Vince had done to her, she remembered that great block of ice in her belly. It kept freezing her intestines and her throat, and sent surges of ice shards into her veins.

She'd find him someday, she promised herself repeatedly. And she'd skin him alive and duct tape his intestines to his stomach and his stomach to his throat and watch him howl. God, how she looked forward to that. She dreamt about that hideous red duct tape. She was a lawyer, but long before that she'd been a *soldado* for the Sinaloa Cartel. She'd been cut, beaten, and raped while she worked her way up in the cartel. She killed a man by slitting his throat to earn her soldado rank. All that she'd been through paled in her mind to what Vince had done.

It wasn't just the beating, the theft of her money, or even her forced confession. The three years she'd spent in her native Mexico, soldering for Mexico's biggest drug and arms cartel, made her immune to beatings, or losing money. She could even live with the fact that Vince had turned her into a snitch for the US government. It was the *indignity* of being strapped to her desk chair with red duct tape. She hated when the FBI stormed into her office and photographed her before cutting the duct tape off. That was seared into her memory. She spent most of her free time digging, searching, planning for the day she'd find him. She fanaticized about black duct tape—fifty yards of it. She dreamed of duct taping his balls to his penis and stretching them up to his face where she would force him to look at how hideous he was. And she wanted him to know how painful duct tape could be.

Now her sources in Baytown had paid off. When she ditched the US Marshal's Office three months ago, she bought a burner phone, with a cell number forwarded through servers all over the world. She'd given the number and a hundred-dollar bill to seven well-placed people in south Texas. It was simple. Call me. Leave me a message. She wanted to know the second any of them learn anything about Plankton Resources in federal court, or the state court case against Vince Manchester for duct taping her to her own desk.

"Julia," the croaky voice of the constable at the Baytown Justice of the Peace's office said on her voicemail, "I got some news for you. The Harris County District Attorney's Office thinks that guy, you said his name was Vince, is somewhere in Houston. They dismissed the case against him, right, almost two years ago. But now they are refiling it. Maybe today. He has a lawyer. You know him. Travis Danders. Remember?"

Julia called back within the hour.

"Jesus, are you sure?" Julia said.

She was using her burner cell, the one she'd acquired via UPS from Belgium. It was an unlocked phone, good anywhere in the world, and untraceable. She kept it in a locked strong box, along with two handguns, ammunition, and cash in dollars, euros, and pesos. The strong box was concealed in a hole under one of the large Saltio tiles in her bedroom at her sister's home in Monterrey, Mexico. Jesus Cantron was one of many low-level employees Julia had paid small sums for small favors over the years. He knew little about her, or her case. All he had was the number of the burner phone she'd given him, and that she paid well for little bits of information.

"I'm sure," Jesus said. "I been watching the docket in the Harris County court for that case where you're a witness.

I guess you're a witness. Remember you tole me to watch it for you? I been watching every week and . . ."

"Jesus, shut up and just answer my questions. When did they refile the case?"

"Dunno for sure. But it's refiled. I read the docket in Judge Rockling's court."

"And it's against Vince Manchester for assault, battery, kidnapping, theft, and burglary, right?"

"Dunno how many counts, but they have your name as the victim, and your old Baytown law office as the place of offense, or whatever that name is. You want me to go get a copy from the clerk? I don't think it's sealed or anything."

"No, Jesus, don't get it. Don't do anything more. Just keep your mouth shut about this. I will put a nice gift in your account at the Wells Fargo. You still have that same account, don't you?"

"Yes, I do. And thank you for being always so generous, Julia, and . . ."

Julia hung up. She went back into the house, and spent the afternoon on the Internet looking at lawyer websites in Texas. She found three lawyers, all in small firms, and all with offices somewhere between Brownsville and Houston. One lawyer stood out, but not for the usual reasons that clients pick lawyers. She used the house landline to call Amherst Pipps.

"Mobile Law," a female voice answered, "how can we help ya'll?"

She thought the voiced slithered somewhere between girlish and twittery. Julia always thought you could tell a lot about a lawyer by talking to the people in his office.

"I was just looking at your website, the one where the lawyer's name is Amherst Pipps. Is that you? Is Amherst a girl's name?"

"No, Mr. Pipps is most surely not a girl. He's unavailable at the moment, but I know he'd just love to talk to you. Are you needing a lawyer, or just reaching out to see if Mobile Law can help you? And also . . ."

"What's your name?" Julia asked, in as curt a voice as she could muster.

"Amber Sue is my name, but Mr. Pipps just calls me Orange. I don't know why. Did you say you were needing a lawyer?"

"I didn't say. But say I was. Are you the right person to answer a couple of what I'd call preliminary questions?"

"Yes, ma'am, I surely am, long as you don't ask me for legal advice. Mr. Pipps has a rule against that."

"What are his other rules? Is it a long list? Does he expect to get paid, or is he a pro-bono lawyer, at least sometimes? And how come there isn't an office address on your website?"

"Well, aren't you the one? You will like Mr. Pipps, he has a sense of humor like yours, I'd say. One of his other rules is I don't talk fees with clients. And he does pro-bono work for people who don't need much 'cept talking on the phone. He does not entertain pro-bono clients here in the Mobile Office; he just talks to them on his cell phone, while we're driving the office somewhere. That's why there's no office address on the website. We don't have one. Mr. Pipps is a cutting-edge lawyer—that's his own words, I swear to that."

"You don't have an office? I thought he was practicing in Corpus Christi. I'm looking at your website right now and there's a big red circle drawn around Corpus Christi. No address, but a big circle."

"No, we don't have an office in a building, like most lawyers. Mr. Pipps owns a really big trailer—well, not a trailer; a humongous RV. It's a 2015 Entegra Coach Cornerstone 45DLQ. He put a picture on the website, there on the right side, down at the bottom. Can you see on your computer?"

"Oh, yes. I saw it before, but I had no idea it was his office. Is that his only office?"

"Well, can I ask your name first? Mr. Pipps likes me to make notes."

"My name is Julia, and I am looking for a lawyer. I never heard of a mobile law office before. It looks like it cost a fortune. Is Mr. Pipps an expensive lawyer?"

"Nice to know you, Julia. I don't know what our Mobile Office costs. But my boss says it's less than the fourth floor two-room office he used to have in Corpus Christi. Course, it's also his home. He lives in it, and we have a driver for trips over fifty miles. He meets clients here at all hours of the day and night from Houston to Brownsville. That's our legal territory, he says. People like it—he tells them he makes house calls in his house. He drives his house to your house, so ya'll can meet in PJ's or whatever. That's what he says anyway, but I don't know about the PJ's. You'll just love the way Mr. Pipps talks."

"Well, that's new to the game, I'll give him that. I live in Brownsville. Can he come down here tomorrow?"

"Tomorrow? Let me look at his calendar while we're talking. He'll want to know can you pay his nonrefundable retainer of $1,000. Oh, now that I'm looking, I can say yes. We can come to Brownsville tomorrow morning. Well, actually, his driver, Jingle, will drive him down there tonight. He will sleep all the way and be fresh for you tomorrow morning. About ten a.m., will that do? And he'd like the retainer in cash at the start of the meeting. OK with you?"

Julia said yes to both questions and told Amber Sue to have Jingle park Pipps's Mobile Law Office at the south end of the parking lot in front of the Gladys Porter Zoo. Amber Sue, using her big girl voice, assured her Jingle could find anything in any town, even a zoo. Then Julia called her driver, who would be able to spot Jingle and the big RV from a hundred yards off. She told him they needed to leave Monterrey at five-thirty the next morning. The trip from Corpus Christi to Brownsville was about two and a half hours. The one from Monterrey, Mexico, to Brownsville would be three and a half hours. She'd make him wait a little while she watched the big motor home with her binoculars from across the little pond at the north end of the Gladys Porter Zoo. She liked watching the alligator pond there.

CHAPTER 9

The Harris County District Attorney's Office is one of the largest in America. With over three hundred prosecutors, almost ninety investigators, and a support staff of well over two hundred, it enjoys a national reputation for evidence-based prosecution. Its website bolstered that reputation, proudly acclaiming "a fair process with the goal of obtaining a just result for the victim, the accused, and the community in every case." That promise was about to be tested in the refiled case against Vince Manchester. The lead prosecutor on the case, Grant Lumberson, was old school, tough as a boot, and spoke his mind on every subject. While some thought him a little uncouth, no one underrated his courtroom ability. His boss knew she could trust him to do what he constantly preached to young lawyers in the office: "If the bastard did it, get him tried, locked up, and out of my hair." He was not always friendly, was proud of his vice-grip handshake, and bald as a cue ball.

Lumberson's trial team had four members. They worked together on the forty-plus cases he was in charge of for the major crimes unit. The Manchester case, which they nicknamed the red-duct tape caper, was far from his most important case, but it was about to become the most challenging case he'd ever had. Cecelia Apindia was his second chair. She was twenty-nine years old and favored cowgirl boots in the office, during trial, and on her weekend ranch seventy miles north of Houston. Curley Docs, the trial document technician, had a real last name, but no one in the office used it. He was in his forties, avoided small talk, and had been with the office for nineteen years. He ate lunch alone, in the employee diner, out of a reusable paper bag. He was fastidious about files; he knew exactly where every legal document, exhibit, case file, and extraneous piece of evidence in every case he managed was, at all times. The paralegal on the team, L. D. Podski, was only twenty-three, but no one who'd ever worked with her doubted her competitiveness. She came to the office after dropping out of college half-way through her junior year. She had little money, didn't seem to care about it, had no family, but seemed content, and knocked down every fence she was told to jump. While not permanent, Lumberson's trial team also included a summer extern, a second-year law student from the University of Houston. He questioned everything. The team nicknamed him "Why."

The team had been sitting at the oblong table in war room 2013 on the fifth floor of the office when Lumberson walked in, fifteen minutes late.

"Sorry you had to wait, guys, that horseshit defense lawyer on the 416 gang rape case got his ass handed to him in Judge Bartling's court. Took a while. Goddamn, it's good to see a grown man cower once in a while. So, here's what I want to do for the next hour. It's brain picking time, ya'll. We filed this case more 'n two years ago, dismissed it at the request of the US Attorney's Office, and refiled it day before yesterday. On the surface it's a straight-laced B&E into a shitty lawyer's office in Baytown, with multiple charges of breaking into a commercial office, assault, battery, kidnapping, wrongful imprisonment, theft, robbery, and some financial crimes for throwaways when it comes time to plead out. There's a short-bed pickup load of hard evidence, lots of video evidence, but no prints or DNA. Big point is, we got an untrustworthy victim, named Julia Santerra-Evans . . ."

Why, the law school summer extern, interrupted Lumberson. "Sorry to interrupt, Mr. Lumberson, but I don't understand. The victim is *untrustworthy*? What do you mean? Why is she untrustworthy?"

"It's Grant. That's my name. My kids call me mister, but just to rile me up. We been calling you 'Why' because you ask good questions. And son, you asked the whopper question for this whole damn case. It's one we got to jawbone and then cook up an answer for. I think Cecelia is the best one to answer that question. And, L.D., feel free to jump in here. You know the case file better 'n any of us at this point. Cecelia, would you mind taking notes on your laptop and feedin' 'em into the case file? The boss lady is gonna want to know about this issue—trustworthiness is gonna get a whole new name as we crank this case up the trail towards trial."

"Sure, boss," Cecelia answered, flipping her three-ring binder open and scanning the index. "Grant and I presented this case to the state grand jury just a little over two years ago. It was a straight up Article 21.01 indictment, against Vince Manchester, whose whereabouts were unknown when we filed. We had arrest warrants issued, but did not make an active search for the defendant, a white male known as Vince Manchester."

"Why not?" Why asked.

"Why, you are gonna have a pile of questions about the whys, why nots, whens, and wheres of this case," said Cecelia. "If you don't mind, just hold some of 'em till I finish this sketch for everyone's refreshment. We got arrest warrants from court as soon as we handed up the indictment from the grand jury, but the victim, the Baytown lawyer, was in the gentle hands of the FBI, the US Attorney's Office, the US Marshal's Office, and God-only-knows how many other federal agencies. She was first arrested at her office, a few hours after Vince Manchester broke into her office, beat her up, stole her money, threatened to kill her, forced her to commit a number of federal wire-tap crimes, and then made her confess to numerous and sundry crimes in three states and one or two foreign countries. All of that is summarized and documented in the file. You can read all of it later. We didn't get access to her for three days. When we did, we had her down in our minds both as a victim of many crimes, a perpetrator of many crimes, a protected US federal witness, and a cooperating witness in cases we knew little or nothing about. We never had a chance to deal with much of that because the feds asked us to hold off on our prosecution while they squeezed her dry of the many federal crimes they were investigating involving money laundering, wire fraud, and murders in at least three different jurisdictions. So we dismissed our case and waited for the feds to return the vic back to us. That never happened. She gave them tons of information and then slithered away. She was both victim and villain, so we had to treat her as on our side, and as a federal defendant in crimes far more serious than the ones committed by this Vince guy against her. He hated her. We didn't understand her. We didn't know diddly about him. I could go on and on, boss, but is this sketch enough to get to our problem now?"

"Yeah, that's the back story," said Lumberson. "I want everybody to know that Julia Santerra-Evans is a victim and entitled to the full range of information and assistance she asks for under Article 56.02 of the Texas Criminal Code. I also want you to know we cannot present a triable case in court against Vince Manchester without her personal involvement and her in-court live testimony at trial. So, for openers, who can tell me what kind of a crappy conundrum this is? Anybody?"

To no one's surprise, Why raised his hand.

"Mr. Lumberson, I had a clinic case last spring at the law school where the crime victim was ignored by the prosecutor, who got into a lot of trouble with the judge. So, I guess the conundrum you have is if you give her all her victim's rights, but she doesn't want to cooperate, and we don't even know where she is, how do we even start processing the case?"

"No, that ain't it," Lumberson answered. "We can start processing the case, but we can't take it to trial. Our conundrum is twofold. One, do we treat her as a vic or as a perp? Two, what about the defendant? Who is he? And is he culpable and legally responsible for the crimes we've charged him with? What if there's something really weird about the perp? Is the vic entitled to know that? The victim's rights law is pretty damn strong. Vics are entitled to be represented by their own lawyer. And we are obligated to keep them informed, I mean both the vic and her lawyer, about all court proceedings, cancellations, and rescheduling. As long as we don't know where she is, we don't have any vic rights problems. But if she surfaces, the feds will want her first, and we may not be able to process our case in a timely fashion. The perp defendant is entitled to a speedy trial, but most guilty defendants are in no hurry to go to prison, so they don't care how long it takes before we try a case. Jails are nicer than prisons, ya'll know that, right?"

Lumberson quit talking to twist the top off a bottle of water. Cecelia, turning her head toward him, said, "Whoa horse, what do you mean, something might be weird about the perp? You mean Vince Manchester, right? He's essentially confessed what he did to the vic, on audio and video tape. I know that's not enough, but what do you mean weird? Is he a nut case?"

Her boss screwed the top back on the water bottle, pushed his glasses up, and spent the next fifteen minutes giving them a summary of what he'd learned at the video conference with the feds and their psychiatric expert, Dr. Ahmed Estancia. At the end, he asked if anyone had heard of dissociative identity disorder.

The first to speak up was L. D. Podski, the paralegal. "Like Sybil? Is that what you're talking about? I read the book in a psych class and our goofy prof even found an old copy of the movie. Back in the seventies, right? The one he found was on DVD, which I don't think was even invented that far back. We watched bits of it in class. I borrowed it from him and watched the whole thing. Twice, even. Holy moley, it was great! I like old movies. It had Sally Field and Joanne Woodward, you know. Great actresses. And Sybil, who was real, had a horrific childhood, and she invented a bunch of other people in her head to help her cope. I think she had three different people living in her head."

"No," Lumberson said, "not like Sybil. I don't know the medical part, but the doc that the feds are relying on is a psychiatrist here, on the faculty at Rice. He's also a lawyer. We sparred a little during his lecture, but I've done some reading since. I think he's got the medical part right, but the law part bass ackwards."

"How so?" L.D. asked.

"Well, for starters, he turns upside down the law of culpability. He talks a lot about not accusing one identity of, or trying one identity for, something another identity did. In the case of Sybil, which I looked up on Wikipedia after that meeting, I found out that her docs identified her with sixteen different personalities. And they implied that one personality had no idea what the other one was doing. Dr. Estancia shuts down prosecution on that basis. But the Texas statute is what we go by, not movies or medical theories about disorders or disturbed people. I don't trust those Wikipedia pages since anyone can write what they want. The Texas Penal Code has it in black and white. Section 6.03 pins it down. L.D., pull it up on your laptop, will you? It's code title 2 of the Texas Statutes & Codes Annotated, Chapter 6, Principles of Criminal Responsibility. Read Section 6.03 about defining culpable mental stress, out loud, please."

L.D. clicked away for a minute, then took her fingers off the keys. Rubbing her chin nervously, she read aloud. "Paragraph A. A person acts intentionally, or with intent, with respect to the nature of his conduct or to a result of his conduct when it is his conscious objective or desire to engage in the conduct or cause the result. Paragraph B. A person acts knowingly, or with knowledge, with respect to the nature of his conduct or to circumstances surrounding his conduct when he is aware of the nature of his conduct or that the circumstances exist. A person acts knowingly, or with knowledge, with respect to a result of his conduct when he is aware that his conduct is reasonably certain to cause the result. Paragraph C. A person acts recklessly, or is reckless, with respect to circumstances surrounding his conduct or the result of his conduct when he is aware of but consciously disregards a substantial and unjustifiable risk that the circumstances exist or the result will occur. The risk must be of such a nature and degree that its disregard constitutes a gross deviation from the standard of care that an ordinary person would exercise under all the circumstances as viewed from the actor's standpoint. Paragraph D . . ."

"Hold up, L.D. Let's circle back to paragraph D in a minute. It deals with criminal negligence. Let's all be clear that Texas law applies to a *person* not a personality. It's only applicable to persons who act intentionally. And that is further defined as acting with a conscious objective. Under the law, intentional acts must be knowing acts. And section 603 covers that too. It defines knowing as when the perp is aware his conduct is reasonably certain to cause the result he intends. We don't need to cover the reckless section or criminal negligence. The point here is whether the defendant we've charged is a person who acted consciously, and knowingly. The Vince we're talking about is that intentionally acting, knowing person who broke in, beat up, knocked down, tied up with duct tape, and stole money. What the shrink the feds hired, Dr. Ahmed Estancia, focuses on is *not* Vince, but Vivian. He says Vivian is a host identity and that Vince is an alter identity. I challenged him, saying that they are one and the same person, and there's no way to charge one and let the other one go. Lemme hear what you think about this."

Cecelia looked baffled. Her mind raced and she felt a tightening in her chest.

"Boss, maybe I'm just a simple cowgirl, but I know the difference between a mare and a stallion. Sounds to me like we have a solid case against a stallion, but a defense verdict if a mare shows up at trial. It won't make any difference at the charging stage. We've charged a male with serious crimes. We're being told by a shrink that the quote *host* unquote identity is a female. Same doc, probably smarter 'n hell, says the quote *alter* unquote identity is a male. And we're told that other cops, FBI agents, and maybe lawyers have talked to both the male *and* the female, not knowing they were the same person. We know the male committed crimes because we can watch it on video. But we have no video of the female. She presumably can't be seen if the male is "out" or "present" or whatever 'n hell happens when they shift identities. I'll dig into LexisNexis and see what I can find."

Lumberson slumped further back into his swivel chair.

"Cecelia," he said, "there's one other thing giving me a gut ache about this case. You mentioning stallions and mares reminds me about this other goddamn thing—the vic and the perp. One's a mare and the other's a stallion. Right? But I ain't all that goddamned sure which is which."

She looked at him with a tight grin.

"The hell you say, Grant. Jesus Christ almighty, if you've forgotten the difference, then you have not been spending enough time in the pasture, behind that big barn out at your little ranchero. The difference's obvious."

"I'm not talking about the difference in identity—between the gal named Vivian and the man named Vince. I'm thinking about the difference between the victim of the crime we're prosecuting and the perpetrator of that crime. Ya'll know Julia has a history—a bloody one—the FBI thinks she's a highly paid assassin for the Sinaloa Cartel. Vince has no history—maybe he doesn't even exist, in the sense that he might be an alter for a woman who does. Here's the thing—which one is the victim and which is the perp? I mean this Julia woman—one day she's killing for a living—the next she's tied to her desk by a man who might not exist. So, who's the vic and who's the perp? We need to know a lot more about this Julia before we base our whole goddamned case on her veracity. If she don't show up, we don't have a case—and that might not be a bad thing."

CHAPTER 10

Julia Santerra-Evans and her three-hun-dred-pound passenger, Chaco Hernandez, had taken the same American Airlines flight from Houston to Boise—she in first class, him in coach. They got off separately. She went to rent a car. He walked outside and waited for her to pick him up in the arrivals lane. They spent the next several hours driving round all the RV Parks within a twenty-five-mile circle around the small city. It was inside that circle that Leopoldo Santos, head of the Sinaloa Cartel, had said they'd find a blue Winnebago RV with their target, Stephan Manchester. He'd been clear about how this was to be done. Julia was to drive and find the target. Chaco was to kill the target in a way that would send a clear message to the FBI: we don't just kill—we destroy.

They'd found several dozen fairly new Winnebagos, but only three were baby blue, and only one of had Arizona plates. It had to be the right one, but Julia had an Arizona

MVD picture of Stephan Manchester, so they could make sure before Chaco would nearly cut the man's head off.

The Quinn's Pond RV park didn't have a park manager. But the first space in the little park held a silver Airstream, which had a small garden between it and a Ford 150. A hefty woman in sweat pants answered Julia's polite knock on her door. She said the owner of the blue Winnebago with Arizona plates hadn't seemed to have been living in it for the last few weeks, but had been coming by at least once a week to check on it. She said the park manager ran two parks and lived in the other one, across the pond—a ten-mile round trip.

Julia found a playground with a hot-dog stand about two hundred yards away. With binoculars, which she always had in her backpack, she had a close-up view of the Winnie from the playground parking lot. She'd told Chaco to stay at one of the tables and she'd watch from fifty feet further back. It took three hours of patient watching before they got lucky.

Finally, a white pickup truck with a ladder rack on top stopped alongside the Winnie. A tall man got out, fished around in the bed of his truck for something, and then walked to the RV door, opened it with a key, and went inside.

Chaco ran to the Jeep.

"Is it him?"

"Can't say," Julia answered. "I only saw him from the front at first, then by the time I got the binocs on him, his back was to me. So, here's the plan, Chaco. We will drive over there very slowly. The road is straight, so if he comes out, we'll see him. You sit up front now. Don't do anything till I tell you."

Julia started the Jeep, put it in first, and moved forward as slowly as she could. A truck pulled up behind them and honked. So she pulled over almost into the bar ditch. Now they were only about fifty yards away. There were trees on both sides of the road, but from where they were stopped nothing blocked their view of the Winnie and the surrounding RV park.

"You get out, Chaco. Leave your backpack here. Walk over there, but stay in the trees along this side of the road. I think you can see from in there everything I can see from here. If he comes out, I'll see him through the binocs. If it's him, I'll switch my headlights from bright to dim and back and forth. If you don't see my headlights switching up from bright to dim, back and forth, it means it's *not* him. You got that! No headlights, it's *not* him. But if you see them, then you go. Do him! I'll watch from here. Then, you make sure he's dead; I mean *sure* because you take his fucking pulse, right? Then you just come out and walk toward me. I'll pick you up between here and there. Got it, Chaco? Do you have any questions?"

He didn't even look at her. He shucked the backpack, felt in his right front cargo pants pocket for his wire, and got out without a word. He walked into the edge of the tree line. She could see him making his way toward the Winnie. He stopped about thirty yards away. Chaco was in his silent zone. She trained the 8x lens, slightly adjusted the focus, and panned back from Chaco in the dark trees to the baby-blue Winnie in bright sunlight. She couldn't see his neck from this far away, but she knew those huge veins were pumping, and that he was wrenching his hands into fists and grips. She knew too that he was controlling his breath, easy in, and with pursed lips, easy out. Very slow. Getting ready.

Seven minutes later, the RV door opened. She had the binocs up in both hands and the MVD photo of Stephan Manchester between her teeth. She focused immediately on the man as he stood in the Winnie's doorway, eighteen inches off the ground. Lowering the binocs without taking her eyes off the man, she picked the photo out of her mouth and held it at elbow's length in front of her. It was him! Slowly, not wanting to lose her line of sight to him, she used her left hand to reach for the headlight switch on the dash. Looking down for a fraction of a second, she turned the headlights on and pumped the floor switch, turning the brights up and down.

The man stepped down from the Winnie and walked to the back of his truck. Lowering the tailgate, he climbed up into the back and unstrapped the twelve-foot orange aluminum ladder. He'd just got one strap loose when Chaco, running at a surprisingly fast pace, reached the truck. She hadn't seen Chaco move. But suddenly, there he was, jogging toward the back of the man's truck. Putting his hands on the lowered truck gate, he vaulted up into the back of the truck. Just as he did, Julia saw and heard another loud truck. It pulled up alongside the man lifting the ladder off its rack, and Chaco starting to swing his garrote wire.

Chaco, seemingly oblivious to the other truck, stretched his twenty-four-inch-long strand of wire, holding firm onto the half-inch bolts that slotted the killing tool on either end. He looped the wire from behind, over the top of the man's head, and jerked back. The hapless man tried to scream, trying desperately to get his fingers under the wire and away from his neck. But Chaco extended his elbows out to both sides, compressing the man backward into his own chest. As they stumbled backward together, Chaco leaned back and lifted the smaller man up off his feet and into Chaco's massive chest. As though it was a giant defensive tackle wrapping his arms around the opposing quarterback, the two jostled and bobbed backward toward the open tailgate.

Two men jumped out of the other truck, hollering incoherently. Julia sat, transfixed by the sight of the four men converging at the rear of the white pickup. Chaco ignored the men screaming up at him from the side of the truck and kept sawing into his captive's neck. The wire had flushed down into the helpless man's throat, shredding skin and bone while gushing streams of blood spewed out and backward onto Chaco as he sawed furiously back and forth across a now disappearing Adam's apple.

The smaller of the two men who had jumped out of the other truck appeared to reach for something behind him in his cameo waist pack. The other man tried to grab Chaco's leg from the side of the truck. Chaco kept his backward pressure as he and the man in his steel grasp stumbled backward toward the tailgate. Chaco sawed the wire back and forth from right to left, as the man's throat ruptured and black blood flew up and out onto them all. Much of it spewed over the side of the truck onto the two on the ground.

Although it took less than a minute, it seemed like much longer when Chaco and the man inside the wire noose lurched backward, flying backward off the tailgate. Chaco landed on his back, with the other man splayed on top of him like a bloody sleeping bag. Chaco roared like a wounded bear as he kept sawing through the other man's skin, muscle, ligaments, and eventually bone.

The passenger in the truck reached the now blood-soaked pile on the dirt just behind the tailgate. Shouting unintelligibly, he pulled a heavy revolver from his waist pack and fired three shots into Chaco's head. Other people, hearing the shots, ran to the bloody scene. Three men were in the dirt. One man was nearly decapitated. Another one, lying under the first, had his head almost blown off. The third, the driver of the second pickup truck, was on his knees, vainly trying to separate the bodies. The man with the revolver flipped open the chamber, ejected the remaining rounds into the bed, and laid his gun on the tailgate. Reaching into the rear pocket of his Levis, he flipped his phone open, and dialed 911.

No one noticed the brown jeep with the gray top start up, make an orderly U-turn, and head west, toward the airport. Julia drove slowly. When she got to the pavement, she turned toward town and passed by the brown and white sheriff's SUV with its top rack flashing red and its siren screaming. No one in Idaho ever saw her again.

CHAPTER 11

Travis Danders landed at San Antonio International Airport, with that sinking feeling lawyers get when they are about to cross a big red line. At the core of every lawyer's practice is the strict rule against helping clients evade the law, or allowing them to use their legal advice to commit a crime. He'd spent the fifty minutes in the air mentally tabulating a pro/con list in his head about representing Vince Manchester. On the pro side it could be a sizeable fee and he liked the legal challenge the case presented—two high-profile trials involving big legal issues. On the con side was the slightly nauseating feeling he was being used, maybe tiptoeing into a bar discipline case. He kept telling himself all the way that he could always quit, return the retainer, and apologize to Nancy Lee. The more he played *what if* in his head, the more anxious he became. He'd ordered a Coke and a can of Pringles on the plane, but only drank half the Coke and left the Pringles in the expandable pouch in the seat in front of him.

Once he got off the plane at Gate 8A, he headed for the security exit. Twenty feet before he reached the turnstiles and the security gate, he stopped, put on his sunglasses, and fished the Houston Astros baseball cap out of his briefcase. As instructed, he put it on backwards, feeling stupid and debating whether he should just tell Vince to get another lawyer right there in the terminal lobby. He'd never worn a ball cap backwards. He stopped on the other side of the security gate and looked for his client, knowing that was even dumber than wearing the ball cap backward. I've never seen the guy, he reminded himself. He walked toward the information booth and told the lady with the thick glasses and ruby red lips his name.

"Nice to meet you, Mr. Danders, what can I help you with?"

"Well, I was just wondering whether anyone left a message for me here?"

"Message? No, I don't think so. I came on at eight and there was nothing here with that name on it. Danders, right? That's an unusual name. But no one has left anything for you here, maybe you should go to the second-floor business office and . . ."

She was interrupted when a young black man, wearing a white baseball cap backwards, tapped Travis on the arm and asked if he was the lawyer from Houston.

"I'm a lawyer, yes, and I'm from Houston. Are you Vince?"

"No, my name is Joe. Just plain Joe. Are you looking for a client to talk about a case?"

"Yes."

"Oᴋ," Joe said. "Come on with me. A young boy told me to come here and meet all the planes landing for the last forty-five minutes. Said I would spot you with your cap backwards, a frown on your face, and a brief case. You fit. I'm a Lyft driver. The man that sent me is waiting for you in Room 242 at the Embassy Suites hotel. It's zero point six miles from here. Fares all paid. Both ways."

After Joe dropped him off at the entrance to the Embassy Suites, Travis went to the front desk and told the clerk he was there to meet a man named Vince Manchester, but he'd forgotten the room number. The clerk said he could not give the names of guests out. So Travis asked where Room 242 was.

"Half way down the hall to your left," the clerk said.

"Isn't Room 242 on the second floor?" Travis asked.

"No, all the rooms starting with two are on this floor. Crazy, right? We don't have any rooms starting with one."

He walked down the five-foot-wide hallway and stopped at Room 242. The inside door latch was flipped open, keeping the door ajar. He pushed the door open and walked in. The TV was on, and one of the twin beds was unmade. Realizing the room was empty, he'd turned around and started for the door when the bathroom door opened and a tall, smooth-faced young man stepped out.

"Travis, you look just like your bar photo, but the one I like best of you is the one on the cover of *Attorney at Law* magazine. Two years ago, right? Definitely a pro photo shoot for that one, right? Have a seat, we got business to talk, don't we?"

As Travis would come to know, the confident young man standing before him asked more questions than he gave answers. He stuck his hand out, but his elusive client ignored it and walked past him to the desk by the window. He took the outside seat and pointed to the business chair pushed into the desk. Travis took it, and laid the thin aluminum brief case on the desk.

"Mr. Manchester, it's nice to meet you. It's also nice to know you did an Internet search for me. Don't take this wrong, but my Internet search for you was a blank. No social media, no mention of you anywhere. I am glad you're not a ghost."

"Don't be so sure, Lawyer Man, I could be a ghost, or maybe a host. But here's the thing I want to talk about, now that you're my full lawyer. What we say stays between us—I don't tell on you and you keep my business to yourself."

As Travis eased back into the standard hotel swivel chair, he took care to adjust the back swivel, smile at his client, and open his brief case. This guy is some piece of work, he thought as he arrayed his legal pad, two roller ball pens, and two business cards on the desk in front of him. I have to create a professional relationship right now, or this young man will be impossible to defend.

"Let's start with you calling me Travis and I'll call you Vince. There are a half-dozen important things to talk about in the next ninety minutes. Maybe the attorney-client privilege is the most important, like you say. What you tell me is covered by the privilege. But there are two rare exceptions to that rule. First, if a client gives perjured testimony to a court, the lawyer must take action to remedy that because no lawyer can suborn perjury in court, even if it is his client. Second, . . ."

Vince pushed his chair backward into the blinds covering the window that looked out onto the hotel's enclosed garden. He grabbed the plastic water bottle from the desk, tore off the paper tag, twisted off the top, and gulped the water down, spilling some of it out the sides of his mouth onto his brown T-shirt.

"Well, that's a weak-ass start to our attorney-client relationship, Travis. You say we're on a first-name basis and then you say I'm gonna lie in court. Well you can forget about that, Lawyer Man. There ain't gonna to be no trial. I won't be testifying to the truth or lying my ass off neither. So you can forget about your exceptions to the don't-ask, don't-tell rule you lawyers got. So, what's the second exception to our *c o n f i d e n t i a l* relationship. Let's get that one the fuck out of the way too, so we can talk."

"Vince, I didn't say I thought you would perjure yourself. I was speaking hypothetically."

"Yeah, well I ain't a hypothetical client, even if others are telling you different. You been asking around about me; I know that for a goddamn fact. What's the other exception?"

"The other is that I owe a duty of candor to the court. Sometimes, clients see that as a conflict. But it's not. All defendants in criminal cases are presumed under the law to be innocent. That puts the prosecutor under a heavy burden. They have to prove guilt beyond a reasonable doubt and my job is to put the prosecution to its proof at every step of the trial. So, . . ."

"Travis, Travis, I'm glad you told me to call you by your first name because we're starting to have a problem, you and me. I don't think you're listening to me as close as you should be. I'm gonna say it one more time. There ain't gonna be no goddamn trial, so you don't need to be wasting my time or yours on hypothetical shit. I know about the presumption of innocence and the big-ass burden on your friend Nancy Lee Sustern. But I got questions to ask and neither one of your exceptions to representing me are real, so can we talk about what I want? Then you can tell me whether you can deliver the goods or not."

Vince sat back down, but his eyes narrowed, and he licked his lips. While Travis had no way of knowing it, his new client's blood pressure went up as his heartbeat grew loud in his ears.

"OK, Vince, I get that you are good at scanning for the law on the Internet. Let's get something straight right now. I went to a much better law school than your lawyer Google did. The Internet is a rabbit hole for unrepresented clients to fall down into. You are paying me a handsome fee because I know way more than you ever will about criminal prosecution in federal court. You need to listen to me on legal issues. You can reject my advice, but you do so at great risk. Let's talk about what happens long before the trial you say is not going to happen. Let's talk about pretrial services."

"What's pretrial services? You mean like finding witnesses and talking to them?"

"No, Vince. That's true on our side of the case. But the pretrial services I'm talking about are on the federal government side of the securities and money laundering case. When you're arrested by the FBI, they will take you to a federal jail facility, and then immediately to a federal magistrate. From there the pretrial services department will talk to you. That's a court employee, not an FBI agent. They will gather information about your background and personal circumstances, and file a report with the judge, prosecutor, and me, as your defense counsel. The report will make recommendations about whether the judge should release you and under what conditions. The pretrial officer will not ask you any questions about the case, only about release issues— like, do you have a job waiting, a place to stay, money for bus fare? But remember this. Be honest. You can refuse to answer any questions, but your answers must be true. Lying to that officer could be used against you at sentencing. If you're convicted. It's a separate crime. And . . ."

Vince couldn't stand it any longer. Jumping up from his chair, he started rubbing his forehead with the back of his hand. His face blanched as he moved out of Travis's space behind the small desk.

"You fucking kidding me? No fuckin' way I'm doing this. I ain't going to no federal jail. It's a men's-only jail, right? They strip you down in those places and hose you for lice, too. That's what I heard. No way man, you got to get me a better deal. I can post as big a bond as they want, but I can't go in no jail."

Travis knew he had to maintain control. He could almost see Vince running down the hallway and as far away from San Antonio as he could. He had to keep Vince here long enough to find out what was really going on. As he'd learned to do with hundreds of guilty clients and a handful of innocent ones, he changed the subject.

"Vince, you're way out in front of me. Please sit back down and answer one simple question. Why did you come to Houston?"

Vince sat down.

"Why? What do you need to know that for? Besides I already tole you that. I'm here because of that note Julia Baby wrote. That's what I asked you to do—take the note to the goddamn feds—find out whether they got the goods on me. Find out where she is. They have to tell you where she's hiding, right? They can't keep her a secret from the defense lawyer, can they? And why ain't they prosecuting her for what she did? That's why I'm here. If they ain't gonna prosecute her, then maybe I'll go back to my first plan for the bitch that murdered my dad."

Travis reached into the brief case and took out a plastic shield containing the note.

"Vince, I brought the note with me. I need to understand what's happening here before we can go further in your case. The first line, which I presume Julia Santerra-Evans wrote in long-hand, says that the name Julia Baby came from you. And that you are someone's brother. Is that person named Vivian? Is that your sister?"

"Man, you're getting me really pissed off. I tole you I ain't talking about Vivian. Remember that? You asked me about third-party money and brought her up. I told you no! We're not talking about her."

"OK, for now. The note says you named Ms. Santerra-Evans, 'Julia Baby.' When did you do that, and what were the circumstances?"

"If I tell you, you got to keep it secret, right?" Vince asked, as his hands dropped to his sides and he leaned forward in the chair.

"Yes, our communications are protected by the attorney-client privilege. I need to know why you're here and the circumstances tied to the note you asked me to give to the US Attorney's Office. I can tell from how excited and anxious you are that it's very important."

"I called her Julia Baby cause I knew she'd hate it. And she'd know why too. She's a killer. She killed my dad, and another man too. A poor slob we didn't even know up in Boise, Idaho. And that note you got right there, all wrapped up in plastic, says she's gonna kill me. And if my sister doesn't help her, then fuckin' whore Julia Baby will kill her."

"So, you think Julian Santerra-Evans is going to kill Vivian, your sister? But you are her primary target, right?"

"Fuckin' A right. You got it there in her own handwriting! She says I destroyed her life. The law is after her. She's got bosses in Mexico and Panama. Those are all killers. And if she don't get me, then she goes after Vivian. That's what it says. So, damn right. I'm here because I ain't going to let her kill Vivian. What the bitch don't know is if she kills me, she kills Vivian. That's fuckin' why I came back to Houston."

"Vince, please listen carefully to me. I'm going to go back to Houston, now. As I told you, the federal indictment against you is under seal. I don't know whether they have a warrant out for you, but they probably do. I know there is no state arrest warrant outstanding. Your issue right now is arrest, not trial. Don't tell me anything else now. Don't call me. I will go back to the federal prosecutor and change the conversation. I will have no further discussion with the state prosecutor. Do not call me again. I will call you. Do you understand what I'm doing?"

"Yeah, think so. You're afraid of breaking the law by harboring a criminal, right? And you don't want me to tell you what I did, for some inside legal reason you don't want to talk about. I get that, too. The cell number I gave you is a pass through, and . . ."

"Vince, I've agreed to represent you. But it has to be on my terms. I'll call you when I figure out what is going in the two cases against you. I will try to help you within the law and within my legal obligations to the court."

He reorganized his brief case, got up out of the chair, and walked out of Room 242 and down the hall to the front desk. He asked the desk clerk to call him a cab, not a Lyft driver. Two hours later, he got back to Houston and sent Nancy Lee a text. "Nancy Lee. Need to see you ASAP. US v. Julia Santerra-Evans, et. al. Your office. Today. Travis."

CHAPTER 12

Brownsville is the county seat of Cameron County, Texas, It's on the Gulf of Mexico and sits just a few miles from what old-timers in Brownsville call Old Mexico. It is Texas's sixteenth largest city and lays claim to being the last landfall on the 1,200-mile-long Rio Grande. The river winds its way through town before emptying millions of gallons of fresh water gathered up in three states into the salty Gulf of Mexico. The town is aptly named; the color of the river water matches almost everything in town nicely. The Gladys Porter Zoo was apt because it housed exotic animals and attracted strangers.

Julia Santerra-Evans's driver had been driving her in and out of Mexico for almost a year, but she never called him by name; she just gave directions and assumed he'd obey. He always did, like the good soldier he was.

"Park, over there," she said, as they drove past the parking lot in front of the zoo, pointing to the north end of the lot.

"Si," he said, nodding to her in his rearview mirror.

Once parked, Julia opened her backpack and removed her brand-new, oversize binoculars. She was still irritated about one of her big dogs knocking her old binocs off the coffee table and cracking one lens. She'd only received the new pair by FedEx shipment three days ago. Like most trained shooters, she was right eyed. And while she was used to telescopes on high-powered sniper rifles, she also knew well how vital the two-step process was in correctly focusing binoculars. She didn't start, like an amateur would, with the focusing wheel in the center of the binocular. It ultimately would focus on the big gaudy RV parked at the south end of the lot. That would focus both barrels on the binocular simultaneously. She started with the adjustment ring, the diopter. That little device adjusted the focus on one barrel independently of the other. That's how trained shooters compensated for differences between their left eye, their shooting eye, and their right eye—the aiming eye. Once done, she started slowly thumbing the focus wheel.

Now focused, she felt a little unnerved at how gaudy, almost obscene, the fifty-foot Cornerstone Entegra looked through the binocs. She had a side-profile view—an elongated sheet metal box with four tandem wheels in back, and two single wheels near the front of the driver's cage. Two slide-outs and a black awning faced her. The discordant paint job was right out of a psychedelic painting. Bathed in brown, blacks, grays, and swatches of a moronic yellow streak, the stupid thing gave her an instant migraine. The entry door featured what appeared to be a magnet-driven metallic poster board. She adjusted the focus wheel to blow up the pistachio green-block lettering on the sign.

MobileLaw.com.

We lawyer from here to your house.

Low Fees. High Skills.

We'll Drive All Your Bad News Away.

Amherst Pipps, Esq.

mobilelawyer@AmherstPipps.us

Eres un cabrón, she thought, but you're *my* asshole. Let's see what you got, Señor Pipps. She walked across the parking lot, dressed in loose fitting jeans, a Dallas Cowboys sweatshirt, and rough out boots that had never been brushed. When she got about ten feet from the door to the RV, it swung open and a man who could not have been over five foot five stepped down. He looked momentarily surreal against the glare of the morning sun off his Mobile Law Office. He wore a toothy grin, a tailor-made pin-striped suit, and no tie.

"Ms. Santerra-Evans, I'm Amherst Pipps. How was your drive? Dusty?"

"Thirsty," she answered.

"Coffee or tequila?" he answered, flashing a little silver from the molars at the back of his wide open mouth.

"Yes," she answered, not extending her hand toward him.

He stepped aside, waved her up and into the RV, and said, "After you."

Surprisingly, the inside looked not at all like a mobile home. Except for the driver's cage, the eleven-by-fifteen-foot box she was now in looked exactly a law office, complete with conference table, comfortable chairs (with safety belts), and a five-foot-wide desk with the usual office accompaniments. Leather in- and out-boxes, a laptop computer, an electric clock with built-in dock for his iPhone, a yellow legal pad, and a small bundle of what turned out to be his standard engagement agreement adorned the slick waxed desktop. His college and law school degrees and his bar license were laminated onto the back wall. He pointed that way.

"I live back there. I practice law out here. Have a seat. I'll have Jingle bring us coffee and tequila."

That was the start of a struggle he was bound to lose, she thought.

"So, Mr. Amherst Pipps, how come our paths never crossed in a Texas courtroom? You are a trial lawyer, right?" she asked.

"I am," he answered, flashing more silver at her. "I've tried DUIs, felonies, no capital cases, and some civil cases for serious bodily injury and wrongful death. Are you a lawyer?"

"You know my name. I'm sure your Amber Sue told you that. She told me to bring a thousand dollars in cash for your retainer. But you didn't surf me? Not even look me up on TexasBar.com? You're not a curious lawyer. I am. I mean I'm a lawyer and I'm curious. So I read your profile on TexasBar.com. I have some questions, but first, here's your cash retainer. Want to count it?"

She handed him an envelope. He took it, opened it, took out the money, counted it out loud, and then smiled back at her.

"Yup. Ten slightly used Ben Franklins. This will do for now. What's your legal problem?"

"You don't know that either?" she asked, not waiting for an answer. "Mr. Pipps, what do you know about wire fraud, money laundering, the commodities exchanges, and federal WHITSEC programs? Have you ever read the victims' rights law in Texas? Have you ever appeared before any of the federal judges in Houston? Tried any felony cases prosecuted by the Harris County District Attorney's Office? Are you the least bit curious why I asked you to drive down here from Corpus Christi, to Brownsville? And before you answer, signal your man, Jingle, for more coffee, and one more tequila shot, *por favor.*"

She tossed the tequila shot down, sipped her coffee, and watched Amherst Pipps do a credible job of pretending to have trial experience in federal court. He posed a decent grasp of felony prosecution in state court but little clue about white-collar crimes, commodities exchanges, or how WHITSEC really operated. Perfect, she thought. She listened four or five minutes, then interrupted him midsentence.

"OK, that's enough. You passed. I'm ready to hire you. Amber Sue said you didn't allow her to talk fees with prospective clients. So, what is your hourly rate for criminal defense in state court?"

"I usually do those kinds of cases for a flat fee, paid in advance."

"No deal. You won't have to actually try a case; you will only negotiate some matters for me with the prosecutor's office. I'm not a defendant in the case. I'm the victim. I think it might take between twenty and thirty hours of your time? How much per hour?"

"Oh, well that's different. My customary rate is $300 per hour, but I always require a cash retainer of at least five thousand dollars. That will get you forty hours, not counting today."

"I'll give you a cash retainer for $9,999. You can bill me at $400 per hour. That will get me almost twenty-five hours. If that runs out, I'll replenish the retainer. Questions?"

"Not really, just curious why you picked the figure $9,999 for the retainer. Are you superstitious, or something?"

"Superstitious? Yes, a little. But I'm disappointed by your question. Do you know that you cannot deposit more than that into your trust account without filing a special IRS report? Banks are required to make these reports pursuant to the Bank Secrecy Act of 1970. That old law was amended by the Patriot Act of 2001. It's designed to help federal prosecutors investigating drug trafficking, money laundering, and terrorism. You did not know that, or maybe it just slipped your mind?"

"No, I knew it, but I didn't think it applied to Texas. But now that we're talking about it, how come you are willing to pay me more per hour than I normally charge?"

"Because I want your undivided attention for the next week or two. Will that be a problem?"

"No, ma'am. What's the case?"

"I'm the victim in a criminal assault and robbery case in Harris County District Court. I want your help in communicating with the prosecutors. That's all. Just talking to them for me, because I'm a witness and have victim's rights under the Texas Penal Code. But I'm also one of several defendants in a case involving federal wire fraud, money laundering, securities fraud, and probably other crimes. The two cases, one in state court and the other in federal court, are based on somewhat similar facts. The federal case is under seal, so I don't know the details. I don't need your help on the federal case, just on the state case. Can you do that?"

"Sure. I know quite a bit about the victims' rights law. Had to deal with some of 'em over the years, but naturally I'm usually on the side of the perp, not his vic, know what I mean?"

Julia couldn't tell whether the man was smug or just overconfident. He jutted his chin out when he talked about what he'd done, or could do. But there was something about the way he kept raising his eyebrows when he said stupid things like, "know what I mean."

"Can I call you Amherst? And you may call me Julia. Who do you know in the Harris County Sheriff's Office? The District Attorney's Office?"

"Who do I know? You mean like we're friends, or something?"

"No, not friends. But someone you know that will take your calls, right away, and who you've worked with on prior cases where you developed a little mutual trust and confidence."

"Well, since we're both lawyers, I know you'll understand this. As a defense lawyer it's helpful to develop friends in the Sheriff's Office who will tip you off with information once in a while, in return for favors. Small favors. No cash. No bribes, but little things like dinner guest cards, and rooms at a casino, or something like that. You know, don't you?"

"No, I don't. But you've answered the question. Know anyone at the District Attorney's Office like that?"

"No, they are straight-laced there, 'cept maybe for one contract investigator they use. He works for me too, sometimes. They like him because he's got a nose for witnesses who hide out. And I got a nose for people who know that world. So, once in a while I send him a bottle of whiskey, or a dinner chit for two."

"Alright, this gives me a little hope you can do what I need doing."

"And what would that be, Julia?"

"I want you to exercise my victim's rights for me with the state prosecutors. I want you to find out where the defendant, a nasty piece of work named Vince Manchester, is. Right now. Today. He was a fugitive from justice, but a little bird told me he's back in Houston. I want you to find him for me. Can you do that?"

"Well, Julia, I hardly know where to start. If you're the victim in the crime this man, Vince Manster, committed, why won't the prosecutors work with you? They have to, right? It's the law, right?"

Julia stiffened. Pipps might not have noticed, but she glared at him and began cracking the knuckles on her right hand. Using a carefully controlled tone, she said, "It's

Manchester, not Manster. Vince *Manchester.* He's a bastard
a hundred times over. They need my testimony to make the
state case. But I'm not inclined to cooperate with them.
They don't know where I am. And you can't tell 'em. But
you can represent me and exercise my rights to information.
I want to know what they know—especially the whereabouts
of the creepy, twisted, little shit that tied me up with red
duct tape, beat the shit out of me, and robbed me of several
hundred thousand dollars. Just so you know, he scared the
crap out of me. The biggest thing you need to get across to
the prosecutors is they need to protect me from him."

"Well, I'm sorry. No need for you to get riled up, Julia.
I can help you any way you want. Why ain't you cooperating with them? You're the victim. If he did those terrible
things to me, I'd jump up onto the witness stand to testify
against him and help them put him behind bars for a good
long time."

"Mr. Pipps," Julia said, slowly and in a now calm, lower
tone of voice, "I am an unidentified coconspirator in the
federal case. It was filed under seal. The defendants are
former clients of mine. It's a complicated white-collar crime
case and I'm the primary witness in it. But I'm the victim
in the state case based on some of the same facts. I was a
cooperating witness and protected under the federal witness
security act. You know about WHITSEC, right? But I left
the program because I know that little shit will try to kill
me if he can find me. I want you to find him first. I'll take
care of the rest. Now, tell me you can do that, and I'll give
you the $9,999 cash retainer, right now. If you can't then
we're done here, and you're bound by the attorney-client

privilege to keep secret everything I've told you. Are you in, or out?"

"I'm in. What are the next steps?"

"Go to the Harris County courthouse and read the indictment. Put your snitches to work. Try to find the little shit for me. Call the Harris County prosecutor—his name's Grant Lumberson. He will press hard to get you tell him where I am. Don't tell him. But insist on my victim's rights to information and solid protection from the asshole that red duct taped me to my own desk. And I want a summary of where they are on the case. Can they make the case without me? I won't be a witness. You can tell him that. Straight out."

CHAPTER 13

The day after he met with Vince in San Antonio, Travis went to the US Attorney's Office to talk to his old law school classmate, Nancy Lee, about Vince. He didn't call first, or make an appointment. Given the state of insecurity that afflicts much of America these days, Travis couldn't just open the door to the US Attorney's central office on the ninth floor. He had to press a call button and explain his presence in the hallway outside.

"Yes, sir," a voice of authority announced, "what is your business with the US Attorney's Office today?"

Taking his cue, Travis looked up at the camera, smiled and answered, "I'm Travis Danders, the attorney for Vince Manchester. I'd like to talk to Assistant US Attorney Nancy Lee Sustern, please."

"Do you have an appointment, Mr. Danders?"

"No, but it's urgent. If she's in the office, I'm sure she'll want to talk to me."

"I'm not sure she's in this morning, but I'll check. Hold on, please."

Hold on to what, he thought, but didn't argue.

"Sure thing. I'll be right here."

Two or three minutes elapsed. Travis moved away from the door and took one of the four wooden, armless chairs in the short hallway. Then the voice of authority came back.

"Mr. Danders, Ms. Sustern is in the building, but not on this floor at the moment. She does want to talk to you and asks you to wait. She'll be down as soon as she can."

"Sure thing. I'll be right here," he said again.

Fifteen minutes passed, during which three other lawyers, who actually had appointments, got off the elevator, talked to the voice of authority, and were promptly admitted into the inner sanctum of federal prosecution. He dawdled away the time by checking the weather on his iPhone, the value of all three of his stocks on the NYSE, and five throwaway messages from LinkedIn. Like all trial lawyers, Travis had long ago learned that officialdom in his profession demanded self-control and composure when dealing with opposing counsel, busy judges, demanding clients, and an absurdly crowded trial docket. He knew well the futility of demanding urgency. But he wasn't above sarcasm when someone kept him waiting. Seeing Nancy Lee come through the steel door with the small wired-glass window, he greeted her with a practiced smile.

"Nancy Lee, I do believe. Thanks for seeing me so quickly."

"Save the acridity for the jury, Travis. Call next time, will you? Let's go inside and fight in private."

When they got inside, Nancy Lee led Travis to a different conference room than last week's. This one was bigger and equipped with an audio and video setup, apparently designed for serious prosecutorial business. Travis was surprised to find Wellington Strauss himself, the US Attorney for Texas, sitting at the head of the table. Another man in a dark suit was standing on the opposite side, and a young woman was at the control desk apparently ready to operate the recording system.

"Wellington," Travis said, striding toward the man in the dark grey suit, with his hand stuck out, "nice to see you. And happy that you have time to talk about my client, Vince Manchester."

The US Attorney didn't stand, but took Travis's outstretched hand. He motioned to Nancy Lee, which she presumably took as direction to start the meeting.

"Travis, since our last short meeting, four days ago, we've done a bit of work assessing the curious handwritten note you left with me, and I'm more up to speed on the sealed indictment that addresses your client, among others . . ."

Pulling out a chair, Travis interrupted, "Addresses? What's that? Is my client under indictment? That's what I asked of you. Mind explaining the context for me?"

Nancy Lee, perhaps remembering a small bit of her personal history with Travis, that one short fling while they were in law school, gathered herself and answered him in a soothing, placating voice.

"Travis, when the front desk staff said you were in the building, I was talking to Mr. Strauss about the sealed indictment. He suggested that we talk to you on the record.

If you don't mind, I'll ask Emily to start recording now. You don't mind, do you?"

"I do. I've been on this floor scores of times over the years discussing a dozen or so cases with other prosecutors. I've never been invited to sit with the duly appointed US Attorney for the great state of Texas, and I've never been recorded, at least to my knowledge. What's this recording business about?"

Wellington Strauss was a political appointee. He had been, before last fall's national election, a midlevel partner in a large Houston law firm. His legal experience was in commercial litigation, but with little actual trial experience. He'd handled antitrust cases, some defense work in False Claims Act cases, and lots of political activity for the local GOP. He was a surprise appointment by a president who seemed to have little interest in advancing the rule of law in criminal prosecution. Ambitious for sure, he had taken over the office with a single-minded statement about America's borders, and its duty to protect Texas citizens from terror, "whether domestic or foreign." Among Houston's trial bar, he was a little-known commodity.

Motioning to Nancy Lee to back off, he answered Travis's question. "The recording business, as you called it, is an attempt on our part to ensure an accurate record of discussions with opposing counsel in cases like this one where criminal cartels across the border are active and where federal laws against wire fraud, mail fraud, money laundering, and other violations of federal law are extant. That is why we . . ."

"Mr. Strauss. How do you know I'm *opposing* counsel? I represent Vince Manchester. Are you telling me he's involved with an across-the-border criminal cartel? Which one? I know you have a sealed indictment against someone. Is my client named in the indictment? I came here a few days ago to pass along a note written by a woman whose name is Julia Santerra-Evans. Is she named in your sealed indictment? What are the charges? You may choose not to answer those questions. That's your right, *if* my client is named in the indictment. But until you connect my client to an active federal case, you have no right whatsoever to record my conversation with my law school classmate Nancy Lee Sustern."

The mention of her name prompted Nancy Lee to intervene in what she sensed might become a bad start to the real goal here, which was to gain information about Vince Manchester. She'd told her boss that Travis Danders was a skilled lawyer and one that should be treated professionally. The recording idea was pure politics.

"Travis, we will of course honor your request to talk to us off the record. You asked me a few days ago to look at a note that might become federal business, or might not. And you are quite correct that we obtained an indictment, under seal, that may possibly include your client. I was actually going to call you this afternoon to talk about the case. Can you assure me that your client is, in fact, in Texas? Can we start there, off the record?"

"Nancy Lee, my client's whereabouts are not yet your business, unless of course, he is named in your sealed indictment as a defendant, and subject to a duly issued arrest warrant. Perhaps it might clear the air here if I reminded you about a case this office brought three years ago that I defended. It ended with a sentence against my client who is now serving a term of thirty-seven months in prison. It was the Forero Acevedo case. There were nine named defendants and three unindicted coconspirators who could have been, but never were, actually named in the indictment. It was a conspiracy case to commit money laundering against American and Colombian citizens residing in Bogota. It involved customer accounts in US stock brokerage firms offering accounts that could be used by customers to receive deposits, wire transfers, and other credit, or money, and to disburse the funds through wire transfers and cash or other withdrawals. The allegations included claims that the brokerage firm was authorized to receive funds in foreign currencies that were subsequently exchanged into US dollars in layered transactions involving many other accounts, trades, puts, and calls. Neither you nor Mr. Strauss was involved in that case. Is your sealed indictment *that* kind of case? Is Julia Santerra-Evans a cooperating defendant in the indictment? And if so, what is your interest in Vince Manchester?"

For a few moments, neither Nancy Lee nor her boss said anything. Strauss had been taking notes on a small note pad. Nancy Lee pushed her chair back a little and seemed prepared to engage Travis when her boss exploded.

"Mr. Danders," Wellington Strauss said, "you are not here by invitation. Nothing you have said so far gives you license to lecture us about drug cases. I do not understand why you told us a war story about a Columbian drug case you apparently lost three years ago. But what we are prepared to discuss with you is the location and willingness of your client to submit himself to this office or the office of the US marshal within twenty-four hours. I must advise you, any attempt by you to assist your client to avoid arrest will be treated as aiding and abetting, and . . ."

"Wellington, Wellington, you're new to this, I get that. But I never said anything about drugs in the Forero Acevedo case. Check the notes you took in that snazzy little note pad you have there. It was a money laundering case. Let me ask you again, is my client a defendant in your case? Is Julia Santerra-Evans a defendant who is cooperating with the government? If you can't tell me that basic information, then we have nothing to discuss, except maybe why you threatened me with aiding and abetting off the record. Would you like to start the taping machine and repeat that threat?"

Wellington glared first at Travis, then at Nancy Lee, and finally at the unintroduced young man sitting to his left. Sticking the leather note pad inside his suit coat pocket, he ceremoniously pushed his chair back and walked out the conference room door.

Travis said, "Well, that went well, didn't it?"

Nancy Lee waited until the young recording system operator left before responding.

"You never change, do you? But do you still drink coffee? How about a cup on me? At the Starbucks in the ground floor lobby in ten minutes?"

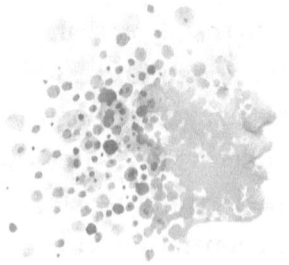

CHAPTER 14

Travis ordered two grande mocha Frappuccinos from the tall, lightly tattooed barista at Starbucks. As good luck would have it, they were ready and on the little round table by the door when Nancy Lee walked through it.

"'Well, that went well'? That's how you meet the new US Attorney for the first time? Travis, you're losing your touch—creating enemies on day one was never your style. I told you I'd be back in touch as soon as I learned what the hell Vince Manchester has to do with a sealed indictment I knew nothing about, didn't I? Well, now I know what's going on, at least on our side of the room. You wanna blow that up? Now Wellington by-God Strauss will probably pull me off the case and assign one of his new line-office prosecutors from Dallas to the case. You won't like that, trust me."

"Nancy Lee, he's a stuffed shirt. His cufflinks have cufflinks. Christ almighty, did you see the way he holds on to that piss ant little leather notebook? He can't even get mad convincingly. How do you work for a guy like that?"

"You don't. Travis, he's a civil, big-firm lawyer who's never tried a case. And never will. He has no interest in how we try cases, only in which ones we file. And then his only interest is in the optics, not the actuality. If we look tough, that's enough. He has two chief deputies—two! One is our boss—he's a courtroom warrior. The other one, who is a woman, runs interference for him in the political world. So don't waste any more time on him. Focus on your client, and before you ask any more questions of me, let me ask you three questions. Listen to them very carefully, because I think your answer is no to each one."

Travis had grown up in a military family and knew how important it was to work with others and listen before you speak. Taking a long sip of his iced coffee, he made it easy. "Fire away."

"First question, do you know anything personal about your client? Second, do you know why he picked you to deliver the note to our office? Third, do you know what he really wants out of you? Now, I'm not asking for details on any of these three questions. A simple yes or no on each one will be fine."

He'd forgotten why he liked her in that criminal procedure class they took as first year law students. She was quick and plain spoken. Plus, he knew she said a lot when she thought it was her turn to talk.

"No," he said, loosening his tie and nodding at her.

She studied him and pushed her Styrofoam cup away. The midafternoon coffee-break crowd at the Wells Fargo

Plaza main lobby was crowding in and the noise level picked up appreciably. Nancy Lee moved her chair a little closer to his.

"No? I'll take that as a no to all three questions—you know nothing personal about him—don't know why he picked you—don't know what he really wants. Didn't think you did. So, let me tell you about the indictment and a few things we need to know. I'll also give you the name of someone you probably ought to call as you plan your next steps with Mr. Manchester. Everything I say comes from a serious investigation into many things we think your client knows nothing about. But we think he should know, and you are in the best position to tell him. The indictment is sealed because it is against several individuals whose names we know, but who cannot be located to serve arrest warrants. It's a classic conspiracy case. Your client is an unindicted coconspirator. There is no arrest warrant out on him. We think he would want to cooperate for reasons we're not yet prepared to discuss with you. And most important, your client may not be who you think he is, which explains why I asked you what you knew about him personally."

"Wait a sec. He's not *who* I think he is? I already answered that one. I don't know anything about him personally. I've met him once in person and talked to him several times over the phone. Why are you so cryptic? What do you mean, he *might* not be who I think he is? He's a guy with enough money to retain me and seems to be in enough trouble to need me. What exactly are we talking about here, in Starbucks, that we could not talk about upstairs in your office?"

"We're talking down here so we can talk in public, but still talk about legal mysteries I'm not yet up on. Let's talk about the note. The Julia Baby in that note is Julia Santerra-Evans. You'll learn, if you stay on this case, that she's the lead cooperating witness in the case. She, like your client, is an unindicted coconspirator, but at an entirely different level than your client. Vince, your client, abducted her, beat her, stole from her, and forced her to run to our office for protection. But she, like your client, disappeared less than a month after someone, we think it was your client, beat the crap out of her, stole a pile of money, and coerced her into several confessions, on tape, of other crimes. So this case is a giant Ferris wheel. Only it's not in an amusement park. It's in federal court."

"Ferris wheel? Nancy Lee, you always were inventive. I remember you using large concentric circles drawn in red ball point on legal pads to connect elements of law and procedure. Remember that?" he asked, as he drained the bottom of his frappe.

"Yeah, I do," she said with a smile. "My dad was an engineer and could never explain anything to us as kids without drawing lines, circles, and squares, to explain how something worked or how something could be made. I use his technique even today. Upstairs, on the whiteboard in my office, I have what looks kind of like a Ferris wheel representing this case. It has maybe fifty cars rocking inside the rim of the wheel. Inside each car is a name of a party, or an event, or a legal issue. In my mind, as I put people or issues in cars and watch the whole thing turn in a continuous circle, I try to remember they are all going at the same speed and that each one will come to a stop only when the entire rim stops turning. Right now some cars seem like they are mounted on the outside of the rim, and have separate motors to independently rotate the car to keep it upright. Know what I mean?"

"No. No idea what you mean. How about telling me which car Vince Manchester is in and which part of the legal procedure you connect him to?"

"He's in the first car. Julia Santerra-Evans is in the second. The next ten or fifteen cars are charges, but only in the federal case. So, actually, I have two Ferris wheels on my whiteboard. The other one is the state case that Grant Lumberson is handling. You know Grant, right?"

"Yeah, I do. He's a guy you can trust, but he's hard to like—very tightly wound—no mercy—hates pleas—loves the courtroom because he gets to run it."

"Really, I thought the judge was in charge of the courtroom. That's how it is in federal court."

"True enough. But Grant knows the judge can only rule or manage what the lawyers present. He always has the burden of proof and carefully feeds the judge and jury what he thinks he can prove, beyond a reasonable doubt. Lots of other prosecutors, without his deep experience, throw crap up on the courtroom wall hoping some of it will stick. Not Grant. He can always prove what he says he can. So he's a challenge for defense lawyers, like me. Have you talked to him about his case? You two plowing the same cornfield with the same mule?"

"No, Travis. We're not. But we do engage, at a comfortable distance. You're read his indictment, right?"

"I have. Straightforward B&E. Alleges my guy broke into Julia's law firm, tied her up in duct tape, banged on her some, and stole lots of money. What's in your case? Can't be the same stuff, right?"

"Different stuff, but there is a connection between the two Ferris wheels in my office. It's another ride, in a different amusement park. I call it *Pirates of the Caribbean.* You know, like Disneyland? We took a trip out there when we were kids. I remember it because it's about a band of pirates and their troubles and exploits. You know, 'Yo Ho, A Pirate's Life for Me.' Here's the thing. The one in Disneyland is not a Ferris Wheel. It's a fake riverboat ride. But it helps me see the federal case and the state case and what joins them. The little boats have characters in them, along the shore, and at various places in the song. Your client is there, in a boat by himself. He's pretty quiet. Julia is in a different boat, singing like a bird. The state depends on her to make the case against Vince Manchester. It's routine crime stuff, you already know that. But both of them are also in the Ferris wheel, the federal case. Some of the cars have complicated legal issues, like money laundering, wire and mail fraud, illegal commodities trading, and theft, lots of theft. Julia was singing there too, but now she jumped off when the Ferris wheel slowed down at the off ramp. Your guy's still there, in his rocking cart, spinning endlessly around the wheel."

Vince sat, wondering whether the feds were serious about his client, given the charges and the difference between what his client was actually facing in the state case. So he asked an abstract question.

"You said there were empty cars on the Ferris wheel but didn't say there were empty boats on the Pirates ride. What might be in the empty cars on your Ferris wheel?"

"Well, let's speculate about that. You know from the note you gave me that Julia talked about a sister. I think it's Vince's sister. Does she exist? Should she be in one of the Ferris wheel cars, and what legal issues are linked to her? There's a much deeper question too. Does Vince exist? Is he real? You met him. So did Julia. But is there more there than meets the eye? Pun intended, Travis."

"Holy shit, Nancy Lee. What 'n hell are you suggesting? That my client's a cross dresser? Maybe transgender?"

"Travis, I'm raising these issues because I can count on you to track them down. You may never call me back. I don't care. There are legal issues in this case that I can't talk to you about yet. But I'll give you the name of an FBI agent in Phoenix, Arizona. That's where Vince might be from. It's Sally Lin. She's at the FBI field office there. My guess is she will talk to you because you are in a position to help her. You might create your own carnival ride, who knows?"

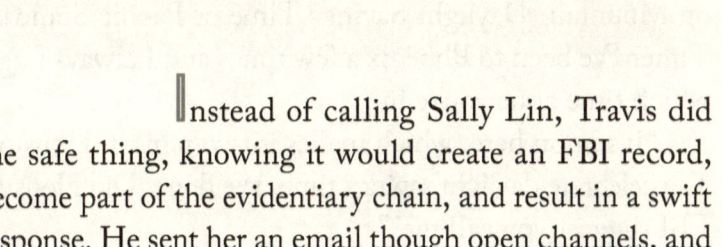

CHAPTER 15

Instead of calling Sally Lin, Travis did the safe thing, knowing it would create an FBI record, become part of the evidentiary chain, and result in a swift response. He sent her an email though open channels, and in unencrypted text.

To: sally.lin@fbi.phoenix.gov

From: Travis.Danders@Danderslaw.com

Re: Vince Manchester

Agent Lin,

I represent Vince Manchester in two pending cases in Houston, Texas, involving Julia Santerra-Evans and her former client Plankton Resources LLC. I would like to talk to you. Please send me a secure telephone line. I understand our call will be recorded. Call at your earliest convenience.

Travis Danders. 832-481-1973

Twenty-three minutes after he hit send, his direct line lit up on his office phone. It was a number not widely known in the legal community. He wasn't surprised the FBI used it. The caller ID read, Phoenix FBI Field Office.

"This is Travis Danders."

"Mr. Danders, this is Agent Sally Lin. FBI Phoenix field office. I have Agent Standusky on the line. We're being recorded. I'm returning your email. I'm curious how you knew to call me regarding your client Vince Manchester."

"Afternoon, Agents Lin and Standusky. Say, are you on Mountain Daylight Savings Time or Pacific Standard Time? I've been to Phoenix a few times and I always forget which time zone you're in."

"It's noon here, which makes it two p.m. in Houston. You celebrate daylight savings time. We don't. Did Houston FBI suggest you call me?"

"No, I got your name from Nancy Lee Sustern. She's the lead prosecutor on the Plankton Resources money laundering case in federal court in Houston. She was sure you would be interested in talking to me."

"Yes, I've talked to Ms. Sustern, but only once, on a conference call with other agents. Your email says you represent Vince Manchester. Can you confirm that for me on this phone call?"

"I can. He is."

There was a pregnant pause on the line. Most lawyers want control of the dialogue in an official phone call between an investigator and a defense lawyer. Lin knew that and had assumed that Travis would, on his own schedule, volunteer information about a call he'd asked for. When he said nothing more, she spoke up.

"Mr. Danders, do we still have you?"

"Not sure you'll ever have me, but I'm still on the line. I confirmed my representation. I assume you want to know more, but if not, I sure have some questions for you."

A shorter pause ensued, as both sides to the legal dance jockeyed for position.

"Fine with me. Yes, I do have preliminary questions. Where is your client, and are you willing to turn him over to the authorities in Houston?"

"Attorney-client privilege on your first question, Ms. Lin. And if you can tell me whether there is a federal warrant for my client, I'll discuss with you what we can do about that. I trust you're not working on the state prosecution team, are you?"

Standusky couldn't stand this jockeying for position so early in the game.

"Mr. Danders, you emailed us and asked us to call you. Before we can talk, we need to know the basics. What makes your client's physical address in Texas a privileged matter?"

"Because I can only know where he is based on what he tells me. All my communications with him are protected. You know that much, right?"

Before Standusky could take the response as an insult and return the favor, Sally Lin interceded.

"Of course you should assert the privilege. We don't want to know anything about your communications. Let's start with this, instead. I have some knowledge of the federal charges that might involve your client. I was in Houston when Mr. Manchester called the local FBI office, gave his name, and told us where we could find Julia. We went to her office, found her duct taped to her desk and suffering from a head wound inflicted by a man she said was Vince Manchester. He kidnapped her, robbed her, and forced her to make illegal wire transfers in Panama. That's what she told us in the first interview after we scissored off the red duct tape. I sat in on some of the debriefing over the next few days. And I have met with his sister, Vivian, here in Phoenix. We can talk about all of that, except for matters dealing with the charges in the federal or state court that implicate your client in criminal activity, or conspiring to commit such activity. Why you don't ask your questions, and let's see where we might have mutual interests?"

"Fair enough. As I mentioned, I got your name from Nancy Lee Sustern. She implied that there is something odd going on with respect to my client and his sister. Not sure of her name, but what can you tell me about his sister?"

"He doesn't have a sister."

"Well, there's a note that I think was written by Julia Santerra-Evans. It contains a threat against my client, who is described in that note as the woman's brother."

"Yes, that came from Julia, the cooperating witness in the Plankton Resources case. Nancy Lee is lead counsel on the case. But, Mr. Danders, we don't think that woman, her name is Vivian Shortfield, is Vince's sister. We think Vince Manchester and Vivian Shortfield are the same person. They are not sister and brother. There is only one person, a young woman who was diagnosed in early childhood with dissociative identity disorder. Do you know what that is?"

Travis felt a little numb. All of a sudden he had a sour taste in his mouth and his hands felt clammy.

"My firm handled a case years ago, about an act of bank fraud that involved a man who said he suffered from multiple personality disorder—is that the same thing?"

"Yes, more or less. There is a nationally famous expert on this condition in Houston. He's on the Rice medical school faculty. Interestingly, he's also a lawyer. His name is Dr. Ahmed Estancia. Now, I can also tell you that I met Vivian Shortfield twice. Once was a short coffee meeting. The other was a formal interview in our office here in Phoenix. That interview was secretly recorded. We think it was arranged by Vince. We've been told that Vivian is the host identity and Vince is an alter identity."

Travis rocked back in his chair at that. He could instantly hear what Vince had said to him in San Antonio day before yesterday. "Don't be so sure, Lawyer Man, I could be a ghost, or maybe a host." Jesus Mother of Mary, he thought, was Vince trying to tell me what Nancy Lee had hinted at and now this lawyer, Sally Lin, is confirming? Am I representing a man who is really a woman? A woman who suffers from this dissociative disorder? He told Sally Lin to hold the line a sec; he needed to get a bottle of water from the office fridge on the other side of his desk.

"Ok, I'm back. Sorry for the little hold up. I'm a bit wobbly—are you sure that the man I know as Vince Manchester is actually a woman known as Vivian Shortfield? I mean who says so?"

"Mr. Danders, we have good reason to believe Ms. Shortfield was diagnosed with a dissociative disorder when she was nine. She's twenty-one now. We don't know for sure if she ever had the early diagnosis confirmed, or has had any psychotherapy for her condition. But our theory is that she may not aware of her condition and may not be aware of Vince. We're not sure, but experts doubt that he's aware of her. We brought in an expert consultant. Maybe you should do the same."

After he hung up, Travis tried to take his mind back to exactly what Vince had said about the "ghost, or maybe a host." Nothing else came back. Then he remembered the drama when Vince blew up at the thought of being jailed while awaiting bail. He'd freaked about being in what he described as a male jail. And he seemed petrified of being stripped. *My God, maybe what he was saying is that he's a man in a woman's body.* He looked down at the legal pad next to the phone. As he always did when talking to law enforcement, he took notes. In underlined script, he had written *Ahmed Estancia — Shrink/lawyer*. Opening his iPhone, he asked Siri for Dr. Ahmed Estancia's number.

CHAPTER 16

On the six-hour drive back to Houston from Brownsville, Amherst Pipps made notes on his iPad about contacting Grant Lumberson on his new client's behalf. Using his Pages app, he made four tabs in her case file. Tab One—things Julia wants to know about the state case against this guy Vince Manchester. Tab Two—things Julia wants Mr. Lumberson to know about her. Tab Three—rights she wants to protect. Tab Four—confirm that, win or lose, since the state case is independent of the federal case against her former employers and clients, what happens in the state case changes nothing in the federal case. He wasn't sure Julia was right on this fourth point, but she had done criminal law cases and seemed confident that one case did not affect the other.

On Tab One, he listed in order of importance the things his client seemed the most anxious about. First, did they ever serve Vince with an arrest warrant and, if not (as she suspected), when did they expect to arrest him? Second, if he's not in custody, could they proceed to trial without him (she said that was *in abstentia*). He was doubtful about that. Third, since she gave sworn statements to them more than a year ago and testified before the state grand jury under oath, could they use that sworn information to make the case against Vince without her presence in court? Fourth, does Vince have a defense lawyer, probably from the public defender's office? And what is his lawyer's position on the case—is a plea agreement likely, or will the case go to trial? Amherst was thinking these things should be covered first, since none of them seemed difficult or controversial to him.

On Tab Two—Julia's position he was supposed to convey to the prosecutor—he had only three notes. First, tell the prosecutor she would not testify in person in court and would not be available for personal discussions, although she might talk on the phone with them. Her preference was to have him do all her talking for her. Second, remind the state she's the *only* victim. Her office was broken into—she was beaten and humiliated—her property was stolen— she was imprisoned—she was forced to confess to things she never did—she hated the man who did this to her—and she wanted full financial restitution as part of any plea deal or sentence the judge handed down at the end. Third, she was a lawyer and entitled to be treated as an officer of the court. That was important to her.

Tab Three was simple. Julia had instructed him to remind the prosecutor she had statutory rights as a victim. He downloaded a copy of Title 1 of Texas Statutes & Codes Annotated, Arts. 56.01 to 56.30, Rights of Crime

Victims. From there he copied and pasted Julia's victim's rights onto the tab. Not all of them, because some didn't apply to her, like the ones that applied only to capital cases where the death penalty was possible. Just reading that section of the statute reminded him of something Julia had said that made him nervous— "Forget the death penalty under Texas law. He'll get the law of Sinaloa—it's quicker than Texas and isn't done with a stupid little needle." He listed the ones he thought she wanted enforced. One: the right to receive adequate protection from harm and threats of harm arising from cooperation with the prosecution. In particular, she wanted protection from Vince Manchester; two: the right to have the magistrate take the safety of the victim into consideration as an element in fixing the amount of bail; three: the right to be informed by the prosecutor if the case has been canceled or rescheduled; four: the right to information about the procedures in criminal investigations by the District Attorney's Office concerning the general procedures in the criminal justice system, including general procedures in guilty plea nego- tiations and arrangements, restitution, and the appeals and parole process; five: the right to receive information regarding compensation to crime victims; six: the right to prompt return of any property of the victim held by a law enforcement agency or the attorney for the state as evidence when the property is no longer required for that purpose.

As he read over his notes on Tab Three, Amherst wondered whether he needed to call his client before the meeting with the prosecutors and tell her about a case he found from the Texas Supreme Court that dealt with

victim's rights. It was the *Stahl* case. The court recognized
the Victims' Bill of Rights but said that even though the
list was comprehensive, the legislature had *not* included
an absolute right by the victim to give testimony. Did that
mean because she had no right to testify, they could not
make her testify? She knew more about this than he did,
so he decided not to call her about the case.

Tab Four gave him pause. As he thought about her
directions to him, he was unsure what exactly she was getting
at by insisting he inquire about the differences between the
federal case and the state case. He mulled it over while Jingle
drove through Corpus Christi back on Texas Highway 77
to Houston, and he began to feel a little overwhelmed. He
was at his best where the issue was mostly money—so much
for a whip-lash in a car crash—so much for getting stuck
with a bad used car—so much in alimony from a husband
lying about his bank accounts, and so on. He'd handled cases
for guilty criminals who almost always plead out and did
their time without all these questions Julia was asking. He
rocked back and forth in his seat-belted passenger seat trying
to get at whatever Julia was so bugged about. She insisted
the state case was solely against the guy who'd robbed and
beat her up. The federal case, she said, was much bigger. It
was a money laundering case against some of her former
clients and employers. She was a witness there too, but she
didn't care about her federal victim's rights, only her state
court rights. So why did she want him to *confirm*—that's
the word she used—with the state prosecutor that a verdict in the state case would have no impact on the federal
case? *Impact?* That was her word too. What the hell was

she getting at, he thought. He vaguely remembered some post-trial consequences from law school, like *res judiciata*, estoppel, double jeopardy, and stuff like that. So, on Tab Four he noted short descriptions from legal websites of what these terms meant.

Res judiciata = claim preclusion. Means already judged. Final judgment in one case precludes trying it again on the same issue with the same parties. Shit, he thought, this can't be what she means. It's for civil cases, not criminal cases.

Estoppel = stopping a person from making claims or going back on his word. It could keep someone from bringing a civil case. Nah, this can't be what she's worried about. She's not a claimant in either case.

Double jeopardy = a constitutional defense. Yeah, this might be it, he noted. He was proud he remembered the nut of it from law school. He'd never had a DJ case and was glad of it. It was mostly about constitutional law, a course he barely passed. Double jeopardy keeps you from being tried again on the same or almost the same charges. The facts needed to be the same; he remembered his con law prof going on and on about that. Didn't make any difference whether you won or lost. You couldn't be tried again on the same facts and law. He did more research and found a famous supreme court case which laid it out. "The prohibition is not against being twice punished, but against being twice put in jeopardy; and the accused, whether convicted or acquitted, is equally put in jeopardy at the first trial."

So what Julia might be getting at here is, what happens if Vince goes to trial in state court and wins? Does that screw up the other case, where she is also a cooperating witness?

That's when it hit him. Shit, what if she's a defendant in the other case? She told him it was still under seal. What if she cut a deal in the federal case and now was not cooperating in the state case? Could that be it? Can they make her cooperate in the state case by telling the feds? Could the feds and the state be working together on these two cases? Jesus Christ! The more he thought about Tab Four, the more his brain sizzled. Who was she, anyhow? Of a sudden, he saw danger everywhere, for himself, his mobile law practice, his license. No matter how hard he'd tried since law school to work with other lawyers, the more they'd screwed him. Same thing for landlords in office buildings. And clients, too. They were rarely happy, even when he won the case. It was never enough, and always cost too much. But *this* client! She was paying more than his normal fee. She didn't want much, just for him to get information and pass other information along. He'd be in and out of this case with a couple conversations. That's what he thought as he closed his iPad and went back to playing video games. His two other cases needed a little research. But they could wait. He played *Call of Duty* all the way back to Houston. He loved advanced warfare video games. This game let him pretend he was in a compelling battleground of the future, using new tactics with sophisticated weapons. Beats divorce cases, he thought.

CHAPTER 17

When the Texas lawyer, Travis Danders, hung up, Sally and Standusky stared at one another for a moment before he snarled at her.

"Well if this isn't a shit pile, I don't know what is."

Sally had been working with him for three years. He was older and had little patience for nuanced investigation, or cases with impaired witnesses or defendants. His FBI mind was narrowly focused on the crime, not the mental state of anyone involved. He was fond of saying, if the perp's a head case, they ought to send him to the psych unit. If not, he belongs in jail. There's no halfway house where the perp gets to vacate and medicate while normal perps do their time in eight by ten cells.

"Actually," Sally mused, "I think it's absolutely fascinating. Just think about it. This Texas lawyer has a client he seems to know almost nothing about. He thinks he's representing the *host* personality. But if our investigation is right, he's representing an *alter* personality. I mean, you and I saw the host personality at Starbucks. Then we interviewed her here. We both wrote 302s on her. We had heard small bits of talk about Vince but weren't sure he existed. Now we just talked to a lawyer who is sure—he's met Vince and is representing him in two cases! I knew about the investigation because I was part of it. Like everyone else on the Texas team, I was flabbergasted to see that lawyer, Julia Santerra-Evans, wrapped in red duct tape to her desk and her chair and screaming about that bastard that did it to her. That turned out to be Vince. We have still and video evidence of what he did. But what was his mental state at that time? This is the case of a lifetime."

"It's the nut case of a lifetime, I'll give you that," Standusky said as he stuck his notes in a folder. "I'm gonna write a soft 302 on the phone call. You go tell the boss. And do me a big favor. You don't want me to go back to drinking Wild Turkey for dinner do you? Well, then keep me out of this bats-in-the-belfry case. If they want you to go back to Texas, that's fine by me. I'll babysit your cases here. Don't let the host or her alter slip across the Rio Grande and infiltrate us again in Arizona."

Sally went directly to Marcus Stanza's office. He agreed she should immediately call the Houston FBI and brief them.

"Send the 302 if you want to on this guy Dander too. Tell 'em I'll give you temporary duty to Houston if they think you can help. I'm still tender about the scam the woman played on us—little miss perfect Vivian. Didn't you tell me it was her brother that beefed up that hidden recorder in the back pack she planted in our office?"

"Yes, boss. But he wasn't her brother. He was her alter personality. And he's the guy that Travis Danders, not Dander, is now representing. Well, that's not right, is it? They are the same person, only different personalities. The medical community calls it dissociative identity disorder. The patient community calls it multiplicity. I think the investigative and legal aspects are fascinating. I'll let you know if they want my help in Texas."

They did. She called Slate Blakey at the FBI-Houston Field when she left the boss's office. They asked her to come to Houston ASAP. She did.

CHAPTER 18

When Sally Lin's Southwest Airlines flight set down at Hobby Airport in Houston, she couldn't help the sense of déjà vu. It'd been two years since she'd been temporarily posted here. That time she missed actually seeing Vince by a few hours. She saw the videos later, but it wasn't the same as seeing him live and in person. Now, she was about to step off an airplane where, so the FBI believed, Vince was waiting with his lawyer—the intriguing Travis Danders.

Now that she had eight very satisfying years in FBI major crimes behind her, she was self-assured and proud of her record. But Manchester had nearly stumped her, and a dozen other intensely focused agents. Her left brain was signaling that it was time to nail this case down tight. But she no sooner thought it than that old bewilderment came back. Was Vince Vivian? Or was it the other way around? Was Vivian Vince? The only metaphor she could think of on the plane was the mirror in the tiny onboard restroom. Who did Vivian see when she looked in the mirror? Her own reflection, or a gauzy face just behind her, waiting?

She texted Slate Blakey and said she was on the tarmac and would be in the office in forty-five minutes, by Uber. But when she cleared the security gate that led into the main Hobby Airport terminal, she spotted a vaguely familiar face in the crowd of locals welcoming their families to Houston.

"Agent Lin, nice to see you again. Slate asked me to pick you up. Do you have checked baggage?"

She remembered his face, but not his name. He saw the question on her face. "Names, Marco, I'm part of the team on the Plankton Resources indictment."

"Right, Marco, nice to see you too. I don't have checked baggage. All I need for a week or two in Houston is in this overhead carry-on, or available at Target. Are we going straight to the office or do I have time to drop this off at the La Quinta Inn, the same one I stayed in last trip?"

"We're not going to the office. There's a meeting in ninety minutes at the US Attorneys' Office with the AUSA in charge of the federal case. Slate's there now. They want you there right away."

On the twenty-five-minute ride to downtown Houston, Marco answered her questions about the sealed indictment. It was against thirteen defendants: three corporate entities, seven individual officers, and two unindicted coconspirators, identified as Persons A and B. There were over fifty-seven counts, but many were duplicative counts for different major illegal commodity trades and wire frauds on different dates for different clients. The unindicted coconspirator factiously named as Person A was actually Julia Santerra-Evans. Person B was Vince Manchester.

"Thanks, Marco, for the summary. I'm unclear about the legal strategy of not indicting either Julia or Vince. What's going on there?"

"Course I was not in on the strategy, I'm just a line investigator. But my take on it is this. Julia was so deep into all the money laundering and wire fraud in the case that she flipped and became our principal cooperating witness. But they wanted to keep her on a short leash. She was not indicted but named in the indictment fictitiously, just in case she bailed on us. Which she did. Vince Manchester, the guy with the red duct tape, didn't do anything illegal in the Plankton Resources business schemes, but he did force Julia to execute two wire frauds by laundering money in Panamanian banks. He was complicit. But the real case against him is not the federal indictment; it's the state indictment. It's driven by his assault, kidnapping, and robbery claims. He took more than six-hundred thousand in cash. He may have taken some bearer bonds too. We're not too sure on that."

"Julia would know, wouldn't she?"

"Yeah, I guess. I haven't read the whole file—that would take a week. But I think they told me she confessed the first day in custody, and the next day started saying she was coerced and had told us a lot of things that weren't true. Then, later she clammed up on some things and wanted a lawyer. Anyhow, his state court case is plain old street crime. Her case in federal court is a complex financial crimes case."

"But, Marco," Sally said, "I thought your office confirmed her role in the Idaho murder of Jason Bloomington, and the Washington, DC, murder of Stephan Manchester? What happened to those cases?"

"Well, you'd have to ask Slate, but my guess is they let Idaho handle its murder and DC handle the other one. Our Texas case is aimed at the company Plankton Resources. It's a big company, even by Texas standards."

CHAPTER 19

Travis spent forty-five minutes with his most trusted law partner, who tried to convince him they should not take this case. The partner, Conner Kilmer, had been Travis's first associate when he started the firm thirteen years ago. He'd made Connor a partner nine years ago and trusted his judgment, especially when it came to the kind of ethical dilemma driving Connor's belief they should withdraw immediately before the multiplicity problem got worse.

Connor Kilmer had made law review at Baylor Law, was a member of the bar association's ethics committee, and had defended a half-dozen lawyers in disciplinary cases. He knew more about the bar's ethical rules than anyone in the firm. They weren't big enough to have a real ethics committee, but everyone deferred to his judgment on ethical conflicts of interest and debatable clients and cases.

"Travis, goddamn it, you're just being stubborn on this. Would you just listen to me? We cannot represent a client in a serious criminal case unless the client either does not have any mental impairment, or his mental impairment has been fully evaluated by a doctor. Only then can we be sure the client has the ability to make what Ethical Rule 1.14 says are "adequately considered decisions in connection with the representation.""

"Connor, you told me to read the rule. I did. It's not much help. It says if our client has mental problems we should, and I quote, 'maintain, as far as reasonably possible, a normal lawyer-client relationship.' What does that even mean? Normal? Normal for what, a stable, mentally fit client, or normal for an impaired client who is quite clear about what he wants and what he expects from us, as his lawyers?"

"Yeah, but Travis, you're talking about Vince. You told me that others think the real client is a woman named Vivian, who has a dissociative identity disorder, and that Vince is an alter personality. She's the host identity and Vince is her alter. That's what you said."

"That's what the FBI agent in Phoenix said, not me. But whether it's Vince or Vivian, there is a real person. I've met him twice. He's real. The feds and the state have indicted him. They think he's real. He's signed a fee agreement and paid us a retainer. That's real."

"You don't have to listen to what the FBI say, Travis, you have to listen to what the Texas Supreme Court says. So, let's go through the fine print in ER 1.14 Do you think Vince's ability to make decisions is impaired in any way?"

"Nope, if anything he makes decisions lickety-split. Might be a thin decision, but he makes it quick and loud."

"Alright. Here's another one. Are the decisions he's made so far in his own interest?"

"Yes."

"No reason you can think of to suggest he needs a guardian or a conservator?"

"No. And before you ask, he seems aware that I will be making independent judgments about what the best course of action should be in his two pending cases."

"OK, those are the easy ones. You suggested I look up the term dissociative identity disorder. I did that. I don't even pretend to understand it, but one article I read talked about classic presentation. That is when a person exhibits two or more distinct personalities and no ability to remember their actions while in the separate personality state. Sometimes it's called a host identity and an alter identity. Did Vince display anything like to you, on the phone, or in person?"

"More than once, he talked about us, or we."

"Like the royal we?"

"No, not like that. Just in communication and . . ."

"Travis, that's a key element. When representing a client with any kind of mental disability, a lawyer has a special and often very difficult responsibility to communicate so the client can know and decide what's best for him in a case. In a multiplicity case, you have to be absolutely sure which identity you're communicating with."

"With Vince, that's not an issue. He is insistent, demanding, cock-sure, no matter what."

"OK, Travis. That's enough easy stuff. The real issue may be competency. If he was psychopathic and that condition were a defense to a criminal case, who has the right to raise the defense? The lawyer, or the client?"

"Connor, do you lie awake nights thinking of questions you know I can't answer? What do you mean 'the right' to raise mental competency as a defense? That's always the lawyer's job, right? Clients, even perfectly sane and well-educated ones, don't know what particular defense they have to a particular case."

"Fair enough," Conner said, as he got up and paced around the room. Travis knew that was a sign of worry. He'd seen it often. "What worries me is this. Court cases confirm that the insanity defense is the prerogative of the client, not the lawyer. Particularly with an insane client, the law demands the lawyer discuss the options, the consequences, the impact, and allow the client to decide whether to plead insanity in a criminal case."

"Come on, Connor, this guy may or not be an alter personality, but he's not insane. Where are you going with this?"

"Travis," Connor said, as he took his seat, "if he was insane, you'd have to talk to him about it, right? So, if he is afflicted with a dissociative disorder, you have to talk to him about that."

"But I don't know that he is. The FBI thinks he has something, but they don't know what . . ."

Connor looked at his watch, thinking about the difficult call he had to make on another case later that afternoon. It was a call from a lawyer who needed help because his wife was psychotic and he was afraid what she might do to their oldest son, who was a juvenile delinquent if there ever was one. But thinking about that case prompted him to ask a new question about their client, Vince.

"Travis, you're not worried about Vince harming himself, or anyone else are you?"

"Harming himself? Nah, he is a little weird, and he has a history with the vic, Julia Santerra-Evans. But I don't think he would hurt her."

"He already *has* hurt her, right? And you said he hates her. Anything about that bother you?"

"Look, Connor, I've met him twice, had two phone calls with him, and that's it. I really have no idea whether he's a nut case, but I am worried about dissociative identity disorder. If he's just an alter personality, and he's focused on protecting the host personality, then who 'n hell knows? He's mad as hell and protective as hell. That's all I know."

"That's enough. I don't mean you have to believe them. But you are obligated to figure out whether you really *are* representing the host personality; that's for sure. And you have to figure out whether the host personality can be held criminally responsible for something his or her alter personality did. Let's do *this*. You dig into the diagnosis. I'll dig into the defense, assuming Vince is a dissociative identity disordered client. I mean, think about the arraignment in court. What do you say when the judge asks Vince if his true name is Vince Manchester and he says no, your honor, it's Vivian Shortfield? Or, what if he is an alter personality and lies to the judge about it? Or the real nightmare—what if he doesn't know he's an alter, or a host personality? Are these personalities aware of each other? You better have answers before you go to court and appear for whoever your client really is."

CHAPTER 20

There was nothing interesting about the conference room on the second floor of a government building that had aged poorly. A picture of President Trump on the wall, hanging slightly askew, and the obligatory metal trash bin by the door, set the stage. The Harris County District Attorney's Office had a hundred first-rank trial lawyers in five divisions. None met with opposing counsel in their private offices. Defense lawyers were not allowed on those floors. There were five small and three large conference rooms for jousting with opposing counsel on the second floor.

Grant Lumberson always asked for Room 2091 because it was smallest one, had a squeaky door, and no windows. Afflicted with pale greyish skin, he looked his age when seated behind a plain conference table, his mouth tight and his eyes lidded. He hated meetings where he had to sit still and resented listening to people drone on. It wasn't impatience, it was insistence. He was so bold in the court-room that judges sometimes wondered whether he would ultimately be consumed by his own ego. He was big, nearly six foot five, and thick in all the right places. And today he was ready for Amherst Pipps, who had dared to call and ask for a private meeting with "whoever was in charge of the case *State of Texas v. Vince Manchester*."

When the summer intern, a thin, dark-skinned young woman, ushered Amherst Pipps in, she quickly turned around and closed the squeaky door.

"Have a seat, Mr. Pipps," Lumberson said, pointing to the seat at the end of the table facing him. "I'm the guy you wanted to speak with. Name's Lumberson. Been here since the eighties when Reagan was president. Why are you here?"

"Thank you, Mr. Lumberson. We haven't met before, have we?" Pipps said, as he opened the cover of his iPad, and turned it on.

"Not likely. Never seen you in the courthouse. Far as anyone in this building knows, you've never tried a case. That true? No trial experience?"

Pipps was a seven-year lawyer. He'd only tried two cases in state district court and four in municipal court. None lasted more than two days. He was good with small cases but felt an intense desire to either throw the iPad at Lumberson or storm out of the room. Rubbing his hands down his pant legs, he quickly decided on sticking to his plan for this meeting, hoping to avoid letting Lumberson set the agenda with his little insults.

"I represent Julia Santerra-Evans. You know her, right? You interviewed her in the presence of the US Attorney two years ago. You have her sworn grand jury testimony about your case against Vince Manchester. I'm not here to discuss my trial experience, I'm here to establish her rights as a victim under Texas law, and . . ."

"Ah, hell, Pipps, didn't mean to rile you. We all got to start somewhere, don't we? Tell you what, I'll start over. Where is Ms. Santerra-Evans?"

"I'm not at liberty to say. I am here at her express direction and as her legal representative in the case you are prosecuting for her. Now, . . ."

"Whoa, Hoss. What's 'not at liberty mean,' between us lawyers? You're her lawyer, right, not just a legal *representative*?"

Pipps felt a little drip of sweat run down the back of his neck and reached back to press his suit coat down over it.

"Yes, I am her lawyer. She has the right to a lawyer, doesn't she?"

"Sure she does. Hell fire, Pipps, she *is* one. You knew that right? Why don't you just tell me straight out why you're here?"

"I'm here, as I said, at her express direction. As the victim in this case she has statutory rights under the victim slash protection act and has directed me to pose certain questions, as is her right under the statute."

Lumberson, with over seven hundred prosecutions behind him, smiled. He'd faced down scores of newbie lawyers in his time and knew that when one hid behind a statute, it was because he didn't know the actual facts.

"Pipps, you are exactly right about the statute. Had I known that's why you are here, to talk about her victim's rights, I would have sent you back downstairs to the front desk. We have victim's rights coordinators down there trained to do exactly what I think you're asking for. On your way out, just stop by the desk. One of the girls there will point you in the right direction. Anything else on your mind?"

"Yes, we need a status update on the case. And she asked me to tell you she won't be here—that is, physically here—for the trial. You have her sworn testimony. She is understandably worried about being harmed by the defendant. He kidnapped her and beat her up. She's scared of him. That should suffice . . ."

"OK, Pipps this calls for a second whoa. I notice you keep fiddling with your device—that's what they call 'em these days—a device. What is that, an iPad? You aren't recording are you?"

"No, I'm not. I'm taking notes. My client has several specific issues she wants me to discuss with you."

"Why isn't she here? She has to be here for the trial—live testimony will win this case—dead words on a page will bore the jury. She's a live wire—I know. I spent nearly two days, over at the federal detention center two years ago, with her. She was madder 'n holy hell at getting duct taped to her own chair and desk. You know about that, don't you?"

"Mr. Lumberson, I cannot discuss confidential information with you. You know that, don't you?"

Lumberson knew a dodge when he saw one. So, he pushed his chair back from his end of the oblong table, walked around the other end, and took the seat next to Pipps. Leaning toward the facial tic just under Pipps's left eye, he crossed his arms across his huge chest and let out a long slow breath.

"Pipps. Don't challenge me about the lawyer's duty to keep his client's secrets. Her location is not covered by the attorney-client evidentiary privilege. You don't have to tell me if you don't want to, but don't hide behind a courtroom privilege that only applies *in* the courtroom. It does not apply here, in our office. You better come straight with me on her location, right now. She's ducked the US Marshal's protection services, as might be her right. The feds don't need her all that much in their financial crimes case, but I goddamn sure do need her in our case. You tell her that. And if you don't want me to start thinking about obstruction of justice, you better tell me where she is."

Pipps was not experienced at this level, but he was a lawyer and felt it was time to show it.

"Mr. Lumberson, I will not tell you where she is. The court file says she's not under subpoena or subject to a warrant of any kind. She is not legally obligated to be present at your trial against Mr. Manchester. But none of that impairs to the slightest degree her rights as the only victim in the case. You can send me an email detailing the case status. She is legitimately worried about her own safety and has a right to know where Mr. Manchester is. I presume you have him under an arrest warrant, but I do not see it in the file. Is he in custody?"

Lumberson, leaned back in his chair, uncrossed his arms, and clasped his hands behind his neck.

"Alright, Pipps. I'm warming to your style. Don't let an old warhorse like me get under your skin. Here's the way I see it. Manchester is on the loose. We have no goddamn idea where he is. We've refiled the indictment. There is no pending trial date. I'll send you an email if any of that changes. You need to talk to your client about her responsibility to this office, as a lawyer, and as a crime victim. She has to cooperate with us, just as we need to keep her informed. Give me her address and I'll have the girl's downstairs communicate with her by letter. We'll copy you. I don't use email very much, but I'll get my second-chair lawyer to do that with you. Go talk to your client and get her to talk to us. It's a two-way road, but right now, it's all uphill. We done here?"

Pipps closed the cover on his iPad and got up. In one last effort to look like a tough lawyer, he said, "We are done here."

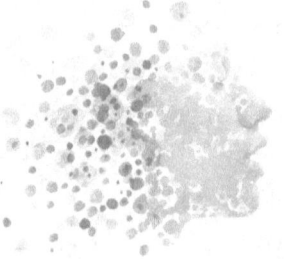

CHAPTER 21

Sally Lin's driver/escort stopped at the La Quinta Inn. She checked in, left her bag at the reception desk, and went back to the car for the short ride to the US Attorney's Office in central Houston. Marco didn't go in with her.

"Slate will either bring you back to our office or drop you off at your hotel."

The reception desk in the main lobby was apparently expecting her when she asked which floor the US attorney was on.

"Are you Agent Lin?"

"Yes."

"Here's your visitor's tag. Please attach it to your lapel. Wear it at all times on the nineteenth floor. Welcome to Houston, ya'll," the blonde with giant white teeth said.

Slate Blakey, wearing a similar name tag, met her at the doorway to a very large conference room on the nineteenth floor. He opened one of the large glass double doors and ushered her in. She was stunned by the technology. And the view. The doors opened into a rectangular room at least twenty-five by thirty-five feet with a curved glass wall at the end showcasing other tall buildings glowing in the west-facing afternoon sun. The shiny Philippine mahogany table was round and looked like it'd seat at least two dozen people. The technology was unlike anything she'd ever seen in a government office. Small monitors were built into the table facing each seat. Each had a keyboard, mouse, and swivel stick. A built-in thirteen-inch monitor faced each chair. A dozen were occupied, and their monitors were lit up. The meeting had obviously been in session since coffee cups, napkins, water bottles, and yellow legal tablets were spread around. Everyone turned to look at Agent Lin when Slate ushered her in.

"Folks," Slate announced, "this is Sally Lin, one of the few people to ever see Vivian Manchester, and a temporary member of our Houston team when we first became aware of Vince Manchester's attack on the lady he called Julia Baby."

Nancy Lee walked from her seat in the middle of the circle toward Sally with an outstretched hand.

"Great to see you again, Sally. I think you will like working with this group. But instead of taking time for introductions right now, since we are deep into the quagmire this case has become, would you mind sitting next to me and taking questions from all of us? Everyone, please identify yourself when you ask a question. Sally, please sit next to me. You can see my monitor. Everyone, Sally's good with names; she'll remember yours. I'll start."

Nancy Lee moved the mouse on its little US government pad. The screen in front of everyone went blank. Then as she manipulated the mouse, a photo showed up on everyone's individual screen in front.

"Sally, you see the man in this photo? It's grainy, but I think you might have seen it two years ago. Who is this?"

"Well, it has been two years, but I think this is Vince entering Julia's office front door. I remember how he looked back at his own video camera from across the street at the Berkley Apartments. We all thought at the time he was making sure we knew it was him crashing into her door a minute or two later."

Nancy Lee made everyone's screen go blank again and put a new picture up.

"Who's this?" she asked, looking at Sally.

"That's Vivian Manchester. Sitting in our FBI conference room in Phoenix, a little over two years ago. I interviewed her with my FBI partner, Standusky. We snapped this picture of her, with her permission, at the start of the interview."

"OK, enough with the photos. Here's why you're here, Sally. There's a lot of confusion in the records of four different FBI field offices on this point. Are these two people, Vivian and Vince, related in any way?"

"Related? No, I don't think so. I think they are the same person. The pictures are of the same person but taken at different times. The first picture is of an alter personality who uses the name Vince. The second picture is of the host personality, whose name is Vivian. Vivian is a victim of childhood trauma. She was diagnosed about eleven or twelve years ago with a mental disorder now known as Dissociative Identity Disorder, or DID for short. That's the current clinical name—it was formerly known as Multiple Personality Disorder."

"Why was the name changed?"

"My lay understanding is that the original name pointed to a person's *personality*, while the later classification focuses entirely on one's sense of self, or *identity*."

"Are you sure about the diagnosis? Or is it based on your investigation, rather than a confirmed diagnosis by a qualified psychiatrist on the record?"

"The original diagnosis was made by psychiatrists when Vivian was about nine years old. We have copies of her parent's notes and medical records at that time. We think Vivian has the originals. We're not sure."

Nancy manipulated her computer again, this time typing directions from her keyboard. A new picture appeared on the monitors around the table.

"Who's this?"

Sally said, without hesitation, "That's Julia Santerra-Evans. It was taken by security cameras at the Boise Airport. We and other agents used it to identify her as being present in Boise when a man named Chaco Hernandez killed a man named Jason Bloomington, thinking he was killing Vivian's father, Stephan Manchester. There's another photo of Julia taken in Washington, DC, the same year, in a different airport. We linked her to the DC murder of Vivian's father. I assume both murders are open files, but they could have progressed to the charging state without me knowing about it."

"So, Sally, you are the only one in this room who has seen and interacted with Vivian Manchester and looked at the documentation about her dissociative diagnosis. You also interviewed a doctor about her condition and talked to witnesses in Arizona who knew her father. And, lastly, you're the only one who as read all the 302s on witnesses in three states and the District of Columbia. We thought it would be helpful to us going forward with the financial crimes case because it was handed to us by Vince Manchester. If he is her alter, we have important decisions to make as we try to take the case forward. That's because without Vince Manchester, we would never have known about Julia Santerra-Evans, and there would be no state case based on what Vince did to her as revenge for what he, or Vivian, believed Julia did to the father, Stephan. So here's the first and hardest question. Is there only one person—the girl we think of as Vivian, who is also the boy we think of as Vince?"

Without even so much as a blink of her eye, Sally answered, "I believe Vivian is the host personality. She was very real—on the phone, in person, and in the eyes of all the other people who knew her in Arizona. Her father was very real too, and we know a lot about him from people he interacted with. That's not the case with Vince. People saw him move—but we think they actually saw Vivian move, dressed and acting like a boy. No one, except a stationary store owner, remembers a boy. Vivian's high school classmates and teachers did not know her well, but they *did* know her. None of them ever heard of a boy in her family. Most importantly, if you assume for purposes of the federal financial crimes case that Vince was not a real person but rather an *alter* of Vivian, then he makes sense. There's no record of a boy except during times when Vivian was under extreme stress. She was in Washington, DC, only after the high stress period of the murder in Boise. Then when her father is murdered in DC, we have only glimpses or sightings of Vince, not Vivian. Do I know for a certainty? No, I do not. Only a psychiatrist could really tell you, and that's impossible because she's never been diagnosed or treated as an adult."

An older man, wearing a black blazer, blue button-down shirt, and a muted maroon tie raised his hand toward Nancy Lee.

"Yes, Your Honor, do you have a question? Sally, this is a senior DOJ lawyer from DC, who was once a state court judge in Delaware. Martin, what's your question for Sally?"

Without turning toward Sally, he said, "I do have a question, but first I'd like to make a comment about judges. If either the state or the federal case gets even close to trial, counsel for the government better make sure the assigned judge is aware that Vivian, or Vince, if they testify, either as a witness or a defendant, or maybe even a cooperating witness, is in fact a DID patient. He or she will also have to know to a certainty who you're putting on the witness stand—Vivian or Vince. Now, Sally, my name is *Marteen*, spelled m a r t i n. I'm Spanish on my father's side and Irish on my mother's. That's why I drink tequila shots with Guinness by the pint. Here's my question. In your work on the other cases, the original one from Baltimore, the murder in Boise, the murder in DC, and the two cases here in

Texas, did you ever treat Vivian as a suspect? Or did you consistently think of her as a witness?"

Sally was rarely lost for words. She hoped everyone who worked with her thought she was smart and devoted to her job. She got up early, worked late, and never ducked a dumb assignment. But this question threw her. Her initial words signaled confusion.

"Vivian a suspect? Suspect of what? Even her father was not a suspect, even though he had walked away from witness protection and the US Marshal's Office. I guess you could say he was suspected of some unknown connection to a man he worked for, who was later killed in a Learjet that exploded over the Gulf of Mexico, not far from here. But Vivian, his daughter? No, we never saw her that way. Now that you mention the alternative, we never thought of her as *just* a witness either. Personally, I always thought she might be a victim, but I could never pin that feeling down. She seemed to love her dad and never seemed to be forced to move from place to place. I felt sorry for her, especially after I interviewed her on the record. She was quite believable when she told us all she wanted was her dad's rucksack back. At the time, we didn't know anything about Vince."

"And," Martin continued, "once you found out about Vince, did you ever think of him as her brother?"

"No, I didn't. But of course, my thinking was colored by what was found in her dad's rucksack. That's where the dissociative diagnosis came from. Talking to Dr. Socorro also helped me understand. And listening to Dr. Estancia at that video conference just a short time ago was persuasive. But what difference does my opinion make?"

"All the difference in the world, Agent Lin. I'm a DOJ lawyer now, but I spent fifteen years as a trial judge in some very complicated financial crimes cases. We have to know who we are prosecuting and why. And we have to disclose all of it as possible exculpatory evidence. If Vince is an alter personality, and unless Vivian was fully aware of what he did, then some important parts of the financial crimes case will be dismissed by any good judge. Much of the evidence was the product of a coerced confession under extreme stress. Julia thought Vince would kill her unless she gave up her coconspirators. If the defense finds that out, they will make sure the jury knows the whole sordid story of the duct taping, the beating, the robbery, all of it. None of that should come in evidence in the federal case, but it's relevant to Julia's credibility. So the jury cannot be left in the dark about whether Vince is really a person or whether he's an alter of a woman we will never be able to put on the witness stand."

Nancy Lee, pointing to the iWatch on her right arm, said, "It's after five. We've been at it for a long time and our guest is working on a different clock. Let's go around the table quickly with comments and then wrap this up. We all have a lot of thinking to do."

There were no more comments.

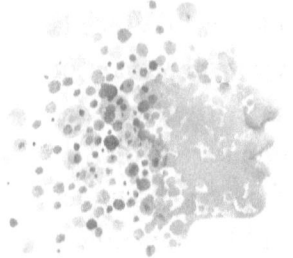

CHAPTER 22

On the drive from his office in central Houston to Rice University, Travis thought about his early morning look at Rice University's website. He regretted never being curious about Rice. It had been in the heart of Houston, the nation's fourth-largest city, for over almost 130 years. It was, the website said, a "comprehensive research university that fosters diversity and an intellectual environment that produces the next generation of leaders and advances tomorrow's thinking." That sounded like exactly what he needed—tomorrow's thinking. He'd read Dr. Ahmed Estancia's seventy-plus-page *curriculum vita* and one of his published medical articles about dissociative identity disorder. Nancy Lee had said he was the real deal in both medicine and law.

His secretary had made an appointment, calling it a medical-legal consultation. As he sat in the small outer room facing the faculty lounge, he looked over his notes and the few articles he'd copied on dissociative identity disorder.

"Mr. Danders," an absurdly thin young man said, "Dr. Estancia is still on the phone, but asked me to tell you he hopes to be with you in just a few more minutes. Can I get you anything while you wait? Warm water, grocery store coffee, anything?"

He hadn't even noticed the guy approach. Losing my situational awareness, Travis thought, as he shook his head sideways toward the emaciated student wearing a mustard colored T-shirt with the word RESIST in all caps on it.

"I'm just *dandy*, thank you," Travis said, wondering if the student would get the pun he'd emphasized.

"OK, I'll come back for you real soon, ya' hear?"

Fifteen minutes later, when Travis' nose was back inside his notes and articles, a deep voice bounced of the wall behind him.

"So sorry, Mr. Danders, so sorry. It's par for the academic course to keep students waiting, but one should never keep a fellow lawyer waiting. I'm Ahmed Estancia, please come on back to my office. Don't mind the mess of books; I just moved into this office two years ago—it usually takes me five to get a new office spruced up."

Once settled, they exchanged business cards. "Professor, my situation is both legally and medically challenging, especially from an ethics standpoint, and . . ."

"Why don't you call me Ahmed, and I'll call you Travis? Will that be alright? I'm sure you know a good bit about me, and I can say I've reviewed your bar profile, your firm's website, and did a quick news search for your name on

LexisNexis.com. You are well known in trial lawyer circles in Houston. You must have a very unusual case to call me for a consult. Let's get straight to that, shall we?"

"Yes, let's. I went to law school with Nancy Lee Sustern. Now I'm on the other side of one of her federal prosecution cases. She said I ought to talk to you about it. Do you know the case I'm talking about?"

"No, not any specific case. I did a short video conference with her and some other lawyers several weeks ago. But none of them told me anything about the case they had. It was strictly a short lecture and conversation about dissociative identity disorders, writ large. No specifics."

"Well, I can put some flesh on those bones. I represent a young man who might have this diagnosis. He's a defendant in a pending state of Texas assault and battery case. He's an unindicted coconspirator in a financial crimes case pending in federal court. He's never been arrested in either case. And . . ."

Dr. Estancia waved his hand, interrupting Travis's narrative.

"Excuse me. You say your client is a male and he *might* have a DID diagnosis? Are you guessing? Is there a confirmed diagnosis somewhere in a medical record? Is he under treatment?"

"Ahmed, I don't know. It's pure speculation on my part. That's why I'm here. If he is what the government lawyers think he is, then my legal representation of him has to be in accord with our legal ethics standards. That's why I'm here. You're a lawyer and a psychiatrist. Who better to talk to than you?"

"Travis, it would be better for you to talk to your client's psychotherapist, if he has one. If he doesn't it would be better for you to get one for him, and then ask that doctor for advice, if your client gives permission. Now, assuming that's impossible, given the urgent nature of your problem, let's talk about what doctors call acuity and lawyers call urgency. Medical ethics demands that doctors do no harm. Legal ethics demands that lawyers not put their clients at risk of harm. Is that why you're here, medical advice about keeping your client out of harm's way in the judicial system?"

"Exactly, yes, that's the core of my problem."

"Then, it's easy for me to help you. Get your client to a qualified psychiatrist. Get him diagnosed. Get him treated. Keep him away from the judicial system pending diagnosis and risk assessment psychiatrically. Then, when you are no longer guessing, deal with his legal problems."

"Don't mean to offend you, doctor, but that's too easy. I believe he is an alter. I don't think he's the host identity. Can we talk about that?"

Dr. Estancia held his left hand up, as he reached with his right for the old-fashioned corded phone on his desk. Punching the dial and waiting a few seconds, he said into the mouthpiece, "Please tell Simon and Candy that I have to cancel lunch. And I think there was a student who said he needed something before that. If he's out there, have him come back later this afternoon. I'll be tied up for an hour or two."

When highly experienced lawyers engage subject matter experts, the discussion is almost always an oral dissertation interrupted by engaged dialogue. That's what happened for the next ninety minutes in Professor Estancia's office. His assistant brought tuna fish sandwiches, chips, and bottled water. Dr. Estancia held forth and Travis took fifteen pages of notes on his yellow legal pad.

Travis learned that the goals of treatment for dissociative disorders were aspirational and often unsuccessful. At the top of the list was an effort to help DID patients "safely recall and process painful memories, develop coping skills, and, in the case of dissociative identity disorder, to integrate the different identities into one functional person."

Ahmed emphasized that "there is no drug that deals directly with treating dissociation itself. Rather, medications are used to combat additional symptoms that commonly occur with dissociative disorders."

Travis asked about psychotherapies. Ahmed told him they were used to treat dissociative episodes by decreasing symptom frequency and improving coping strategies. Travis probed for specific strategies and learned about CBT. Ahmed described it.

"Cognitive behavioral therapy helps change the negative thinking and behavior associated with depression. The goal of this therapy is to recognize negative thoughts in DID patients and to teach coping strategies. That's quite different from DBT, which is dialectical behavioral therapy."

"How do they differ?" Travis asked.

"DBT focuses on teaching coping skills to combat destructive urges, regulate emotions, and improve relationships while adding validation. Involving individual and group work, DBT encourages practicing mindfulness techniques such as meditation, regulated breathing, and self-soothing."

"How long would something like this take?" Travis asked.

"Years, perhaps decades," Dr. Ahmed answered.

"We don't have years," Travis replied. "What else have you got in your psychotherapeutic bag of tricks?"

"There's one more. I'm not a fan of it, but other psychotherapists use something called eye movement desensitization and reprocessing. The medical acronym is EMDR. They say it alleviates distress associated with traumatic memories. The literature says it mixes CBT techniques of relearning thought patterns with visual stimulation exercises to access traumatic memories and replace the associated negative beliefs with positive ones. But I've not used it."

"Ahmed, what else should I know about DID patients?"

"There's a great deal more, if you and your client get past the accusatory phase in litigation. Let's start with how opposing counsel might argue against any defense grounded in your client's condition. I call it science versus prosecutorial myth. Number one on that list is the prosecutor's position that multiplicity isn't real; it's junk science. Fact is, DID in several iterations has been recognized in healthcare since its inclusion in the 1980 release of the *Diagnostic and Statistical Manual of Mental Disorders*; that's the DSM-III. It's still recognized now in the DSM-IV. The symptoms are real. People who appear normal do experience them. Next, you might face a prosecutor who argues that the only mental illness protected by law is schizophrenia. Because they rarely see dissociative identity in criminal cases, they often confuse it with schizophrenia. They are totally different diagnoses. Schizophrenia is a psychotic illness. It presents as delusions, hallucinations, and paranoia. Prosecutors see that as easy to fake. Schizophrenics also display disorganized thoughts, speech, and movements. They withdraw socially. But dissociative patients do not present with any of those. They are hallmarked by alternate personalities and dissociation. I don't know of any study that suggests DID patients hallucinate their alters. Now, as you might guess, some DID patients may also present with symptoms related to actual psychosis, such as hearing voices. But that's where the comparison with schizophrenia stops."

Travis took his roller ball off the yellow page, shook his right hand in the air, and blew out a little air.

Ahmed said, "Taking notes is stressful, as well as tiring. It may feel better to raise your hand up, like you just did, but I'd recommend letting your hand drop to your side, and shaking it at the floor. Better blood flow that way."

Travis drank the last few swallows of his water bottle. Ahmed took the hint and asked his assistant for more warm water.

"Real Texans don't need their water cold, right Travis? By the way, were you named Travis after that splendid soldier at the Alamo?"

"That's what one of my uncles always said, but my folks never really confirmed that. I guess I hope I'm not because he died young."

"Yes, he did. At twenty-six. His first name was William, but they called him Buck. Did you know that in addition to being the commander, a lieutenant colonel, of the Republic of Texas, he was also a lawyer?"

"A lawyer? No I didn't. Hope he was a defense lawyer."

Dr. Estancia beamed at Travis.

"He was, he was. He defended a mud fort in a lost cause deep in the heart of Texas. Hope you don't suffer the same fate. Now, enough history. You surely have more questions."

"I do, I do, professor. Are DID patients mostly violent? I mean is violence a common element in their presentation?"

"No, the data doesn't support that. They are no more likely to be violent than anyone else. There are very few documented cases linking crime to DID. I know; I've done the research. But they always are traumatized. Sadly, they are more susceptible than the general population to re-traumatization."

"How so?"

"They often experience subsequent abuse and more violence."

"The host personality or the alter personality?

"Travis, I'm almost always talking about the host personality. We don't diagnose or treat alter personalities. Remember, the patient with a dissociative disorder *is* the host. Rather than extreme emotional reactions to the world, people living with DID *lose contact with themselves*. That's what dissociative means. The host personality loses track of his or her memories, sense of identity, emotions, and behavior."

"Can it happen any time?"

"Yes, and unlike personality disorders, DID patients may show symptoms at almost any age."

"Ahmed, I'm representing a man named Vince. I think he's an alter personality, like I said. Should I suggest to him that he come see you?"

"Ah, now you've asked the most important question. I've told you we don't treat alters, but that doesn't mean we can't, sometimes, rarely, but sometimes, interact with an alter primarily to get the host to emerge. That's what we call it—emerge. Honestly, I've never first seen an alter and later seen the host personality. The mere thought raises goose bumps in my brain."

"Doctor, you need a refresher course in anxiety. Goose bumps are signs of anxiety; they happen on your forearm, not in your brain."

"Speak for yourself, Travis. My brain gets goose bumps all the time. When I can't make a proper diagnosis, I get galloping goose bumps in the ventricles of my brain. It's like rust. I can only scrape it off by a deeper examination."

"Do you think I'm crazy for trying to diagnose my client as an alter personality?"

"No, I think you're a good lawyer, digging into the psyche of your client, looking for the best way to represent him. It may not be in his best interest to go to court. Maybe he should disappear. Maybe his host identity will emerge. Here's a wild guess. Imagine yourself walking arm-in-arm into a courtroom to present your client before a magistrate on a pending charge. He's an *alter* identity when you walk in. But a very different personality, the *host* personality, is suddenly standing beside you when the judge asks for your client's plea. That could happen, you know."

CHAPTER 23

Travis had tried calling Vince on his throw-away cell phone for two days. The same female voice inside every cell phone warned him, "Voicemail on this phone has not been set up." Right, he thought, I've got a client whose voicemail is as unavailable as he is. But do I even have a client?

He thought they'd established an agreement where he'd call, Vince wouldn't answer, and then moments later Vince would call him. But after the awkward meeting in San Antonio, nothing seemed to work.

At home, after the eleven o'clock news was over, Travis was in his study, taking a second look at a brief due in a week. His home phone rang.

"Yo, Travis, my lawyer man. You been ringing me on my old phone? I chucked it a few days ago. This is a new number. Log it in. Say, what's up? You making any progress keeping me on the outside?"

"Vince, thank you for calling me, but how did you get this number? It's unlisted."

"No such thing, lawyer man. Unlisted is for weebs who don't surf the right net. Like they say, ain't no secrets in satellites. On to business—you got any information for me yet?"

"Vince, listen to me. I need you to come to my office and talk in person. We have serious things to talk over and . . ."

"No, that ain't gonna work. I been sniffing around and there's shit-slinging going on at the fuckin F Bee Eye. I smell a capital R, little a, and touchy T. There've been some meetings and I think they were about me. You catching any of that? Anyway, it's way out of my comfort zone in downtown, lowdown Houston. Know what I mean? I can drive to San Antonio if you want. You know I don't fly, don't you? Highways, river bottoms, and steel rails—I do them, but not airplanes. Know what I mean?"

"There is a lot going on, Vince, but we need a face-to-face to discuss it. San Antonio is too far, not to talk, but the airports, taxis, and all that take too much out of the day. Can I meet you in one of Houston's suburbs, or exurbs? Beaumont's about a ninety-minute drive from here. What say we meet there tomorrow morning? I can think of a couple places . . ."

"Hey, here's what I can do. I'll meet you there, but not in the morning. Say 'bout three in the afternoon. I'll pick the place. When you get to the outskirts of town, pull over and call me. I'll tell you where I'm at. Someplace I can slide in and slide out. Know what I mean?"

Travis didn't, but said that would be OK. He left his office the next day at one o'clock, figuring he'd be on the west end of Beaumont by two thirty. He liked being early. Probably because he'd grown up in a busy, active family. In a house with four siblings, his parents had to plan on getting somewhere way earlier than usual just to arrive on time. When he crossed the Beaumont city line, he pulled over into a Circle K with gas pumps. He filled up, bought a cup of coffee, and called Vince's new cell phone. As he expected, there was no answer. And as he'd hoped, Vince rang back almost immediately.

"OK, you're here, right?"

"Yes," Travis said, fitting the Styrofoam coffee cup down into the cup holder in his Ford Expedition. "Where are you?"

"OK, here's the plan. Go to Lamar University. You can find that on your iPhone, right? Go to the Dishman Art Museum. There's lots of student-types here. Remember what I said about sliding in and out? Well, this is just the place for that. I'll be watching for you in ten. What kind a car you driving?"

"I'm in my Ford Expedition. It's white. The license tag is . . ."

The line went dead. Travis used his iPhone maps program to lead the way. When he got to the Dishman Art Museum, he parked, got out, and waited for his phone to ring. It didn't. But Vince showed up, eating Doritos and carrying a bottle of water.

"Let's sit in your car, Lawyer Man. Mine's trashed. Want some Doritos?"

For the next twenty minutes, Travis engaged Vince in a back and forth about the federal case, the state case, what it meant to be an unindicted coconspirator, and why the federal system didn't operate the way state courts do. Then, when Vince quit looking all around as they talked in the middle of a small university campus, Travis asked about multiplicity.

"Vince, have you ever heard the term identity disorder?"

"You mean like when a dude gets a new identity and it ain't working like it should? Like over the Dark Net when you want your identity to disappear and you can be whoever you want? That's what you're saying?"

"No, Vince, I'm talking about a mental health issue. It's called dissociative identity disorder. Some people are afflicted by it from childhood. I want to talk about Vivian. Do you know that name?"

Vince was in the passenger seat. The Ford Expedition is a large, roomy SUV with seats large enough for one 250-pound football player, or two teen age girls. He'd been slouching, but when he heard Vince's question, he leaned forward toward the dash and jammed his hands into his armpits, like he was trying to hug himself.

Lowering his voice to a whisper, he said, "We're not talking about her. Tole you that last time. Shut up. Shut up. Shut up."

Vince reached down, turned the AC blower up a few notches, and held his breath. They just sat there, Travis looking at Vince and Vince looking at his Just-Do-It high tops. Two minutes went by.

"That's all right, Vince. I think I know who she is and I respect your rights here. Can you tell me this—do you ever feel like your life's wasted because you're not who you want to be? Like you were living for someone else all the time?"

Vince said something, but then his voice sputtered, and he started to shake from side to side. Not rapidly, just even, shoulders going from one side to another, but not looking up, or over at Travis.

"Take a drink of water, Vince."

He did.

"Pass me your Doritos, Vince."

He passed them.

"Tell me what time it is, Vince."

"Can't. Time is skewed. Time to be out."

"How long have you been out, Vince?"

"I never know. Can't remember. Don't know when. Mostly when she's scared."

"Does she know Julia, Vince?"

"Shit no. Just me."

"All right, Vince, I want you to lean all the way back in the seat. Tell me why you came back to Houston."

"The note."

"The note Julia wrote? Right, Vince?"

During the next few minutes, Travis realized that if he used Vince's name as part of the question, he would get a simple answer. When he left the name out, Vince froze up, right there in the big Expedition seat. He didn't learn much more, but now he knew for sure. He was talking to an alter personality. He leaned back in his own seat and was silent for a good five minutes. Then, turning to the man still pushing back and forth against the plush leather seat but who stared ahead without seeming to see anything, he tried to bring reality back.

Raising his voice, Travis said, "This is a beautiful little university. Did you go to college in Arizona?"

Vince turned his head and said, "This fancy-ass car is killing me. Besides, I got to get back to my own ride. Places to go, Lawyer Man, places to go."

He got out, leaving his Doritos and his bottle of water in the car. Travis watched him go back into the art museum. It probably has a backside parking lot, Travis said to himself as he carefully wrapped his unused handkerchief around Vince's water bottle and placed it the large glove box between the seats. He pulled out into the main street and dialed Nancy Lee's cell phone.

CHAPTER 24

Julia had heard nothing from Amherst Pipps in three days. She was thinking of him as her toy lawyer; when she wrote a note about him she called him Pipp Squeak. She called the website number for mobilelaw.com.

When Amber Sue answered with her Texas-style cherry hello, Julia cut her off after three words.

"Can it, Amber Sue. This is Julia. Pipps was supposed to call me two days ago. Did he have that meeting with big-bear-in-the-woods Lumberson, like I told him to? He better have. Is it on his calendar?"

"Miss Julia, I cannot discuss Mr. Pipps . . ."

"How old are you, anyhow? Do I call you 'Miss Amber Sue'? You can call me Julia. I ain't formal. If I was, I'd be offended. Don't you know young women these days are Miz, not Miss? Hell with it, just put him on the line."

"But I can't, Miz Julia. He's indisposed at the moment."

"You're in the Mobile Law Office, right? And he's back in the shitter behind that paneled wall, right? OK, we all got to go sometime. Have him call me right goddamn back, you hear!"

Three minutes later, Julia's cell lit up. She let it ring five times then clicked the little green image of a phone on her oversize screen.

"Pipps, you feel better now? Hope so. Why have I not heard from you about your meeting with Lumberson?"

"Good afternoon, Julia," Pipps said, hoping his tone of voice sounded mildly annoyed but not condescending. He'd been grinding his teeth ever since that humiliating conversation with Grant Lumberson. He knew his dentist would probably notice and suggest more dental shaping. "Yes, I did meet with Mr. Lumberson, day before yesterday. I could not call you yesterday. I was on the road and the cell phone coverage was pitiful, just pitiful. Anyhow, we did talk and . . ."

"Don't tell me. The old bastard would not let you ask all your questions and ended up giving you a lecture about real lawyers in real courtrooms in real cases and all that shit he's known for. The main thing was telling him I would not testify, but I wanted protection from that maniac. You got that much done, right?"

"I did."

"And you learned there's no arrest warrant out, yet, for Vince Manchester, right?"

"There is no clarity on that, Julia. The court record does not list one and . . ."

"Goddamn it, Pipps. You did ask Lumberson whether he'd asked for one, right?"

"He was very difficult, very close-mouthed about the case. I got the feeling that he's talked to Mr. Manchester's defense lawyer, Travis Danders, and . . ."

"The feeling? Why would he be talking to Vince's lawyer if there is no arrest warrant outstanding? Why would a defense lawyer call the prosecutor if his client was not either under arrest or subject to an arrest warrant? A good defense lawyer would just lie in the weeds, right?"

"Well, I haven' talked to him myself and . . ."

"Goddamn it again, Pipps. I gave you instructions, didn't I? I never said talk to Vince's lawyer. Don't be running all over Houston saying you're my lawyer. I hired you not to represent me, but to find things out for me. But now there's more to talk about. In person. I want you to come down to Brownsville again. Next Monday, same place, but before noon. You can do that, right?"

"Well, I'll have Amber Sue check for calendar conflicts. I'm in Houston now, not in Corpus Christi like last time. It's a long drive and there's costs for transportation, too, and . . ."

"Pipps, you are on a four-hundred an hour fee agreement with me. Of course, you can charge that same rate for traveling to meet me. Gas for the big-ass buggy, too. This time, it's gotta be more private. Don't bring Amber Sue. And send Jingle on an errand before I get there. Same south end of the Gladys Porter Zoo. Eleven o'clock sharp. Got it?"

"All right, Julia. I'll be there. But I'll have to charge you the hourly rate both ways. Round trip, OK?"

Pipps waited for an answer but only heard a dial tone. He didn't take it personally. He was not all that comfortable talking to her anyhow. Twelve hours travel time and one or two more for the actual meeting was a good fee. He'd charge her the state mileage reimbursement fee. That would bring in 64 cents per mile times 355 miles; $227 dollars. And there would be meals, too. Could he charge for Jingle's time? He wondered. The calculating felt good, better than thinking about what else she would make him do. But as long as he was getting cash by the hour, who cares, he thought.

CHAPTER 25

Vivian waited for her noon phone call from her dad. When it didn't come by twelve-thirty, she dialed his number at the Sand Oaks Retirement Community in northeast Washington, DC. No answer. She called again five minutes later. Stay calm, be aware of your surroundings, don't panic, she kept telling herself on the bus ride to his retirement home from the DC YWCA across town. Like her dad, Stephan Manchester, had insisted, she got off the bus two blocks before it passed the cross street to the home. Seemed a normal day in residential Washington until she got a half block away and saw the yellow crime-scene tape cordoning off the curved entryway. She ran past the big oak trees and stopped dead in her tracks. Two fire trucks, an ambulance, and several police cars blocked her way.

Trails of smoke lazily drifted out of the giant hole in the left wing of the building. Bricks were widely scattered on the lawn, and one tree only a few feet away from the wall lay splintered ten yards out onto the lawn. The blackened bricks around the burned-out hole in the wall told her everything.

"That's my dad's room!" she screamed as she pushed her way through the crowd of onlookers and ducked under the yellow tape, trying to get to the front door. A blue-uniformed police officer grabbed her from behind and held her tight to his chest. Screaming and kicking backward at her captor, she wailed at him.

"Lemme go! Let me go! That's my dad's room. It's . . ."

Another officer, a black female, barked at the man still holding her from behind. "Let her go. I've got her now."

Vivian felt his arms drop just as the lady dressed in black SWAT clothes reached for her. Too late. Vivian dropped to the pavement with a thud. It seemed like just a minute, but it actually took the paramedic almost ten minutes to revive her. When she came to, she was on a gurney in the back of an ambulance headed for the closest hospital. The lady SWAT officer was seated across from her in the back, with two hospital-garbed EMTs.

It was hard for Vivian to focus, and her head throbbed like she'd been run over. The EMT's words came in slow motion. She heard most of it.

"You fell and hit your head. Try not to move. You're in a neck brace. Just in case. Can you see me? Hear me? Try to squeeze my hand. We'll be at the hospital in three minutes. IV line in . . . soon . . ."

Her dad's voice seemed to ring in her head between spurts of sound from the EMT, the siren blaring above her, and the black SWAT lady holding her hand. Do not tell them anything. Can't trust anyone. Just be quiet. Be still. Vince will be close by. She closed her eyes, and her mouth.

Vivian stayed in the trauma room inside the huge ER at George Washington University Hospital for four hours before she got up the courage to speak.

"Where is my dad?"

One of the green-garbed nurses heard her from the other side of the curtain that surrounded her bed. She'd been awake the whole time, but kept her eyes shut and moved as little as possible. Her head ached and she felt the small bandage over the cut on her forehead. But she could move all her limbs and her brain worked. Actually it was on fire with what became organized thinking once they took her off the ambulance's wheeled gurney and plopped her onto a bed. She knew her dad was dead, simply because he was not here. They must have her name from her Boise driver's license in her purse—they had been calling her name all afternoon. Vivian, can you hear me, can you open your mouth please, can we get you anything, your vitals are fine, you only have a cut on your head, no damage, X-ray is perfect, can you talk, there are some people here who want to talk to you, are you ready to talk, can you talk?

Within a minute, the curtains parted and the nurse came in with the black SWAT lady and a man with a gray beard and dark suit carrying his hat and a small brief case. "We need a private place to talk," one of them said. The nurse accommodated. They rolled her into a small treatment room with a fetid smell. A large, round plastic tub with a floppy top used to discard bandages and used medical equipment took up half the wall space.

Gray Beard said, "Ms. Shortfield? That is your name, right? Shortfield? We have to talk to you about . . ."

Vivian grimaced but spat her question at the man.

"Where is my dad? Is he dead? Why won't anyone tell me?"

"Is Stephan Manchester your father? If so, we can tell you. But we have to know who you are and why you collapsed at the Sand Oaks retirement home earlier today."

"He is my father. I was coming to visit when I saw the police cars and the hole in the wall in the same wing where he lived and . . ."

The SWAT lady shooed the stern-faced man away, put her hand on Vivian's hand, and moved closer to her.

"Vivian, just hold onto yourself, my dear. I'm gonna give it to you straight. Your father is dead. He was blown up in an explosion at his retirement home. The man with me, Agent Burlein, is from the FBI. They are taking over the investigation, but I'm the one who picked you up off the pavement. And they are letting me talk to you with them so I can report to my boss, the DC police chief, what happened to you. I know they gave you some pain medication. Are you thinking straight, or is the medicine still working on your brain?"

"I'm OK," Vivian mumbled. "Can I please have some Kleenex? And some water. I fainted because I saw the black bricks and knew there must have been an explosion. Who did this?"

Agent Burlein responded. "We don't know that yet. Can you think of any reason why someone would want to kill your father?"

Vivian glared at the man. Still holding onto the woman's hand, she answered his question while looking into her eyes.

"They killed him by blowing him up. Just like they did to his old boss at Hurlitt International. He showed me the newspaper about it. You know that, don't you? They blew up a Learjet flying over the Gulf of Mexico just to kill my dad's friend, Fritz Goshkervic. Then they tried to kill Dad in Boise. Are you going after them now?"

"Ms. Shortfield," the man said, moving closer to the end of the bed so she had to look at him, "this is not a conversation we can have in a hospital room. I'll talk to your nurse and make sure it's medically permissible for you to be checked out of here. I will escort you to the FBI office downtown and we can continue the interview there. We won't need DC police assistance there," he added, looking at the SWAT lady.

Vivian shook her head slowly, took several deep breaths, and said quietly, "Are you arresting me for the death of my father?"

"No, of course not. But we still . . ."

"Then, I'm not going to the FBI office or anywhere else with you. I would like you to leave my room. I want to talk to this lady. I'm sorry, ma'am, but I didn't get your name."

"That's all right, my dear. My name is La Fonda Wilsea. I'm a police sergeant with the DC police. We would also like to talk with you, but only if you want to help us. We can wait until you're feeling better."

"No, I want to answer your questions now. But the FBI has never been helpful to me, or my father. So, as soon as he leaves, I'll answer your questions."

Sgt. Wilsea said, "All right, if you feel up to it. Let me talk to this gentleman out in the hallway. While I'm out there, I'll get you some fresh ice water, or would you like a soft drink?"

"Dr. Pepper would be nice," Vivian said.

When Sgt. Wilsea came back into Vivian's cubicle in the ER, Vivian was gone. The nurse said they never saw her leave, and she didn't go out past the triage nurse at the swinging-door entrance from the lobby. All they saw was the young man who'd been in visiting her. He walked down the hall and out the ER front door.

"Who was he?" the SWAT lady asked.

"Dunno," the nurse said. "We didn't see him come in; we thought you sent him to talk to her."

"Describe him," she insisted.

"Just another DC kid. Levis, hoodie, sun glasses, Baltimore Orioles baseball cap—looked brand new. In a hurry."

Vivian was gone. The boy in her room was gone.

CHAPTER 26

Jingle drove Pipps down to Brownsville from Corpus Christi late on a Sunday afternoon to meet with Julia at eleven o'clock on Monday morning. The Gladys Porter Zoo was closed on Mondays. For this trip, they towed Jingle's 2007 Hyundai Veloster behind the RV. Jingle's nephew, wife, and two boys lived north of Brownsville; he wanted to spend the night with them. Pipps loved spending the night in the master suite at the rear of his treasured mobilelaw.com RV office. He told Jingle to come back to the zoo parking lot by noon. He was sure the appointment with Julia would be over by then.

The blast shook the neighborhood around the zoo and generated several dozen emergency calls into the Cameron County 9-1-1 Emergency District at exactly 11:04 that morning. Dozens of cars driving by and scores of homeowners heard the blast and then the sirens. The press, never far behind major 911 calls, made it to the fiery scene by eleven-twenty. The zoo didn't open until Thursday because investigators took three days to slog through the debris, remove body parts, and put everything under microscopes and scores of forensic testing. Very little of Pipps's Entegra RV was recognizable. The burned-out chassis looked like a pinpoint strike from a secret drone flying at five thousand feet and dropping a radar-guided three-hundred-pound bomb. The crater was forty feet long and fifteen feet wide.

Although Pipps didn't know it, the Gladys Porter Zoo's main entry had security cameras covering the main entrance to the parking lot and the front gate. There was no coverage of the south or north ends of the parking lot. The Brownsville police and fire department responders screeched through the main entrance six minutes after the explosion. They could be seen on the digital recording security tapes pulling through the main entrance, making sliding turns toward the south end of the lot, and then disappearing out of view. Smoke could be seen on the video, but there was no audio.

Early video and digital reporting popped up on local media outlets by noon. KTLM, the local NBC affiliate, and KFXV, the Fox News outlet, had reporters and camera crews there all day. Democrats learned about the explosion and fire from KTLM. Republicans heard the suspicion it was a terrorist act, given Brownsville's location on the Mexican border. By four o'clock, at least one representative of the ATF was on site.

The Bureau of Alcohol, Tobacco, Firearms, and Explosives, commonly shortened to ATF, is the federal agency primarily responsible for administering and enforcing the criminal and regulatory provisions of the federal laws pertaining to destructive devices, bombs, explosives, and arson. The FBI and the ATF work together on bomb explosion cases. If the initial investigative findings suggest murder, the FBI becomes the primary team, and the ATF provides logistical and forensic support.

Jingle, Pipps's driver, heard about the explosion from Fox News and raced to the zoo parking lot as fast as his aging Hyundai would go. He was the first one to tell a police officer holding the crowd behind the yellow crime scene tape he knew the owner of the RV. The cop was surprised that it was an RV. He thought it was a semi tractor and trailer. He took Jingle to the dark canvas tent set up as a temporary command post by fire, police, and the first ATF officers on the scene.

By two p.m., the ATF officer on site contacted Pipps's secretary, Amber Sue. She confirmed her boss's cell phone was not answering. She said his meeting was supposed to be eleven that morning with his client, Julia Santerra-Evans. That was enough for the combined police team to kick the investigation from accidental to possible arson. A quick Google search revealed Pipps as a criminal defense lawyer. The public sites had little on Julia Santerra-Evans, but FBI Houston had many files and investigations involving her. They said she was a cartel lawyer involved in a big federal case in Houston. Local police called in the FBI around two p.m.

The six o'clock news had reported two bodies in the burned-out RV, but no identifications were announced, pending notification of next of kin. Identification by autopsy would take weeks. They had bits and pieces of bodies. Charred skulls, spines, pelvises, and leg bones were visible once the shattered debris was carefully disentangled from body parts.

By midday on Tuesday, arson and explosion experts had confirmed the source of the fire and explosion. It was a bomb, set off below the truck chassis. That explosion blew up the gas tank, which fed thirty gallons of gas to fuel a fifty-foot tall fire ball. The passenger and living quarters up on top were gone. The engine was found ten feet away from the chassis. Determining the origin of the fire and its cause would take months to reduce to writing.

Nancy Lee Sustern and Slate Blakey got text messages just in time to watch the TV reporting Monday night. They notified Lumberson and Agent Lin. All four helicoptered down to Brownsville early Tuesday morning. Everyone at the crime scene knew this was criminal interference, rather than error, or arson by Pipps. By Wednesday morning, the FBI and the Harris County Attorney's Office were rethinking their cases. One body was presumed to be Pipps, the other his client, Julia Santerra-Evans. Final identification would be confirmed after the autopsies.

Meanwhile, Agent Lin ticked off, for the benefit of local law enforcement, and the ATF officers, the four linked murder cases that Julia Santerra-Evans was involved in. A bombing over the Gulf of Mexico. A garroting in Boise, Idaho. A bombing in Washington, DC. And now a bombing in Brownsville, Texas. There appeared to be only one common connection—Vince Manchester. Federal and state all-points-bulletins went out immediately. Nancy Lee Sustern and Agent Lin were tasked to find and interview Travis Danders as soon as their helicopter landed in Houston Wednesday morning.

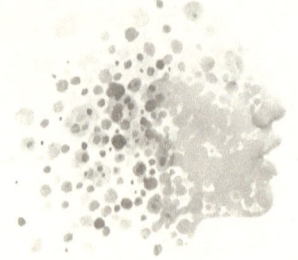

CHAPTER 27

Travis spent nine billable hours on Monday meeting with clients preparing for a mediation in a wrongful termination case, which arose out of his forty-two-year-old client's wrongful arrest on a shoplifting case. He didn't get back to his condo until after eight and skipped the local news. So he didn't know about the explosion at the zoo in Brownsville until he opened his Tuesday morning copy of the *Houston Chronicle*. He read the headline and the first paragraph before turning the page. It didn't identify the dead or the owner of the RV. Even if it had, he didn't know Pipps, or that he had any connection to anything Travis was working on. But he got a text from Nance Lee at 11:45 Wednesday morning that got his attention.

"Travis, this is Nancy Lee. It's 11:45. Wednesday. Call me immediately. It's about your client Vince Manchester. We have just issued APBs for his arrest and detention. Call now. FBI agents will be at your office soon."

He got the text while gassing up his Expedition on the way to the office. He'd spent the morning at home, going over a new case file involving a high-profile bribery case involving a member of the Texas state senate. He was supposed to fly to Austin on a red-eye tonight for a breakfast meeting with the senator on Thursday. He texted back.

"Nancy Lee. Am driving downtown fm home. Shud be in office—twenty mins—I'll call fm there—Travis."

He took fifteen minutes to get to the office, park in the underground lot, and take the elevator to the fourteenth floor. He went in the front door. Two new faces were sitting in the waiting room. Both got up as he let the door swing closed behind him. His receptionist, Becca, stood up quickly, looking like a home invasion was in progress.

"Mr. Danders, I just tried your cell because these are . . ."

He looked at the man and woman who were getting up from the soft leather seats.

"Mr. Danders, I'm Agent Sally Lin. We met by phone ten days ago, but it's nice to see you in person. This is Agent Widnor—he's with the FBI field office here. We would like to talk to you about . . ."

"Let me guess," Travis said, flashing both agents a nodding smile, as he walked toward them. "You're here to talk about my client, Vince Manchester. And yes, Agent Lin, it's nice to place a face. I just got a text from Nancy Lee Sustern. Will she be joining us?"

"She's on the way. Should be here in a few. Can we meet in private? You are willing to talk to us, aren't you?"

"Of course, as soon as we settle on terms. Follow me. Can we get you anything? Water, tourist recommendations, homemade cookies? Becca is a good receptionist, but she's a great baker. Her Texas Cowboy Cookies will pick you up and slow you down at the same time, right Becca?"

"Bet on it, Boss," Becca said, as he led the way to the conference room next to his office. "Should I bring Miss Nancy Lee directly to the conference room? Will she be having cookies, too?"

"Just bring us a plateful, will you? And a Coke Zero for me. Ya'll want water or a soft drink to go with your cookies?" he asked over his shoulder as he opened the conference room door.

Once settled around the six-seat conference table, Agent Lin explained she was tasked to the Houston FBI office temporarily regarding the federal case under seal, the one related to his client Vince Manchester. Travis interrupted her.

"Agent Lin, when we talked on the phone, you gave me some insight about the federal case and my client's alleged role in what happened in Baytown. I take it you're here about those same issues. But like I said, AUSA Nancy Lee Sustern's text informed me of my client's extant arrest warrant. Is he also under an immediate all-points stop-and-arrest bulletin? Do you have a copy of the warrant with you?"

"Mr. Danders, I do. I'm willing to show it to you, but given the urgency of the matter, maybe I should just outline the situation for you; Nancy Lee can fill in when she gets here."

"No thanks, Agent Lin. You're here with a fellow agent. This is looks to me like a formal interview; I trust both of you will be filing 302s on what we say by the end of the day. Let's make a record, OK? Please show me your identification and badge numbers. Here's my card, one for each of you. I'd rather wait until the AUSA is actually here, given the at-risk warning you and Nancy Lee have established. But we can speculate about a related matter, if that's alright."

"Related?" Agent Widnor asked.

"Yes, let's talk about a case you're not involved in—the state case against Mr. Manchester. Maybe you can tell me whether the state prosecutor, Grant Lumberson, has *also* sought and been granted an arrest warrant for my client?"

Agent Lin answered for Widnor.

"Mr. Danders, we were not clear about why we're here. The APB and the arrest warrant issued this morning by a federal judge are not related to the federal money-laundering case *or* the state assault-and-battery case."

"Not? Not related? Are you pressing new charges against my client that I don't know about?"

"Mr. Danders, we . . ."

"Make it Travis, please. So, I am perplexed . . ."

The conference room door opened. Becca came in bearing a wooden tray with cookies, two bottles of water, and a can of Coke Zero with a large glass of ice. Behind her, Nancy Lee Sustern came in, looking a little out of breath.

"Travis," she said, eyeing the cookies, "you know those Texas Cowboy Cookies could be considered a bribe in some circles. We won't charge you if we each get two cookies. Sally and Fred, you're going to love these."

They settled in comfortable chairs, the cookies and drinks were distributed, and all four opened legal pads and prepared to take notes between bites of the oversized cinnamon-topped sugar cookies.

Agent Lin finished her explanation.

"Your client, Vince Manchester, is the subject of a probable cause determination made this morning by a federal magistrate judge authorizing his immediate arrest and detention arising out of the deaths yesterday of two persons in Brownsville, Texas. You may have seen the TV coverage, and . . ."

"Come again? You're telling me your respective offices have determined my client is somehow involved in an explosion yesterday in Brownsville? I know almost nothing about that, except that an ATF investigation is underway. Who got killed? And how in the world do you connect that to my client? Does it relate in any way to the existing indictments?"

In what would become a ping-pong conversation, Nancy Lee answered the question directed at Agent Lin.

"Travis, in a nut shell, here's the connection. ATF presumes the two bodies, which are totally disembodied, so to speak, are those of a Houston lawyer named Amherst Pipps and his client, Julia Santerra-Evans."

"Jesus H. Christ, you gotta be kidding. Julia? In Brownsville? She's got a lawyer? Why, I mean . . ."

Agent Lin waved her hand.

"Maybe I can help here. We're only a day ahead of you, Mr. Danders. The identifications are very tentative but are supported by Mr. Pipps's secretary, a woman named Amber Sue—not sure whether Sue is her last name or her middle name—and his driver, a man named Jingle. I don't have his last name. Both confirm an eleven a.m. meeting on Monday morning at the Gladys Porter Zoo in Brownsville.

The explosion occurred at 11:06 a.m. in the south end of the parking lot. Incidentally, the zoo was closed on Monday so there were no other cars in the parking lot."

Sally wiped her chin with a paper napkin. Travis had noticed Nancy Lee signaling the problem to the well-dressed FBI agent by pointing to her own chin and nodding her head. He took the pause as a chance to slow down this information train.

"Can we go back a bit? Do I understand this meeting to be a *supposition* based on a secretary's notation on her calendar, and the driver's *supposition* about what he thought was taking place? But nobody knows for sure who, exactly, was in the RV at the time of the explosion? Ya'll got a warrant from a federal magistrate judge on that evidence? Really? Mother of Jesus, probable cause has gone amuck, looks to me."

Nancy Lee knew where this was headed.

"Travis, we really need your cooperation. Wait, don't look at me like that. You're right that we're on thin ice here. You could probably get the warrant quashed. Hell, we probably wouldn't oppose you. But we're here in your office because I know you're new to the case and . . ."

"I'm new to the federal money laundering case, in which my client is not indicted, not subject to arrest, and not even remotely connected to an explosion in Brownsville on Monday. I'm new to the federal case, but you two are just as *new* to whatever happened on Brownsville on Monday. So, no. I won't help you until you give me a clear statement of the evidence suggesting my client, Vince Manchester, had anything at all to do with what you cannot even be sure *is* a crime much less an indictable crime on my client's part. You want him arrested? For what? A supposition about a lawyer's calendar? Did Julia actually hire the lawyer—Pipps? I've never heard of him. What's his practice?"

"He's a fairly young lawyer with a mix of misdemeanor and personal injury cases. A few felonies, but no trial experience. We know for sure Julia hired him because he met with Grant Lumberson last week on the assault-and-battery case your client is damn sure involved with. He is indicted in that case, Travis. That's part of our probable cause for his warrant . . ."

"Ah hell, Nancy Lee. You're making it worse. If the connection is the assault-and-battery case, why 'n hell didn't Grant by-God Lumberson take it to state court and get a warrant there? Or is that a federal secret?"

Nancy Lee, pinching her lips together, felt like she was back in law school and Travis was ramping her blood pressure up, or maybe her hormones.

"Travis Danders, don't get your dander up. Remember that poke? Give us a break. We're here because we think this problem is far bigger than any of us could have fathomed just two weeks ago. Save your lecture about criminal procedure. Let's try to see this as a professional and an ethical challenge for everyone, including you! Just let me try and piece some of this together."

"Well, my Coke's all gone, the cookies are gone, and if you can assure me that you'll call off the federal arrest warrant, at least for now, I'll back off and we can talk."

Agent Lin said she'd call her office and put a two-hour hold on the search for Mr. Manchester.

Nancy Lee explained her primary concern. She said, let's assume a maniac is responsible for the bombing in Brownsville, and that his motive was to halt either the federal money laundering case or the state assault case. Travis countered by saying bad people set bombs off all over America. Some are maniacs, but most are terrorists or deranged sociopaths, not maniacs.

This resulted in a change of adjectives. Whoever set off the bomb was just a killer—let's not speculate on his mental state yet. Nancy Lee said, let's assume the target was Julia, not Mr. Pipps. Doesn't that tie in Mr. Manchester even though we don't know how? Both FBI agents cautioned against that. No evidence of any kind about whether one or both *were* targets. Besides, Mr. Danders is probably right— we have bits from two bodies—and circumstantial evidence they were Pipps and Santerra-Evans. Not enough to start framing them as connected targets. What about Pipps's other clients? What about Julia's other enemies? Could be one was a target and the other not. Could be connected to Mexican border issues, or the administration's zero tolerance policy on illegal border crossings.

Travis speculated that it could be about money. Julia had it. Pipps, maybe not. But money, bad blood, and politics were at the root of most violent crime. Nancy Lee posed doubt—we know Julia hired Pipps—and we know Pipps talked to Lumberson. Three days later Pipps and Julia are murdered. That must be connected, she argued. Maybe so, Travis conceded, but Julia's history reeked of drug cartel response—more so than anything remotely connected to his client.

Agent Widnor interjected because, he said, there is a long history between Julia and her former clients—Plankton Resources and others in the money laundering business. Might they be suspects as the Brownsville bombing investigation moves forward? Good reason to cancel the warrant on my client, Travis argued, while agreeing that Plankton's beef with Julia was a possible motive.

Agent Lin returned to whether Vince was an alter personality. Travis did not disclose his own views but agreed that path needed to be fleshed out before anyone goes off half-cocked about motive or opportunity. We don't even have basic forensics yet from Brownsville. Why are we debating the mental health of only one possible suspect? What about Julia's mental health? Some people think she's either a hit lady or a broker for the Sinaloa Cartel. Either way, she might have been the target of people none of us have even thought about.

After sixty minutes of back-and-forth chess moves by legal advocates, they mutually called the game a draw. Nancy Lee said she'd recommend to her boss, the chief deputy ASUA, that the warrant be quashed. Travis said he'd contact his client. He didn't say why. Agent Lin said she'd follow up with Lumberson and that she'd recommend to Slate Blakey she be posted as the primary contact between Houston FBI and Mr. Danders. Travis asked that he be kept informed about the Brownsville ATF investigation. Yes, Agent Lin, agreed, "to the extent they determine the actual identity of the victims and offer a forensic explanation of either a criminal connection, or perhaps just a mechanical defect in the RV."

Travis showed everyone to the door. When it swung shut, he turned to Becca.

"Is Connor in his office, Becca?"

"No. He's in Austin today. But he'll be in early tomorrow. He's got that hearing in the Sharpie case. Want me to try to reach him for you?"

"No, it can wait. I'm going to talk to Grant Lumberson. In his office. But interrupt me with a text if my client Vince Manchester tries to reach me."

"Right, boss. Vince Manchester? That new client, right? He's not called in through me, has he?"

"No, but he's got my cell. He's not very predictable, so he could call the office line. If he does, try to figure out where he's calling from. Don't bother asking him, just try to figure it out."

Becca said, "Figure it out? I'm a baker not a candlestick maker. I use recipes for everything. Got one for finding out where clients are when they are on the telephone?"

CHAPTER 28

Dr. Ahmed Estancia had two offices—one at the medical sciences building on the Rice University campus and the other at the Harris County Psychiatric Center, the largest provider of inpatient psychiatric care in Houston. He saw patients two days a week and accepted clinic patients on Mondays. The Monday after the explosion in Brownsville a new patient walked into the clinic and asked to see Dr. Ahmed.

"Do you mean Dr. Ahmed Estancia?" the beleaguered clerk at the front desk asked.

"I guess so," the woman asked.

"Do you have a scheduled appointment? He sees clinic patients on Mondays, but he's always booked well in advance. What is your clinic number?"

"I don't have one," the tall, dark-haired woman said.

"Oh, then you need to start with the paperwork. The doctors here only see patients who are registered in our clinic—all of them have been seen by our psychiatric nurse practitioners for a workup. Just a sec, and I'll get you a set of forms to fill out."

The receptionist swiveled her chair around to reach a tall set of shelves with boxes of forms. She selected three and swiveled back around to face the front. The tall, dark-haired woman was gone.

Two days later, Vivian got her nerve back up. She looked up Dr. Estancia's name at Rice University and found his office number at the medical sciences building. It was more difficult to navigate, but she finally found a public parking garage four block from the building. She walked slowly, in her new red pumps, to his building, and found his name on an electronic signage board in the lobby. She sat on a ledge outside for an hour. Then when people stopped coming in and out of the building, she went up the stairs to his office at four o'clock. She never liked elevators. It never occurred to her he might not answer the door, so she was not surprised when he she heard a man's voice from the other side of the dark walnut door.

"It's open."

Wetting her lips, she pressed her finger tips on the door after turning the handle slowly. It creaked, but opened halfway. She stood there, thinking maybe she should just run for it.

The male voice said, "Hey, I have open office hours from three to four-thirty, once a week. I'm all alone in here. I don't bite. Come on in."

She was surprised to find a large man squished down behind a small desk covered with blue notebooks, stacks of stapled paper, two computers, and a China tea service. The tray was cluttered with an open sugar bowl and half a dozen small spoons. A small pewter bowl held used tea bags, with discolored tags on little brown strings. The narrow window behind the man's back was shaded and seemed smaller than it actually was because it was surrounded top, bottom, and both sides by shelved books, not all of which had visible spines. A full wastepaper basket was stationed on his right side.

The man was the opposite of his desk. His nearly white shock of hair was combed neatly. His suit coat, lint free, hung like a custom fit. His tie was loose, but barely, like he loosened it only to improve air passage without looking disheveled. He had deep-set eyes, and salt and pepper eye brows. A protuberant but not unruly nose pointed down and just to his right side. She thought he looked like an understanding man; she'd known only a few. While she never trusted her own first impressions, she felt suddenly comfortable.

He got up, almost knocking off the edge a short stack of what looked like typed papers with streaks of red ball point on top.

"I'm sorry, I took you for a grad student. Are you, or did they send you over here from central casting?"

"Central casting?" she asked, pushing up her cheeks and turning her head slightly off center.

He thought he detected a hint of either Irish in the southern part of the Isles, or England in the midlands. Not a brogue—definitely college, perhaps even university, he thought.

"It's something I ask of faculty. Many neurology and psychology teaching adjuncts these days have a common look about them—I call it central casting. I just mean they look like students in the sciences rather than the humanities. I'm Ahmed Estancia. This is my office suite. Housekeeping avoids us both. Have the seat, you can see there's only one."

Like all psychotherapists, he waited to form that all-important first impression from words, not appearances. He could already tell this woman was not here on school business, or to talk about education or a job. He knew her secret from the way she opened the door and because she waited for permission to enter. He knew from how carefully she looked obliquely at him, not straight on. She'd been wounded; a long time ago.

Once settled in the chair, she arranged her purse in her lap. It was the purse of a very private person—zippered, latched, belted, and in leather, not cloth. As he watched her, his mind zipped from outer motivation to inner motivation. When would she mention the wound? When the lie? And how long might it take before she lowered her shield so he could help?

"Would you like some tea?" he asked.

"No, thank you."

"Have we met, somewhere?"

"No."

"Did someone refer you to me?"

"Yes. Well, sort of."

"Sort of?"

"I heard your name."

"May ask from whom?"

"First, can I ask you something?"

"Of course."

"What's a psychiatric nurse practitioner? They're not doctors?"

Dr. Estancia took a moment to think about the question. He could just respond by defining the job—that probably wasn't what she wanted to know. He could answer by telling this young lady how important MSNs were in mental health care—no, that wouldn't be reassuring. He answered by talking about what he guessed she was fearful about.

"Well, some patients like talking to nurses better than doctors because they seem more trustworthy and down to earth. You know, doctors seem so busy and some of them don't take time to really explain things. Psychiatric nurse practitioners have masters' degrees and years of experience in nursing. They specialize in mental health and work under a doctor's supervision. But most importantly, they are great listeners. Sometimes I think the ones I work with at the Harris County Psychiatric Clinic should get flowers every day; they are the nicest people I know."

"I went there. Last Monday. They said I couldn't talk to you first. So I came here."

"Well, I'm glad you did. I'm a psychiatrist, but I'm also a lawyer. Did you know that about me?"

"Maybe I did."

"Sometimes I'm asked to talk to someone who is afraid because of the combination of both law and the past. Both are very scary things. The law because it's hard to understand, and the past because it won't go away. But they can be soothed and even cured if the person really wants that to happen. If you don't mind, I'll just tell you what I do every day. Then I'll ask you a few questions that I think might be on your mind. Would that be OK?"

"OK."

She'd been in his office for only four or five minutes, but her lower lip no longer trembled, and she quit looking all around the room while he was talking. He noticed that she quit gripping the arms of the chair as though she wanted to catapult out of it. Leaning toward her, and trying to smile at her with his eyes, he clasped his hands on the desk.

"Before I tell you what I do, can you tell me your name? It doesn't have to be your real name, and you can give me only a first name, if you want."

"Vinessa."

"Thanks, Vinessa. I've never known a Vinessa before. It's nice to meet you. So, as a doctor, and sometimes as a lawyer, I have to look into the pain that people feel. Life is painful for almost everybody. We all go through painful things, some much worse than others. But lawyers and psychiatrists are often confronted with unbearable emotional pain. A broken arm is very painful, but you can put a splint on it and take pain medications, and usually in a short time your pain disappears. But emotional pain sometimes never goes away, even if you take something, and even if other people can get over their emotional pain easily. Some emotional pain hurts so badly and lasts so long that we call it *trauma*, something that can't be forgotten. It's this last part that is important. *Forgotten*."

Dr. Ahmed paused, and reached into his desk drawer. Pulling out a tin box, he showed it to her.

"Would you like a jelly bean?" he asked. "I love 'em. Especially the green ones, my favorites."

She looked at him as though she hadn't heard him.

"Jelly beans. They are pure sugar, and not good for my waist line. But they give me energy and peace. Want one, or maybe two?"

She shook her head and, for the first time, smiled. She had what his mother always called a "Cupid's Bow," a classically shapely upper lip. The smile, while faint and lasting only a second, was a small psychiatric victory. Placing a green jelly bean on his tongue, he continued.

"Physical pain, when cured with an aspirin, or maybe a pain-killing drug like morphine, is forgotten. But traumatic pain is always there, always on your mind, never forgotten. Lawyers deal with it by litigation, which can sometimes help emotional pain go away—be forgotten. Psychiatrists deal it by psychotherapy. And that involves talking with patients and helping find ways to cope with, and even forget, the trauma that causes so much pain in our lives. It's actually a wound. An emotional one that no one can see. And because none of us want to talk about it, some wounds never heal. They fester. Sometimes they lay low in our heads, waiting for something else to happen. They squeeze our brains, make our hearts beat faster, and make us scared, all over again. Like the wound was being ripped open. When that happens, lots of people deal with it by hiding from it. We create ways to avoid thinking about it, so we don't have to feel fear. Does this make sense to you, Vinessa?"

"Doctor, I read a book a few years ago about disappearing. It said that you are whoever you say you are, even if it isn't true. Do you believe that?"

"Yes, I do. I have patients who change who they are to avoid something in their life. Sometimes it's as small as boredom. Sometimes it's as large as violence. People who the world sees as emotionally happy, but who are privately very unhappy, change their lives and call themselves by new names. It's a coping mechanism, and it works. For a while. But often the wound comes back. It's scratched, or it bursts wide open. How long have you been Vinessa?"

"How did you know?"

"I knew when you knocked on my door but were reluctant to come in that something was wrong. I knew when you were vague in answering small questions. I knew when you asked about psychiatric nurse practitioners. You were here to see a doctor, not a nurse. You've got a serious look about you, but it doesn't seem to consume you. And lastly, I detected a very slight accent, one that you might have acquired for a reason; one that you've cultivated. Vinessa is a cultured name. It's elegant, and you are an elegant-looking woman. But once you were a child, and I don't think your name was Vinessa then."

"Vivian. It was Vivian. When I was nine I did something really bad. I only remember little things about that. Like the rest of my life. Sometimes I forget my life, like somebody else pushes the pause button on me. Then they replace me. For a while."

He got a telephone number and an address he guessed was fake. She said she didn't have health insurance, didn't have a job, and had no close relatives. But she could pay, she promised. He told her that he'd get her a registration number for the Harris County clinic next Monday. Giving her the clinic call-in line, he told her to call them next Monday morning and confirm her appointment. It will be near the end of the work day, he told her.

CHAPTER 29

The zoo parking lot was still yellow-taped off, eight days after the explosion. But no debris was visible. The RV chassis had been towed off. A twenty-by-twenty-foot tent with zippered front flaps was about thirty feet from the black crater that was ground zero for the ATF's investigation. Since all bomb cases were subject to federal jurisdiction, investigating the crime was the FBI's job. Analyzing the debris and the crime scene belonged to the ATF. Criminal charges were the responsibility of the US attorney for Texas. That's why AUSA Sustern and FBI Agents Lin and Widnor were there. Harris County prosecutor Grant Lumberson was also there because Julia Santerra-Evans had been his primary witness in the state's case against Manchester. He brought his chief investigator, a quiet man named Art Casio, along for the update. They gathered inside the ATF tent nine days after the explosion for an onsite status briefing. Sally Lin was on point for the

Houston FBI Field office. ATF's lead investigator, Nathaniel Plotski, did the briefing.

"Before you ask," Plotski said, "let me answer your first two questions. Where is all the debris from the explosion? When will we get a report? The debris, all 3,200 pounds of it, is in Atlanta. We have a large lab there. More than a dozen experts are sifting and cataloguing evidence in this bombing. The report? Best guess is five weeks. But I can tell you we are strongly leaning toward an electronic trigger device that set off a sizeable chemical bomb. It was magnetically attached to the underside of the carriage, within a foot of the gas tank. When triggered, it was powerful enough to penetrate a thirty-four-gallon steel gas tank and spew its fuel throughout the fuselage. The explosion killed both occupants, and the explosive fire reduced everything to pieces no larger than a seventeen-inch laptop computer and weighing no more than two pounds. There were two bodies, we think . . ."

Grant Lumberson interrupted, the first of many times.

"Think? Your team *thinks* there were two? Is there any doubt about how many bodies?"

Mr. Plotski continued, seemingly not the least bothered by the interruption. "Gross examination revealed bone fragments, burnt tissue, cooked blood, and teeth. The vics were adults. We're pretty sure there were only two vics because the body parts add up. But we moved a ton and a half of debris. Lots of body parts were welded to metal, and some parts were so badly burned they looked like burnt leather seats or melded plastic utensils. We have not confirmed gender, but the lab specialists are leaning toward one man and one woman. There is lots of DNA, all of it human. Questions?"

Lumberson would not let it go.

"Yeah, I asked about how many vics, and you said the body parts added up. What's that mean?"

"Sorry, Mr. Lumbsan, I'm a pathology tech, so I think weird sometimes. The provisional lab report reports two pelvic structures, two cranial vaults, and two spines. All blown to bits. None recognizable except under microscope. But the body parts add up to two vics. If we had three cranial vaults, but only two spines, we'd still be digging into the explosive residue."

"It's Lumb*erson*, not Lumb*san*. Sorry for the confusion on my part. I'll be quiet. For a while."

Nancy Lee threw the first softball.

"No doubt this was Amherst Pipps's RV, right?"

"Right. VIN number stamped on the chassis, engine block, and the little tin strip beneath the front windshield. And we found a key chain, mostly intact, with his US Navy dog tag on it. He was enlisted and deployed to Iraq in 2009, between college and law school. His family wants his remains delivered for military burial in the Dallas-Fort Worth National Cemetery. Next?"

"Yes," Nancy Lee said. "I have several identification questions. Other than Pipps's dog tags, what other identification markers are there on the victims? Do fingerprints ever survive a fire as hot as this one must have been?"

"Yes, ma'am. We've got data confirming latent marks are capable of withstanding exposure temperatures about 100 degrees centigrade for several hours. Depends on where you find them. Actual fingers, pretty doubtful. But on metal surfaces that might have blown up, or away?

Yeah, we find lots of them that way. And so you know, 100 centigrade is 212 Fahrenheit. The lab techs search through soot material as well as articles affected by fire. Even though it's probably not the case, we're investigating the possibility of owner-arson. The technology comes out of the misconception that fingerprints are destroyed by the intense heat and black soot deposits arising during a fire. The body parts will be more definitive, because DNA beats fingerprints every time."

"Yes," Nancy Lee said, "but I was thinking more of other people than just the two known victims. Will the investigation include that area?"

"Yeah, sure. Routine. I mean, we don't look specifically for fingerprints, but they show up all the time on objects we knock the soot off of."

Agent Lin asked, "Since you found Pipps's dog tags, do you have a list of other metal objects or things that were not destroyed that might help identify who was in the RV at the time of the fire, as well as prior to the fire?"

"Yeah, sure. It will be a long list. Things like tools, jewelry, kitchen stuff, desk accessories, keys, eyeglass frames, weapons, nails, hairpins, ear rings, flashlight batteries . . . I mean, the list is huge—*huge*. Once you get it, it will take an hour just to page through it."

Agent Widnor asked, "Do you make that kind of a list in every case?"

"No, heck no. But this case looks like a double-murder and it has international overtones, if you know what I mean. So we got instructions from on high to cover everything that might interest lawyers, judges, jurors, and those freaking reporters. But we know how to handle reporters; just tell 'em about celebrities, and they run off to write their stories."

Nancy Lee moved back into the line of questions. "You said this case had international overtones, 'if you know what I mean.' I don't know what you mean. What international overtones does the ATF have?"

"Ma'am, maybe that was a lip-slip on my part. But the guys were thinking, you know, this is a border town. The drug cartels move a lot of merchandise around here. Money talks on the border, you know. And then you know the two people on board, word is they are both lawyers. That's international, right there, know what I mean?"

Sally asked for confirmation on a central point. "Are we certain that this was a bomb rather than an accident?"

"No doubt about that. Our statutory mission is to differentiate accidental fires and explosions from everything else. We examine all explosion incidents in the US, where explosive materials, chemicals, or ignitable mixtures are determined to be the primary cause of an explosion. In this case, the initial explosion caused the gas tank to rupture, spewing fire on the top of a massive explosion. Do you know about BATS? I don't mean flying ones. We say BATS to mean 'bombings, accidental explosions, and undetermined explosion incidents.' The undetermined explosion category is used in ongoing investigations where the cause was either unidentified, pending further investigation, or awaiting laboratory results. We're past that stage now. This was an intentional bombing of a very large, very expensive RV. The bomb was detonated from a distance of at least fifty feet from the unit. We know that because of the bomb blast.

Had the bomber been within fifty feet he or she would have been badly wounded, or killed. We're sure it was detonated because we have bits and pieces of the electrical device that exploded the actual bomb."

"What was the bomb made of?" Agent Widnor asked.

"You'll get a detailed list of everything they used to make this bomb. Bomb materials are widely published on the Internet. For example, rust remover contains nitric, or sulfuric, acid. That can be used to make high-order nitroglycerine. You can buy model engine fuel in hardware stores or over the Internet. It has chemicals with explosive properties a whole lot more powerful than TNT. And if you mix that with an oxidizing agent like ammonium nitrate, the explosive power is gigantic. And, of course, since this is Texas and we are in the desert, we have lots of swimming pools and stores that sell stuff to swimming pool owners. Did you know that pool sanitizer contains hydrogen peroxide? Oh boy, that stuff can be used to make an explosive known as TATP."

Nancy Lee interrupted. "TATP? Wasn't that used in that New Orleans case?"

"I don't know," the ATF guy said, "I didn't work that case. It stands for triacetate tripe oxide. Terrorist literature calls it the 'Mother of Satan.' That's because even terrorists hate to be around it since it's so dangerous to handle. It's what they used to bomb the train station in London."

The grisly meeting came to a close on that cherry note. They packed back into the three-seater, black Suburban and drove to the airport. Agent Lin, seated in the middle row, raised the question they didn't want to discuss in front of the ATF pathology tech.

"So we're facing someone sophisticated enough to make a dangerous bomb, smart enough to set it off without killing themselves, and big enough to send a message, right?"

Nancy Lee, from behind the steering wheel, answered over her shoulder, "Message? That's your take on why this happened? What message? That bombers hate lawyers? The bombers want the two cases we have under indictment ramped up? Ramped down? What? What is the connection between killing Pipps and Julia, on the one hand, and our money laundering case in federal court and Lumberson's assault-and-battery-case in state court, on the other?"

Agent Lin knew she was the only non-Texan in the van. And she was reluctant to opine since she was also the youngest. But she sipped the last of her water bottle and cleared her throat.

"I'm not sure what the message is. But I've been thinking about the messenger. I think the bombers were paid assassins. The did this for money—probably a lot of money. And they disappeared immediately. My guess is across the border, which is less than five miles away. They could have been driving across the Rio Grande about the same time the first responders slid into the parking lot."

Lumberson asked, "You ruling out terrorists?"

"Yes, but it's just my guess. Terrorists do everything to send a message. It's always political, religious, or fanatical for some reason we can't fathom. The DOJ doesn't think this is international largely because no one claims credit for it and because the bomber picked a parking lot closed to the public on Mondays, and at the far end away from houses or street traffic. There was no advance warning and no post-explosion bragging. There has never been a blast like this in a small border town like Brownsville."

Agent Widnor almost agreed.

"I think that's a good call. But what about some other motive—one against either Pipps or the Santerra-Evans woman? Maybe revenge. Payback. Hatred. Money. Blood. Hell, coulda been lust—it was a man and a woman, both a long way from home. They were lawyer and client, I guess. But it could have been more than that."

Lin, encouraged by the give and take, asked the question they were all thinking about.

"What about Vince Manchester? He almost killed Julia two years ago. I think he intended to then but changed his mind on the fly. And, as you all know, I think he's mentally disturbed and protecting his host personality, Vivian. She seemed childlike and had a sweet innocence about her. He seems hateful and violent. We have to think of him as the primary suspect. If he did kill her for what he thinks she did to their father, then Pipps was just collateral damage. It could be that simple."

"Or, if you're right," Nancy Lee said, "it could be just that maniacal. How do we catch a ghost—a person you don't think exists? Who do we look for? Vivian?"

They caught the 4:40 flight back to Houston. When they landed and headed for their separate cars in the parking structure, Lumberson said, "If ya'll catch Vivian, then watch you gonna do? I don't think your button-down federal grand jury will buy any of this bats-in-the-belfry stuff about different personalities blowing up lawyers down in Brownsville."

CHAPTER 30

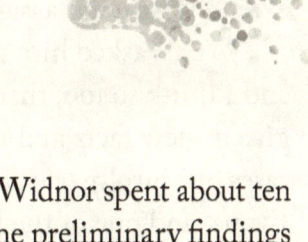

Sally Lin and Fred Widnor spent about ten minutes briefing SAIC Blakey on the preliminary findings by the ATF in Brownsville. He was surprised by how little they learned.

"Well, I shouldn't be surprised, but I am. ATF is a fine investigative agency, but they couldn't investigate spilled milk from a two-year-old's high chair in less than a week. So, telling us it will be another five weeks tacked onto the one they've already spent at the explosion site is probably quick for them. All we really need to know at this early stage of our investigation is how sure they are this was a bomb, not an accident, and who the vics are. So item one, check; it's a bomb. Item two, not so fast. We think it was Pipps and Julia—based on shoe-leather investigation—but they won't confirm pathology pending DNA verification. That's where we are, right?"

Agent Widnor answered, "Right, Slate, but ours is the more important investigation anyhow. We can approach the victims' identities from another angle. And, while we're at it, we can dig for motive, opportunity, and means. I know nailing down the victims' identities is crucial, but identifying the perps is even more important."

"Fred, you're on first on this one. You take the lead. Sally, we really need you on this. Will the SAIC in Phoenix extend your temp assignment on this?"

"Yes, I asked him this morning. He agrees. He thinks, and I think so too, that what happens in this new case will give us new facts and maybe new leads on the other three cases that involve one of the presumed victims, Julia Santerra-Evans, and one of the likely perps, Vince Manchester. He wants a complete sharing of 302s and access to all evidence acquired, but otherwise he wants me to take whatever role you think is the best fit for me from this point forward."

Turning to the investigator, Dish Joandiz, Slate waved his arm, palm up, at the bespectacled little man in Levis and Western plaid shirt with pearl snaps instead of buttons.

"Dish, this is your first look today, right? You never heard of the other two cases—the money laundering federal indictment and the state indictment for beating up a lawyer, who we think is one of the vics in Brownsville."

"Yeah," Dish said slowly, like he always did. "I'm green on the facts, but Sally gave me a nuts-and-bolts look over coffee this morning. She gets here at seven sharp, Slate. Like me. Unlike the younger generation in the office, no offense intended, Sally. I've got an idea or two when you're ready for them."

"All right," Slate said, pushing away from the conference table. "Ya'll work out a tactical plan, send me a one-two-three on it. Give me a time table and a very short list of what other resources you think you need. We will be getting a push from FBI HQ, just because this is a bombing. Had the perp just shot the vics, we'd be free of HQ interest. But there's always a chance that this is international terror, so they'll want frequent status notes. They're big on one-day-later pdfs on all 302s. Got it?"

When the door closed behind him, Fred said, "OK, let's not get hung up on who's lead and who's following, OK? Sally, you're senior, and your insight could make a real difference. Where do you think we should start?"

"At the border crossing closest to the Gladys Porter Zoo."

"The border crossing? Why there?" Widnor asked.

"Well, I've been reading up on explosion technology and explosion materials. I learned last night that the components ATF agent Plotski talked about are hard to come by in *this* country. But it's not that hard in Mexico. Also, Julia has been AWOL from her handlers at the US Marshal's Office for almost a year now. They haven't had a clue where she'd been before she surfaced a week ago, via her lawyer's talk with Grant Lumberson. She's from Mexico, lived there for years before taking the Texas bar exam and hanging out a shingle in Baytown. My guess is she's been in Mexico. And I think we're gonna find out she picked Pipps to be her mouthpiece with Harris County because of his crazy mobile.law persona. She could talk him into driving down to a border-crossing town, which made it easy for her to aim him back up here in Houston and have him tell the state prosecutors what she wanted in their case against Vince Manchester. But I don't know anything about how Mexican nationals, or people hiding in Mexico, cross the border. I know they don't need a visa, but are they searched when they come across? Is there a database we can scan for names and crossings?"

Dish spoke up.

"Well, there's two databases. The one on our side and the one on theirs. I can access our side easily, but it could be hundreds of names, and even then, we don't know who we're looking for."

"No matter," Sally answered. "What we need to know is who crossed the border on the two mornings Pipps met with Julia in his traveling law office, and whether that same person crossed back into Mexico that same morning. We can get the meeting times from Pipps's secretary—I think somebody said her name's Amber Sue. I'll call her. Maybe we can't know exactly who crossed, but the ones that crossed back and forth in our time frame, *twice*, should be high on our radar."

Dish was a small, round-bellied man with an easy way of talking and a grin that got everyone around him grinning too. His arms were freckled and tattooed. Although his thick eye glasses gave him a Mr. Magoo look, there was little doubt about his reputation as a first-class investigator. He had been watching Sally intently, and when she finished her summary of where they were, he seemed to draw back, making himself even smaller than he was. He licked his lips.

"Sally, was the trip yesterday your first introduction to Brownsville?"

"Yes, and I have to say I thought it would be, I don't know, maybe sleepier than it was. It seemed to be bustling, at least from what I saw in the car ride into town from the airport."

"Well, it bustles up and down something fierce these days. It's a border town's border town. In other places the border is harder to identify. In Brownsville, it's the Rio Grande River. Thousands of people cross back and forth every day. A large part of the workforce in Brownsville actually live in Mexico—their side of border is called Matamoros Tamaulipas. They walk over the bridge every day—across to earn a living in the morning, and back across at night for dinner and sleeping. That's my town, in a way. I grew up not far from there, went to college there, and I've crossed that bridge hundreds of times. You were at the Gladys Porter Zoo, right? Well if you wanted to, you could walk from there into Matamoros in under an under an hour—twenty minutes by car. Not counting the wait at the border."

Sally leaned toward Dish, realizing how valuable this man could be.

"I'm sure glad to know we have a real expert because I know nothing about this part of the world. But I think I read, just last year, that the border area in Matamoros was dangerous. Is that true?"

"Now? Yeah, hell yeah, it's dangerous now, but that's fairly new. Compared to my partying days in the 80s and early 90s, today it's like a different planet. These days, most people in Brownsville won't cross the bridge. But there are some who make the trip every day, even from our side to theirs. They make the trip for work, or to visit family. You can save money there on dentists and podiatrists. Glasses and prescriptions are cheap. Lunch is good. But they stay on the main streets, and they don't go alone. And they scat back across before dark."

"What about you? Do you cross over these days?"

"Not so much, unless it's on business, and then I'm usually talking to the *Federales* or some government agency. They have their bureaucracy just like we do."

"All right, Dish! This is great," she said, moving to the edge of her seat and starting to rush her words.

"Do you have trusted sources over there that could cut through the clutter and help us out?"

"Trusted? Can't say I have that in the way you mean it. When I want a bad hombre across the border to know I'm looking for him, I cross over and ask people I know where he is. Even if they knew, they wouldn't tell me. But they will try to sell the fact I'm looking for that bad hombre. They make a few pesos, and I get the word out that he's wanted. Then, sometimes, he makes a mistake and moves somewhere and somebody else spots him. Then they try to sell his location to me. That how it works over there. *Todo tiene un precio.* You speak any Spanish?"

"*Porquito*," Sally answered.

"Well, then, it means everything has a price in Mexico."

"So, if Slate gives you a stack of pesos, you might be able to find out things we need to know in Matamoros?"

"If Slate gives me a stack of ten-dollar bills, I could find out a lot about what's happening in Matamoros. But it wouldn't do any good. If you're right about the Mexican connection, we won't be looking in a border town, especially one as fluid as Matamoros. I'm guessing there's a half-million people living on that side of the Rio Grande—twice as big as Brownsville."

"But do the locals, on both sides, get along with one another? I know you said Matamoros is dangerous, but is that true for Brownsville?"

"Sally, if you drove your car on Brownsville's north side, along the river and close to the country club, you'd be looking right across the border. At that end at least, you'd look at pretty nice, small homes with gardens and ponds, tiled driveways, and lush trees. Brownsville is very safe. Most of the people who live there are of Mexican descent. They all speak some Spanish. What you'd see is how different things are now. Both sides have deep roots in the area, but there is great violence on the Mexican side of the river. On our side, there's a giant shadow coming down from the eighteen-foot-high steel beams of the border wall we built to keep the violence out. You're probably right in speculating that the bombers came across the bridge into Brownsville and then scooted back across while the fire trucks were screaming to put out the fire. If you are, we'll get some clues from the border crossing data. Clues, not convictions. We'll have to dig 'em out further down, maybe in a big city like Monterrey."

CHAPTER 31

Grant Lumberson was furious, and his trial team was taking the brunt. He'd called this late afternoon meeting, asking all five members of the team to come armed with good ideas. Cecelia Apindia, his second chair on the case, recommended they dismiss the charges now.

"Put the case back on the shelf," is how she'd posed it.

The trial technician, Curley Docs, looked like he wanted to crawl under the table. His lead paralegal, L. D. Podski, was smart and politically astute—she knew better than to take sides on this one. So she sat mum, arms crossed, legs crossed, with a faint smile on her face. The young summer extern they'd nicknamed "Why" could hardly wait to ask his banal questions.

"What 'n hell, Cecelia, do you mean we cannot move this case forward without telling the judge about the bombing case in Brownsville?" asked Lumberson. "And to compound that dumb-ass idea, you say we have to tell the judge we can't find Vince Manchester? The judge does not give a shit about that bombing case, even it does turn out that the victim, Julia, is in a box of soot and ashes, waiting for the slow-as-molasses ATF crowd to sift and study the last remains of two people we don't need to try the damn case. You're the best second-chair lawyer in this big-ass office. But I do not understand your due process argument."

Cecelia Apindia had graduated *cum laude* from the University of Texas's nationally ranked law school in Austin. She had offers from big law firms all over Texas but chose the Harris District Attorney's Office because she knew she'd get real trial experience there. Grant knew she would not make prosecuting her career, like he had. She'd get her trial experience and then get hired by a big firm doing white collar crime work for seven hundred dollars an hour. She had a "high mental capacity and is cerebral as all hell," which is how Grant described her to his boss, *the* Harris County Prosecutor.

"Grant," she said, in her methodical don't-you-get-it tone of voice, "due process of law means giving the defendant all exculpatory evidence in advance of trial. We know the victim of these crimes, and the primary witness in the case is *dead*. At least we know she's probably dead, pending that ATF investigation final report. We have a status report coming up in three weeks. The judge already warned us that unless we actually are prepared to go to trial, he wants the case off the docket. We can always seek a new indictment until the statute of limitations runs our. And we have speedy trial rules to deal with as well. You cannot hide the fact that our case is like a tumbleweed in a wind storm. The defendant, Vince Manchester, cannot be served because he might not exist. The victim's lawyer, Amherst Pipps, told us his client, Julia Santerra-Evans, would not testify for us. Now they're both dead—Julia and Pipps—in in the same bombing, down in Brownsville. If we don't volunteer this to the judge now, he's gonna chew you a new one when he finds out. That's my due process argument."

The conversation lulled, giving Why a chance to speak up.

"What's going on over at the federal building? Don't they have the same problem we do? I mean their case. I know it's under seal and all that, but didn't their lead lawyer on the case go with you, Mr. Lumberson, down to Brownsville? Why don't they have to dismiss their case if we have to dismiss ours? Seems to me they can talk to that defense lawyer, the one who represents Mr. Manchester. Maybe he knows something we don't. I mean, who's his client anyway?"

Lumberson looked at the young extern, thought a minute, and then grinned like a tomcat in an alley full of trash cans.

"Well, if that don't beat all! Young man, you just offered us a back door I had not given one second's thought to. Maybe two weeks ago, when I saw Nancy Lee at a bar lunch, she mentioned that Travis Danders was talking to her about this Vince Manchester guy. Claimed to be representing him, but I told her he'd never called me, or tried to make an appearance in our case at all. So, young man, let me ask *you* a question for once. Can a lawyer represent a defendant in a case without disclosing that fact to the judge in the case? Any notions on that?"

"I've never researched it, but who says a lawyer has to enter an appearance in a criminal case where the state has not arrested the defendant? What if the lawyer did not want the case to move forward? I remember my crim law professor asking us in class once how good defense lawyers defend guilty clients. None of us gave her the right answer. She said it's simple. If your client is guilty, just keep on ducking a trial. Without a trial, your client stays free. Maybe that's what Manchester's lawyer is doing."

"Well, I think I need to stoke Travis Danders's fire a little bit. You're probably right, he's ducking me and the judge on the state case because he don't want a trial. Good thinking, Why."

CHAPTER 32

As she promised she would, Vivian called the Harris County Psychiatric Hospital the following Monday and learned Dr. Estancia had enrolled her as a clinic patient and that she had a 4:15 p.m. appointment that afternoon. She went to the hospital in a taxi, two hours early, and spent most of the time in the hospital's small medical resource room. The sign on the door said it was open to patients and families. The man behind the glass-topped desk said he'd be happy to help find books or pamphlets on medical subjects. She said her niece was having mental troubles and was there to see a nurse practitioner. The man said, "I've got just the thing for you. It's short, only about six pages. You can have a copy to give to your niece." The title was, *Raising the Psychological Drawbridge*.

"What does that mean, a drawbridge?"

The man was not wearing a name badge but said he was a docent, just helping out where they sent him.

"I'm not a doctor or anything, but my mother was a patient here before she died. So I come here on Mondays, their busiest day, and do whatever they ask me to. This little booklet helped me and my mom. We know from experience that seeking help from a psychologist or a psychiatrist is a fearful thing. You know you have mental problems, but you're not crazy, right? So, this little booklet tries to get you to cross over your own fear, like it was a moat around an island, or something. If they let the drawbridge down so you can get help, you've still got the fear, right? The doctors and nurses here are very friendly, they want to listen to you, and they have an optimistic outlook on life. My mother didn't. This hospital turned out to be a bright spot in my mom's life. Sure hope it helps you."

Vivian took the booklet and went down the hall to the clinic's main waiting room. It was full of people. Most had someone with them. Vivian knew some were troubled, like her, and the rest were family. That caused her more trouble. Her problem *was* her family—the alters in her life. As she read through the little booklet, she was struck by the phrase, *emotional shielding*. No matter the diagnosis, the unnamed author said, the actions and decisions made by people with mental health issues are steered by fear of rejection and abandonment. To avoid situations that aggravate those feelings, many patients hide behind their true emotions, like they had a shield against the bad things that happened. And, as Vivian finished the booklet, she came to recognize herself in what they said. When my emotional shield goes up, it transforms me, she thought. Instead of protecting me, or healing me, my shield keeps me from a life of balance and fulfillment. Can it be that simple?

The last line in the booklet made it seem that way: "The patient who recognizes his own psychological condition, and wants to achieve self-actualization, can accomplish the goal for all mental health: personal fulfillment, no more guilt, no more fear." She put the booklet inside her purse, zipped it up, set the latch, and hung the strap across her chest. An hour later, a young woman wearing hospital scrubs and carrying a clipboard called her name.

"Vinessa DiAmonte, Vinessa DiAmonte, are you here?"

"Yes," she answered, and followed the dark blue scrubs down a maze of hallways to Dr. Estancia's clinic office.

CHAPTER 33

Grant Lumberson went back upstairs to his office, still fuming a little over his team's consistent view they had to tell the judge about the missing defendant and the missing victim. He'd rather have waited until the final ATF report, but they were probably right. He asked his admin, who used to be his secretary before political correctness invaded Harris County and secretaries became administrative assistants, to call Travis Danders and get him to come over for a talk about the case.

"Which case?" she asked.

"The goddamn case we indicted Vince Manchester on. Which case did you think I meant, just coming back from a team meeting on that goddamn case?"

"Well, is his number in the file? I don't remember his name anywhere."

"His number is on the goddamn State Bar of Texas website. He is not in the file because he is ignoring the damn thing and he represents the defendant. Good Lord, what's the legal world coming to, anyhow?"

A half-hour later, his admin, wearing her hurt face, buzzed him. He picked up.

"Yes."

"Travis Danders has his own law firm. His admin says he will call you first thing tomorrow. I have his email. Should I email him for you to confirm he'll call tomorrow?"

"Yeah, that'd be good. And Louisa, sorry I snapped at you. This goddamn case has got me off my feed."

She hung up and sent the confirming email, copying him and the rest of his trial team. Next morning, when the call came in, Louisa asked him if he wanted to take the call or wait and call back when she could round up the trial team. "No, not necessary," he said. "Send him through."

"Mr. Lumberson, this is Travis Danders. I'm sorry I haven't had time to call you yet about my new client, Vince Manchester. I'm just barely getting into the case, and from what I hear, there may not be any case. I presume that's why you called me."

"Well, that's alright. I know about busy. Been busy myself. You know about that bomb that went off down in Brownsville, week before last, right?"

"I do. Last week the AUSA on the federal case came over to my office, and we talked about the foolishness of seeking an arrest warrant for my client on the bombing of Julia Santerra-Evans and her lawyer, Amherst Pipps. You know anything about that, the arrest warrant, I mean?"

"I didn't call to talk about the bombing, or the US Attorney's Office. I want to talk to you about the state case against your client, Vince Manchester."

"Mr. Lumberson, . . ."

"Call me Grant. You might not remember, but you were on a case eight or nine years ago, fresh out of law school. I was prosecuting a pervert and your old law firm pled him out. I think you were second-chairing that case, right?"

"No, Grant, that wasn't me. There was a guy in my class, Travis Fuller. He joined a two-lawyer shop in town and they did a lot of contract work, especially in sex trafficking cases. Might have been him you're remembering."

"Spect so. Anyhow, about our case, what's your thinking on it? Something we can plead out, or do you have a defense I ain't heard about?"

"Your case?" asked Travis, with a whistle in his voice. "Far as I can tell, your case blew up in Brownsville. No victim, no case. That's pretty much it, right?"

"We can make the case on her sworn testimony before the grand jury and a pile of crime-scene evidence we have on tape, including videos of your client."

"Grant, if her sworn testimony is offered to prove the truth of her words, it's hearsay. If it's not offered for that, it's irrelevant. Your videos show—what? —my client going in and coming out of Julia's office? Not probative. Your crime-scene evidence is fruit of the poisoned tree since it came from a witness who was herself a swindler. But most importantly, Grant, everyone in Houston is glued to their TVs about the Brownville bombing. Gruesome deaths always draw an audience. You're going to ask a Houston jury to convict a nice young man, *in absentia*, who allegedly robbed a mob lawyer who got herself blown up, along with another young lawyer, who I suspect you've already talked to. You probably ran him out of your office, am I guessing right about that?"

"Well, Travis, I did have a visit with young Mr. Amherst Pipps. Hate to speak ill of the dead, but he was not too impressive. Didn't know shit about trial work. But you just said your client was a nice young man, who'd be tried *in absentia*. Is that what you think? *In absentia*? We haven't found him yet, but the feds are on his case. We'll find him. If we don't, I'll be straight with you. We'll just dismiss the new indictment and wait it out. If he shows up anywhere in Texas, we'll round him up. Then we'll have a real trial. As for Julia's testimony being hearsay, that won't work in state court. She's the victim, dead or alive. And her testimony will come in evidence and sink your client. That's the nub of it."

"Well, Grant, call me back when you find him. Anything else we need to cover on this call?"

It was one of those times when experienced trial lawyers both think the conversation went well.

CHAPTER 34

Dr. Estancia's office at the county-run hospital was not like his academic office at Rice University. This twelve-by-twelve-foot square all-white room didn't have a desk. It had a round vinyl-topped table with folding metal chairs in one corner, and in the other corner were two old stuffed leather chairs, separated by a coffee table. A computer stand attached to the wall held a seventeen-inch monitor, small keyboard, and a mouse. All were black. He got up from one of the two leather chairs.

"Good late afternoon, Vinessa. I'm sorry to run late. Did they give you a set of written questions at the desk?"

"It's OK. Found the little library off the main hall. A nice man said he was a docent and gave me a booklet to read."

"Yes, his name is Oliver. Nice man he is. He loves greeting new patients. Now, about that paper they asked you to fill out, the one with a dozen questions and only a little space to write the answers. Don't bother to fill that out. I only use it to start conversations. Let's start with the first three. It asks if a person ever hurt you. Did someone hurt you?"

"Chester. Well, he didn't mean it. He just wanted to swim in the big lake. He drowned."

"How old was Chester?"

"They never said. Maybe five or six. I was nine."

"The next question asks, what happened? You already answered part of it. Chester drowned. What else happened?"

"He drowned because of me. I told him not to jump in. He did anyhow. So it was my fault."

"Who said it was your fault?"

"Me."

"No one else? Were your parents there?"

"Up the hill."

"How far away was the big lake from the hill where your parents were?"

"It was dark."

"Dark when Chester went in the lake?"

"Dark when I came out of the cave."

"Were you scared? Scared of the dark in the cave?"

"Scared to see Chester. He drowned."

"All right, Vinessa, let's put the form away now and . . ."

"Oh, Doctor Estancia, thank you ever so much for agreeing to see me. I liked your other office better than this. It's so cold in here. Could you turn down the AC for me? And I'm sorry about the forms they gave me out front. Was I supposed to fill them out?"

"Vinessa, does the name Chester mean anything to you?"

"Chester?"

"Yes, Chester. I think he was a little boy about five or six. Is that right?"

"The only Chester I ever knew was a doorman at the Savoy in London. Is that the man you're talking about? He was probably sixty-five or seventy, two years ago, when I first met him."

Dr. Estancia quit asking direct questions. He had penetrated Vivian's emotional shield completely by accident. He knew now that Vinessa, the woman who trolled him to his Rice University office and whom he'd invited to come to this clinic office, was probably not who she said she was. She would not have revealed a childhood memory within minutes of coming in his office. The trigger question he'd asked was whether anyone had ever hurt her. The answer didn't come from Vinessa; it came from someone else. A host identity from twenty years ago? He tried another trigger.

"Did you go to Chester's funeral with your parents?"

"They said no."

"Who said no?"

"The doctor. Like you."

"Did he ask questions, like me?"

"Not to me. He just talked to them."

"Your parents?"

"Yes."

"What was your mom's name?"

"He said it was Angela."

"Who said that?"

"My dad."

"What's his name?"

"Stephan. He's dead too."

"What about your mother?"

"Dead, too."

"Any brothers or sisters?"

"Maybe. They say they are anyway."

"Do they have names?"

"Vince."

"Your brother? Is he a big brother or a little one?"

"He never said. But he has a foul mouth and only comes around when I fall asleep. I guess. He thinks he is too smart to live on earth. He lives up in a cloud."

"Is Vinessa your sister?"

Looking embarrassed, Vivian felt a flush creep across her cheeks. She rubbed the back of her neck vigorously.

"Doctor, I'm sorry, I didn't hear you question clearly. You were asking about those questions, the ones on the form? You'll have to forgive me. I can get so addled sometimes. Is that a sign of something? A symptom you could use to help me?"

"Help you do what, Vinessa? What makes you addled?"

"Sometimes everything. Things make me want to run. Things panic me. Then I just quit thinking, quit worrying, quit being; you know, like sleeping off too much red wine. When I wake up, things are better, but sometimes when I wake up, at first I don't know where I am. There are whole days when I can't remember being in my office in Paris, or on an airplane, or a cruise ship. I can't remember getting on, or even ordering dinner. But then I just let it go and things get better. Are you the right kind of a doctor to help?"

On that first visit to Dr. Estancia, he accidently discovered a passage that often takes months of therapy to bridge.

When talking to Vivian, he heard from her both as a little girl and as a young adult. When talking to Vinessa, her heard the voice of a more cultured woman, still young, but more knowledgeable about the world. It seemed possible, at that early therapeutic stage, to draw out the underlying fears, the shame, and Vivian's lies about them. And as a sort of safe place to go, he could rely on Vinessa emerging just by asking about her. Knowing that patients were more likely to be focused on their fears rather than on the psychotherapist as a source of help, he gave Vinessa breathing room.

"Vinessa, I feel sure we can get to the bottom of some of these anxious moments you are having. Could we meet twice a week, maybe for three or four weeks? Then I'd like you to think about some group sessions with other patients. The sense of losing yourself, of not remembering where you were for a period of time, is very real and fairly common. We have a group that works on those realities. Sound good to you?"

She agreed. The front desk helped Vinessa schedule two appointments per week for three weeks and suggested she cut her caffeine intake. She was too much the cultured lady to tell the girl at the desk she preferred white tea. By the time she walked out the front door, headed to the parking lot, Dr. Estancia was dictating his office note.

> Patient is a WF not appearing to be in an
> acute phase of what her ultimate diag-
> nosis, DID, will likely be. Her affect
> is normal, when responding as Vinessa
> DiAmonte. When responding as Vivian, she

submerges into late childhood or early
adulthood, depending on the sensitivity
of the issues. She s not OBCD, not severely
depressed, only mildly anxious. I see
no indicia of bipolar, hypochondria,
paranoia, or schizophrenia. I will see
her twice weekly and move toward group
sessions. Will administer the MMPI next
week. No medications indicated.

CHAPTER 35

When Sally got back to her cubicle at Houston FBI, she called the bar association's Houston office. They said a lawyer formerly associated with Mr. Pipps had agreed to assume responsibility for Pipps's succession plan on file with the bar. His name was Lucias Aring. She called his number and Amber Sue answered the phone.

"Law offices of Lucias Aring, this is Amber Sue. How may we help you today?"

"Miss Sue, this is Agent Lin. I'm with the FBI. I hope I'm not intruding. My condolences for the passing of Amherst Pipps. Do I have it right that you worked for him for several years?"

"Well, thank you very much. Yes, I was his office manager for two years and eight months. Now I'm working for Mr. Lucias Aring. Do you wish to speak with him?"

"No, I got this number from the bar association. I understand Mr. Aring is going to wind down Mr. Pipps's law practice, and . . ."

"Wind down? Why goodness sake, Ms. Win, we're not winding down the practice. Mr. Aring is purchasing the practice from Mr. Pipps's sister, Orleans. She's a lawyer too but goes by her married name—Orleans Pipps Newton. She's real nice and says her agricultural practice is on the Canadian border and she is licensed in Canada as well as Minnesota, and has an inactive license down here in Texas, and . . ."

"Excuse me, Amber Sue, but I'm in a bit of a hurry, and this is an official call from our office. We need to take a statement from you, and we'd like you to come to our office for that. Could you come over here this afternoon, maybe about four o'clock? We are investigating Mr. Pipps's death and that of his client, Ms. Julia Santerra-Evans."

"Well, yes, I suppose so. But Mr. Aring is not here right now, and he has all of Mr. Pipps's files boxed and lined up against the back wall of our conference room. Is it legal to tell you what's in the file?"

"We cannot give you legal advice. Is there a number where I can reach Mr. Aring? I presume he will understand our sense of urgency."

Amber Sue gave Sally a cell number for her new boss. Sally called him and he said he'd tell Amber Sue to cooperate fully with the FBI and provide copies of all file documents related to Julia Santerra. He said he'd been appointed as personal representative of the Pipps estate. Pipps's will left everything to his sister in Minnesota, who would not be coming back to Texas, he said. Except for his law practice, a nearly new Corvette, and an IRA, there's wasn't much to probate. Mr. Aring had made an offer for the accounts receivables and whatever digital assets the firm owned. At a quarter to four that afternoon, Amber Sue came to the FBI building and asked for Agent Win. It took a few minutes for the desk to clear that up.

"It's Agent Lin, not Agent Win. She's expecting you. Just have a seat, and someone will be down for you momentarily."

It turned out to take almost thirty minutes because Amber Sue had dozens of questions about the FBI and whether they all carried guns and worked overseas searching for Muslim terrorists. She brought a copy of everything in the Santerra-Evans file, including the billing records. She assured Sally that the billing records were accurate down to the tenth of an hour. The arrival and departure times for the first meeting in mobile.law.com's RV were precise. The scheduled meeting for the second mobile visit was recorded by Amber Sue on the firm's website, but, "since he died and her too," the arrival time was on the schedule, but no departure time was entered. That made Amber Sue tear up for a few seconds, but she got over it quickly.

"Ya'll all probably know exactly when those terrorists blew up Mr. Pipps, don't ya? I did not enter any billable time for the meeting. Should I? I know Mr. Aring is refunding part of the retainer from the client to the sister in Minnesota. Do ya'll need that documented as part of your investigation?"

"No, but someone from this office will be sure to call you if we need anything else."

Nothing in Pipps's files meant anything to Sally to or Dish, the investigator. But the next morning Dish came into Sally's office with a grin on his face.

"I got the full record of crossings back and forth from Matamoros and Brownsville on the two days we know Pipps met with Julia. There were ninety-seven border crossings—that is, back and forth—documented within thirty minutes before and thirty minutes after Pipps and Julia had their first meeting in the RV. On the second visit, there were even fewer—eighty-four—going back and forth within our defined time frame. I excluded foot crossings from these because I can't see a lawyer crossing on foot, both ways, twice from Matamoros to the Gladys Porter Zoo. So, out of all that, there is only one crossing on both days within our time frame. We got the driver's name and a name for the passenger. Probably a fake. It's not Julia Santerra-Evans. My gut's screaming at me, it was her—under a different name. That's understandable since she's on the lam from the US Marshal's Office, right?"

"Way to go, Dish! If you're right, it gives us a track to follow."

"Oh, wait till you hear the rest. This will settle your frijoles for sure. The driver's name is the same on both days. The passenger's name is the same too. That could be a coincidence, except that the driver's name is a known quantity between Monterrey and Brownsville. He lives in Monterrey and makes a living driving back and forth on that 194-mile stretch of black top between Monterrey and Brownsville. He's connected to the Zetas down there, or at least he was a year ago. You don't know about the Zetas, do you?"

"No more than what I occasionally read in the news."

"Well, at one time, the Zetas were to Texas what the Sinaloa Cartel was to California. They were one of Mexico's most feared and violent organized crime threats. They took over Monterrey. But now there's been what up here you'd call a gang war. The Zetas are fragmented. I'm guessing the driver of that black SUV, with its armor plating, is a contract driver, traveling back and forth over the border. His name is *Lil Loco*. That's his gang name. The name on the Border Patrol crossing sheet is Admondo Rosales Torres."

"Carrying what, guns, drugs, what?"

"No, no. They're too smart for that. He probably only carries passengers who are rich and known to both gangs. Rich people in Monterrey buy protection from more than one gang. Some guys work for more than one. Probably a good job for a man who can drive, keep his mouth shut, and carries a big pistola on the Mexican side. Now, though, the group is fragmented."

"This Lil Loco driver; you said he carried a gun? Across the border?"

"No, they don't do that. There are lots of guns in Mexico. He probably has a cousin in Matamoros. Stops there, uses the toilet, and stashes his pistola, Then, on the way back, same thing. Empty the bladder, stick the gun in your belt, and head southwest for Monterrey."

"OK, Dish. This all sounds like a good lead to follow. But what's that saying, 'settle my frijoles,' mean?"

"It's a Mexican take-off from the American 'settle our hash.' Up here it means to subdue or knock someone or something down. But in Mexico they say it when the frijoles in the morning give you a belly ache by lunch time. I got a big knot in my stomach when I found out that Lil Loco and his passenger, a woman, made the first trip across the border, I think to see Pipps, in the black SUV on the CBP records. But the second time, the day of the explosion that killed Pipps and his client, they came across in a Mexican hearse, with a body in the back! When they crossed back, only forty-one minutes later, there was no body. Just Lil Loco and his passenger! Can you guess where that body is now?"

"No, where?"

"It's just a wild-ass hunch. But my gut's telling me it's at the ATF lab in Atlanta, *pretending* to be Julia Santerra-Evans."

CHAPTER 36

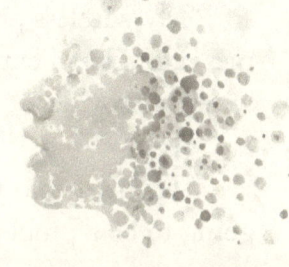

It had been ten days since Travis had any contact with Vince. He'd called every day at nine a.m. On the last nine days, someone picked up the phone, but as usual nothing was said. That had been the way Vince wanted it, but he had always called back immediately. Travis noticed that the return call was not from the cell phone number Vince had initially given him. And more often than not, it was from area codes he didn't even know existed. Vince had proven not only that could be a ghost, he was also a geek of the highest order. But this morning's call reached a recorded voice.

"The number you dialed is no longer in service. Please check your wireless provider for details."

Travis walked across the hall to the office of his partner, Connor Kilmer.

"Got a sec, Connor?" Travis asked, standing in his partner's doorway.

Connor was one of those lawyers who always left his door open unless he had a client inside. "Open door, open mind," he always said. Travis told him about the odd message on Vince's cell phone.

"My wireless provider?" Connor repeated. "That's the message? *Our* client's call-back now says to check with *our* wireless provider?"

"Yep."

"Travis, I told you more 'n a week ago this guy was going to be a problem. Did you check in with Nancy Lee about your concerns and about our continuing lawyer-client relationship?"

"Not exactly. I mean, I did call her. We did talk about Vince. But I was a little vague about whether he was impaired under Ethical Rule 1.14."

"Figures," Connor said. "Ok, let's check with Ginger about this weird message and whether it's from *our* wireless provider."

Ginger was the firm's office manager; she handled IT and everything else on the business side of the firm. She checked with Verizon, the firm's wireless carrier. They confirmed that the number Vince had been using was in fact a line they'd been paying for over the last two months. When Ginger insisted their office had never asked for an additional line number, the carrier gave her a reference number for the added line. She checked the last two bills and discovered, to her chagrin, that they were right. She'd just not checked the lines. The firm had five lawyers and six support staff. Eleven lines, but someone had added a wireless line over the Internet. Someone with their login name and password. Ginger assured Connor she had immediately changed the Verizon password. He told her to change all passwords, in all systems, right now. Ginger was certain that no staff member had added the line. Connor told her not to worry, he knew who it was.

"Travis," Connor said, "we have to bail on this nut-ball client. He defrauded us by hacking into our system, getting our Verizon logon data, and who knows what else? And now you say we've lost track of him. We have no address, no phone number, except the line we didn't know we bought. And to top it off, the victim of his alleged crime is dead, herself a murder victim. It's no stretch that your old girlfriend, Nancy Lee Sustern, is probably lining our client out as the bomber."

"Hey, partner," Travis said, "we don't want to be bringing up one another's old girlfriends, do we? Nancy Lee was a one-and-done while we were 2Ls at UT-Austin. But you're right, this phone hack changes everything. We're not counsel of record in state or federal court, so there's no hitch to unhitch there. But we have retainer money in our trust account and no way to find our client. What do your ethical rules say about that?"

"Travis, old buddy, I went to a legal ethics seminar last week. The lecturer reminded us of a famous legal ethics lawyer, a law professor named Monroe Freedman. Professor Freedman wrote an essay in 1975 that fits our situation today perfectly. He coined the phrase, 'The Lawyer's Trilemma.' Know that that is?"

"No, I don't. And I'm getting the feeling that I don't want to know."

"Well, you should because you've got it, right now, because of this Vince character you took on as a client. Here's the trilemma Freedman was talking about. 'Lawyers are required to know everything, keep it in confidence, *and then* reveal everything to the court.' You ready for that?"

"No, not yet. But I'm ready to follow your direction. What do we have to do now?"

"Number one, we need to inform the authorities, even if we're not counsel of record, that we no longer represent the man, as of today. *Today.* Got it? Number two, we need to spend some of our own money trying to locate our missing and very elusive client. I'll call Dick the skip tracer and put him on it. Number three, the most important part, Travis; we still owe duties of confidentiality to him for the long term. What you could not tell anyone last week still holds for this week. Jesus, how could you take on a new client who didn't even have a street address for USPS mail?"

Travis took the mild rebuke by Connor in good stride. And he called Nancy Lee's admin and asked for a quick appointment in her office. It got set for 8:30 the next day.

"Morning, Nancy Lee," Travis said, as the young extern delivered him to the same ninth-floor conference room where'd he first shown her that mysterious note from Vince.

"Morning," she returned without the barest hint of a smile. Pointing to a seat on the opposite side of the table, she sat back in her chair, coupled her hands on the table, and waited for him to talk.

"I called Grant Lumberson earlier this morning and left a voice message on what I'm about to tell you. I'll follow this up for both of you with an email later today, so there's something in your file. For reasons I cannot reveal, I am no longer representing Vince Manchester. Let's call it a conflict of interest that we cannot reconcile. Connor told me to tell you it's an ER 1.7 conflict. Said you'd know what that means."

"Sure, I know what it means. But which part of ER 1.7 are you bailing out under? There's two parts. You know that, right?"

"Two parts? Connor's the ethics committee in our firm. He doesn't always spout subparts. But he's looked at our situation and insisted I come here and tell you in person. We cannot any longer represent Mr. Manchester."

"Not good enough for me, Travis. We've confided in one another. I lifted an arrest warrant at your request. So you owe me a better explanation. Subpart 'a' of the conflict rule involves a conflict with another client in the same case. Is that it? You're withdrawing because Manchester conflicts with another client in your firm?"

"No, we have no conflict like that."

"Ok, subpart 'b' says you cannot represent a client if his interests conflict with a third person or with the lawyer's own interests. Which is it, a third person or your firm's own interests?"

"Connor says I cannot give you details, but I can say the conflict is inside our firm."

"Travis, you've lost contact with him, haven't you?"

"That's privileged."

"Sure it is. But you just told me why you're bailing. He's gone underground—your ghost of a client. Travis, I trust you. I think you're here in good faith. So, I'll give you something official to put in your ongoing file about Mr. Manchester. We are investigating the bombing in Brownsville. I'm sure you know all about that. We have no identifiable suspects, and we're not technically sure about the victims, that is, by autopsy, or DNA results. But we're pretty sure that Amherst Pipps and Julia Santerra-Evans are the two victims. We're damn sure the explosion was a bomb, not an accident. We will take the case to the sitting grand jury when we have ATF handoff. That will take several weeks. Your former client, as of today, is suspect, but not before the grand jury yet. If he does surface, or if we find him before you do, I'll give you a call. Anything else you think we need to talk about?"

"Why is he a suspect if you are not sure of either the victims or motive for the bombing? Could have been terrorism, right? Why would Vince be suspect in a terrorism case?"

"He's suspect because we are pretty sure his nemesis was a victim. Remember the note you brought to me? Remember what you told me about why you were even in the money laundering case? Vince Manchester tried to kill Julia Santerra-Evans once. She hates him. The feeling is probably mutual. This does not look like a terrorism case, so far. When that's ruled out by ATF, we'll take your client to the grand jury. We won't tell you about it because you're withdrawing, as of today. Right?"

"Right," Travis said, hoping he looked more convincing than he felt.

CHAPTER 37

The FBI office in Brownsville, at 2305 Hudson Boulevard, doesn't look like a federal office building anywhere else in the US. It is a single-story building that looks like a dentist's office. Featuring a white stucco façade, front porch entryway, Spanish tiles on the roof, and palm trees surrounding the front parking lot, it feels residential. But it's all law enforcement inside.

The conference table had twelve seats, with six computer monitors and heavy security. No windows and the single entry door is sheet steel. Inside, one wall has four TV monitors. The ten-foot-wide white board was filled with pictures and diagrams. Amplifiers were evenly spaced between chairs, connected wirelessly to a desk-size telephone console which managed communications over the FBI-only network.

The Brownsville agent in charge, Oscar Simpson Benavidez, sat at the head of the table. Flanking him were Dish Joandiz from the Houston office, and another

Brownsville based agent, Mari Dominquez. Slate Blakey, Sally Lin, and Fred Widnor were on the speaker phone. Oscar opened the meeting.

"Good afternoon, Slate, Sally, and you too, Fred. I'm sorry to change the time of this update from this morning to early afternoon, and now to dinner time up there in Houston. But Dish has been grinding away for hours and hours now, and he's been telling me since breakfast to wait just a little longer. He's given me a thumbnail sketch, but he's ready now to update the investigation. Go ahead, Dish."

"Ok, everyone. The weather's fine in Brownsville, the sluice line for good information has been solid all day long. I gave you the news yesterday about nailing down two possible suspects—a man and a woman—who crossed the Matamoros border within the tight time frame for the meeting between Mr. Pipps and his client down here in Brownsville. The client's name was Julia Santerra-Evans. Her body and Mr. Pipps's body are not yet DNA-certified, but that's our working assumption. So, here's the names of the two people from Mexico, both Mexican citizens, who crossed on those two days. Now, yesterday I told you the driver's name was Admondo Rosales Torres; his gang name is Lil' Loco. I don't think I told you the passenger's name because it didn't seem important then. Her name *wasn't* important then, but it certainly is now with what I found out earlier this afternoon. The passenger was Isabel Santerra Reyes. That's the name on her passport, and the one on the CBP's border crossing from Matamoros, Mexico, into Brownsville, Texas, and then back again on the return trip."

Sally Lin's voice over the amplifier sounded like she was a little out of breath.

"Well, so both the passenger and Pipps's client share the same middle name? It's a common Hispanic name, isn't it? Santerra? Why is it important?"

"Because this morning I discovered why Lil' Loco was driving a hearse across the border instead of the armored Suburban he usually drives on trips from Monterrey to Matamoros. He was transporting the body of a woman who'd died three days ago in Monterrey. I have the death certificate—it's for Isabel Santerra Reyes. Get it? *Her* body in the hearse and *her* name on the passport the passenger used to cross into the US! That ought to knock your socks off. But that's not all. My source in Monterrey says Isabel was a twin. She's been sick for about a year and her twin sister was living in her house taking care of her. My guess is the twin sister is Julia Santerra-Evans. She could hide in plain sight in Monterrey by not using her American name—Julia Santerra-Evans. She essentially became her twin sister, who rarely left the house because of her illness."

Slate Blakey asked, "But how could she be a passenger in the car crossing the border for the meeting with Pipps and also get blown up in the explosion with Pipps? Something's wrong here."

"That bothered me too, boss, but I checked on the rules for transporting a deceased person's body into the United States. It's really simple, if you have the right documentation. You need certified copies of a Mexican death certificate, a permit from the health department, and the embalming permit. These original documents must be presented by the person traveling with the remains at the port of entry into the United States. But you don't have to declare where the body will be buried or cremated."

Sally jumped back in. "Does the CBP keep copies of those records?"

"They do. I have 'em. Right here. I just got them a half-hour ago."

"Scan them and get them up here ASAP. I'll get them into circulation so we can find out where they buried or cremated Julia's sister. If they did. And we need an address in Monterrey for Isabel, or Julia. Is everybody worrying about what I'm worrying about?"

Sally almost shouted. "Oh my God! Maybe the body inside Pipps's RV wasn't Julia's. Maybe it was her twin sister's body. Maybe because she was a twin, Julia assumed her DNA and her sister's was the same. So, when the final ATF report comes back, it could identify her sister's body as Julia's—same DNA."

"Where you going with this, Sally? Why the switch, if there was one? What does it get Julia?"

"Slate, maybe it gives her a final goodbye to the feds on the money laundering case and gets her off the hook for testimony in the state case. And, as a bonus, the US Marshal's Office will quit looking for her. But there is an even bigger motive for her to want to be believed dead."

"Like what?" Fred asked.

"Like Vince Manchester. She hates him. This might bring him out into the open if he believed she was dead. Who hides from a dead person?"

"Good lord, Sally, if you're right, what's that make poor Amherst Pipps?"

Dish spoke up. "It makes Pipps collateral damage and puts Julia back on the hunt."

Slate took over.

"All right, everybody. Let's not get too far afield here. Dish, I want you to go to Monterrey. I'll alert the US consulate there—work out of that office. If possible, work with the federal police, but be careful. Monterrey is not cop friendly, nor are the *Federales* always to be trusted. Fred, you revive the full file on Santerra-Evans; if she's still alive, then she is our prime suspect in the death of Amherst Pipps. Sally, I want you to make contact with Grant Lumberson, Nancy Lee Sustern, and Travis Danders. Give all of them our speculation—make sure they understand it's just speculation since we don't have a final ATF report yet. But they should all be considering the possibility, however bizarre it sounds, that (A) Julia is a suspect in Pipps's murder, (B) Vince might not be a suspect in the bombing case, and (C) he might actually be Julia's next target. Maybe they should consider protected witness status for him? Let's do a status meeting tomorrow at four p.m. And everyone, document your files over FBI SecureNet so everyone knows what you know. Clear?"

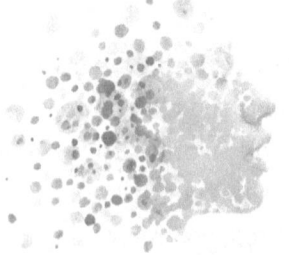

CHAPTER 38

Vinessa parked the white Honda rental in the open lot, not the parking garage, of the Harris County Psychiatric Hospital. She didn't like hospitals, but she hated parking garages. So closed in, partly dark, never clean, and given to sudden noises. The three-block walk to the mental clinic and Dr. Estancia's office was nice, she thought. Good air, a big sky, and never much wind.

She had the last appointment of the day, the one she liked best because the waiting room was not crowded—no one paid much attention to her.

"Good afternoon, Vinessa, it's good to see you. How was your weekend?"

"I don't celebrate weekends. I read somewhere that America's labor unions invented the weekend. Is that true, doctor?"

"You know, Vinessa, I think that's probably true. Before and after the First World War, factories employed thousands of workers six days a week. Sometimes eleven hours a day. Children too. Unions get the credit for the forty-hour week and the weekend off work. What kind of books do you read?"

Vinessa paused before answering the question. She'd read enough about psychotherapy to know that doctors didn't want to know things like this. They wanted to know why people don't read books that scare them.

"Books about young people. When they do funny things. You know, happy books?"

"Like what? What are you reading this summer?"

"Nothing."

"Newspapers, magazines, *People* magazine, maybe? Most of my patients read *People* magazine."

"I don't like celebrities, they're mostly fake."

"OK, Vinessa, I'd like to talk to you about transactional analysis. We find this helpful with patients who sometimes get locked into a storyline in their minds. Once locked in, a storyline is hard to shift or change. People, lots of people, behave a certain way because the storyline in their head demands it. If that happens, people ignore the real events in their world because they don't fit the one in their head. Do you understand what I'm getting at?"

"No."

"Well, that's normal. It's hard to explain, hard to understand, but we have clinical studies that confirm a basic principle of the brain and how it controls our behavior. The ability of anyone to shape what they see and remember in their little part of the universe is grounded in their expectations. People who expect to be lucky, or liked by everyone, or who are good at some sport, remember times when that was happening to them. They were lucky. They were liked by others. They were good at a sport. Their experiences reinforce their belief about luck, friends, and sports. And the studies also show that people who expect bad luck, the loss of friends, or not playing basketball very well expect those results. Can we talk about how you feel about those things?"

"I guess so."

"OK, we talked a little last time about when you were nine and something bad happened to a boy named Chester. Remember?"

"Remember what? What happened? Or do I remember you talking about that to me last week?"

"Remember what happened to Chester."

"I remember telling you I don't want to remember that."

"Does it hurt if you remember that far back? Do you think about it often?"

"No, it does not hurt. Does not hurt! He's the one who got hurt, got drowned. He did it, not me. I don't like people accusing me. You better stop, or it will make me lose time."

"Lose time? You mean not remember what happens? Is that losing time?"

"Maybe."

"When you lose time, Vinessa, does Vivian remember for you?"

"Yes."

"So, Vivian is a good person, she has a good memory. But does she lose time too?"

"Ask her, not me."

"Vinessa, I have to write some notes right now. I'll just be quiet. When I finish, I will ask Vivian about losing time."

Dr. Estancia shuffled a stack of papers on the corner of his desk and tapped on the edge with his rollerball pen. He tapped methodically, at an even pace for a minute. He watched Vinessa. She slumped forward in the soft leather chair, pressed her palms to her eyes several times, and parted her lips.

"Vivian," Dr. Estancia said.

"Yes. I know who you are," Vinessa said.

"Who am I?"

"You're the doctor we found at that university in Rice, Texas."

"Did you find me by yourself, or did someone help you?"

"Vince, I think. We don't like how he talks, but he knows things and is braver than we are."

"Do you remember Vince? I mean, is he always in your brain?"

"He's not in my brain. He's Vince. We don't talk. We look."

"Look? What do you mean, look?"

"When we lose time, we look when time comes back. Sometimes we can see he was there, while we lost time. Not always. No, not always. But sometimes. He left your name. He left that note."

"A note? Who left a note?"

"He did."

"Vivian, I'm sorry, but I don't know who you are talking about. Is it somebody who wrote the note?"

"No, his name's in the note. That's why he left it for us."

"His name's *in* the note, or he *wrote* the note? Can you tell me that?"

"He got it from us. His name's in it. Vince. It says Vince is our brother. But he is not!"

"Can you tell me what the note said?"

Vivian looked at him wide-eyed. Instead of sitting slumped in the chair, she sat up ramrod straight and rocked back and forth slowly. She clicked her teeth together then clasped her knees tightly together. In a hoarse voice Dr. Estancia had never heard, she screamed at him.

"Fuckin' A, Doctor Man, I can spit the note right in your face—Julia Baby wrote it—she's a bitch—tole my fuckin' lawyer that already—she said, 'You do not know me, but your brother Vince called me 'Julia Baby.' I mean you no personal harm, but I intend to find and kill him. He has destroyed my life'—fuck her! I'm glad she's dead. Glad! I shoulda killed her myself. Fuckin' A."

Dr. Estancia shuffled the papers again on his desk, waited a full minute, and watched as his patient's face paled, her arms returned to her lap, and she quit nodding her head.

"Vinessa, I've finished writing my notes. I want to talk to you about something else, OK?"

"Yes, of course, doctor. Could I have some more water, please? Or preferably, some tea. Would that be too much trouble?"

"No, Vinessa, not at all. Let me just put some water in my little electric kettle. It'll only take a minute."

"And, I need to go to the ladies'. In England, they call it the loo."

"Sure, it's just down the hall, make a left turn, and you'll see it."

He waited twenty minutes. Fearing the reality of what he might have done, he went to the ladies' room. No one as waiting outside it. He waited for a full minute, checking his watch, then knocked loudly on the door.

"Hello? Anyone in there?"

No answer. He turned the knob and eased the door open. "Hello, hello," he repeated. There was no one there. Cursing himself for moving too quickly and not recognizing fragility when it was staring him in the face, he went back to his office, opened a browser on his laptop, and searched for the law office of Travis Danders. It was almost 6:15 but he dialed the number anyhow. Maybe lawyers still worked late, he thought.

The Danders firm's electronic receptionist announced the office was closed but offered a name index for lawyers and staff based on first or last name. It rattled off several names before announcing, "For Travis Danders, please dial one-two." He did.

"Travis, here, who's this?" a live voice said.

"Mr. Danders, this is Ahmed Estancia, you came to my office at Rice University about three weeks ago. Do I have the right lawyer?"

Travis picked up the handset from his desk, clicked off the speaker, and said, "Dr. Estancia, yes I'm the guy who asked for a little free advice on a case I was handling. Thanks again for the advice. Are you calling about that matter, or something else?"

"Mr. Danders, so glad I caught you after working hours. Have you got a few minutes to talk to me?"

"I remember you're also a lawyer, doctor, so you know the grind. It's seven to seven most weekdays for me. What's up?"

"Well, Travis, you came to me asking abstract questions about dissociative identity disorders. You said you'd called me because a colleague of yours had suggested it."

"Right, Nancy Lee Sustern. She's an AUSA here. I'm on the other side of a case she's prosecuting. I could not give you any information about the actual case, but we talked about that diagnosis. The shorthand is DID."

"Yes, that's it exactly. You know about the sociological theory that says all of us are within six degrees of separation from one another, right?"

"Vaguely, doctor, but what does that have to do with this case?"

"Because, Travis, I suspect that between us, there's only one degree of separation. Let me explain. After my call from Ms. Sustern, I lectured her and several other lawyers about a pending case but they didn't give me any specifics, no names. It was entirely abstract. Then you came to my office with another abstract set of questions, again no names. Then, a week later a young woman came to my office, seeking consultation about a very specific set of circumstances. Now, when you and I talked we agreed that both doctors and lawyers owe clients and patients a strict duty of confidentiality. We also talked about the ethical demands of our profession. In medicine, it's to do no harm. In law, it's to never place a client in harm's way. And now, . . ."

"Doctor, sorry to interrupt, but I'm getting a terrible feeling that you're trying to tell me, without actually telling me, that my client is your patient. Am I getting warm?"

"Travis, you're most intuitive. We cannot say what our ethical rules prohibit, but we both face an ethical challenge of enormous reach. What I want to tell you is something that I think is in your client's best interest. I hope you can reciprocate by telling me something that is in my patient's best interest."

"Maybe, doctor, but I should tell you that my client—I'll use his first name here, Vince—he has disappeared. And I have told the authorities at the US Attorney's Office and the Harris County District Attorney's Office that I have withdrawn from Vince's legal representation."

"Well, my lawyer colleague, that knocks out the last degree of separation. My client has disappeared as well. She did so because I asked her about a man named Vince. That ended our relationship. We were talking about her dissociative issues, about her sense of self, and about memory. Then something happened. Remember our conversation about host identities and alter identities?"

"Yes, of course. I was vague with you, but I think I said my client might be an alter rather than a host."

"You did. I was struck by how intuitive you were, especially given the fact that you knew so little about DID. Well, since neither of us has a current professional relationship, and since we owe continuing duties to former clients and patients, I have to tell you what I'm worried about."

"Which is?" Travis asked, knowing that his voice would give him away.

"I worry that Vince is an alter of my patient. That he's emerged. And that he intends to kill a woman named Julia. I learned about her because my client has a note she wrote. Do you also know about a note, and a woman named Julia? If so, she is at risk of death. Can you suggest a course of action for both of us? Don't we have an obligation to tell someone about Vince looking for Julia to kill her?"

Travis, not a man easily stunned, felt a sour taste in his mouth.

"Yes, doctor, we do. And I think that once we figure that out, it might be in our former client's slash patient's best interest if we kept talking, at least in the abstract. I mean your patient could return for more psychotherapy and my client could show up in need of more legal representation."

They traded cell phone numbers.

CHAPTER 39

Travis called Connor the next morning on his cell. He'd forgotten that Connor was somewhere on Galveston Bay, drifting in a small fishing boat he'd rented on Galveston Island. Connor would rather fish than eat, and he loved eating.

"Hey, partner," Connor said when he saw Travis's number and face on his caller ID.

Travis told Connor what he'd learned from Dr. Estancia. Connor readily agreed they had to alert the authorities since a bona fide psychiatrist had alerted them to their client's potential for violence and their best judgment that Julia Santerra-Evans was his target. But he said, do not call them, or communicate in person. Do it in writing. We must have a written record, and let me look at the draft *before* you hit send, Connor insisted. Travis's draft was, to his way of thinking, sufficiently terse, but a clear warning. The "TO" line included Nancy Lee Sustern, Grant Lumberson,

Sally Lin, the Cameron County Sheriff's Department, the Brownsville Police Department, the Harris County Sheriff's Department, Houston Police Department, and US Customs & Border Protection—Brownsville, Texas. In the subject line, Travis typed "In re Vince Manchester." The text read:

> TO WHOM IT MAY CONCERN:
>
> The law firm of Danders & Associates (address and contacts) respectfully informs you that a white male, in his mid-twenties, who may identify himself as Vince Manchester, is a former client of this office. We have withdrawn and no longer represent Mr. Manchester. In our opinion, he may present a danger to the health and safety of a woman named Julia Santerra-Evans. This firm has recently notified counsel of record in two pending cases in US Federal Court for the District of Texas and the Harris County District Count that we no longer represent Mr. Manchester. We will not reveal the particulars in either case. We have no knowledge of the whereabouts of Mr. Manchester. Our prior representation of Mr. Manchester is and will continue to be subject to the confidentiality requirements under Texas statutes, applicable case law, and the rules of the Texas Supreme Court.

Travis sent the draft to Connor, who texted back a minute later. "OK by me." Realizing that Connor, as usual, was right to insist the warning be done in writing, Travis turned back to his computer and typed a comprehensive memo to the file. He posted it in Vince's digital file, printed a copy for the paper file, and sent copies to Connor, and

May Nguyen. He detailed his four phone calls with Vince, their three personal visits, and his mounting concerns about Vince's presentation, his insistence on control, details of the meetings he had with other counsel, and the meeting with Dr. Estancia at Rice University. The next afternoon, Connor came to his office with an ashen look on his face.

"Hey, partner," he said once he'd closed the door to Travis' office. "I just read the file memo you wrote in the Manchester file. It gives me the willies."

"Why? You approved the notice, and told me we needed a record. What did I say to spook you?"

"It's not what you said, it's who you said it to."

"Just the file, I didn't send the file memo to anyone outside the firm."

"Well, you know how May is about computer security. We hired her as both office manager and IT lady-in-total-charge, since neither one of us knows much about computer systems. You know she thinks our website and our internal computer systems are always at risk to hackers. She just left my office and said that we have cookies and several intrusions in our system. From a hacker named 'VVV.' She's afraid your file memo is now in the hands of our former client—Vince. He got into our communications portal to get that free phone line. And to chart the meta data in the phone system. Now it looks like he's been browsing around reading client files, including his own."

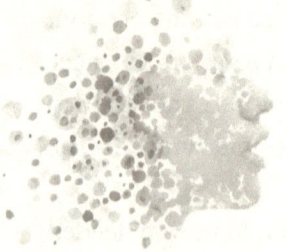

CHAPTER 40

The text from Nancy Lee to Travis was summary. Travis sensed she sent the text rather than call because she was unhappy about his terse email regarding withdrawal from the cases involving Vince Manchester.

It said, "Travis. FBI Agents Lin and Widnor are in my office. Can you join us ASAP?"

He texted back he was on the way, drove the eleven blocks from his office to hers, and made it in twenty minutes. Another extern met him in the hallway and escorted him to the small conference room.

"Travis," Nancy Lee said, without getting up when the extern opened the door for him, "sorry to be so abrupt, but we have to talk to you. I got your email yesterday about withdrawing from your representation of Vince Manchester. I don't suppose you're willing to tell us why you withdrew?"

"Don't suppose I will. You know I can't. You didn't ask me to come here ASAP to ask me that, did you?"

"No, but it was worth trying. Actually, your withdrawal made us think you need to be given information we would not share publicly; it's something we think you need to know. It's about Julia Santerra-Evans. You already know her lawyer Amherst Pipps was killed in that Brownsville bombing. And you know the working assumption is that Julia was also killed. We ask only that you do not share what we're about to tell you with the media, or with your former client, Vince Manchester. I take it you're not in ongoing contact with him now that you've withdrawn as his lawyer. Right?"

"Right, no contact. At least nothing direct. What's this all about?"

"Do you agree not to tell the media? It's important to protect the ongoing investigation into the bombing."

"Sure, I don't try my cases in the press. Why should I try yours?"

Nancy Lee turned to Sally, "Would you summarize for Travis where we are on the bombing?"

"Yes, now Travis, this is a one-time thing. We won't necessarily keep you updated as we go forward, but we think it important that you know about something that, while not proven, is quite possible. We think Julia Santerra-Evans may *not* have been killed in the bombing. In fact, she is a person of interest in our ongoing investigation. We don't have a warrant on her or enough evidence to get one. We think one other person is involved. We would not have told you this, but for your abrupt and unexpected withdrawal. It was my idea to reach out to you because I think it's possible you could be of help to us."

"Sally, we've talked before. It was in my client's best interest then. But now I've withdrawn and we're in uncharted territory. Not at all sure I can help, or that I should offer to help. You're going to have to be more direct. What kind of help?"

"Well, you know from our first telephone conversation almost three weeks ago that I've been involved in other FBI investigations concerning Mr. Manchester and Ms. Santerra-Evans. I think I told you when we talked on our first phone call that I was here in Houston when Mr. Manchester called the local FBI office, gave his name, and told us where we could find Julia. When we cut her out of the duct tape and gave her a little first aid, she told us your client broke in, robbed her, and tied her to her own desk with *red* duct tape. She hated that. I sat in on some of her debriefings, her multiple confessions to many crimes, over several days. And you probably remember that I'd interviewed Vince's sister, Vivian, in Phoenix more than a year ago."

"Right, and I told you that I got your name from Nancy Lee. She suggested I call you because you had information you were willing to share about my new client, Vince."

Nancy Lee joined the conversation.

"Travis, I suggested you call Sally because I'd just talked to her and learned that FBI Phoenix was way ahead of FBI Houston as far as Vince and Vivian were concerned. Sally confided in me that their investigation doubted that Vivian was in fact Vince's sister. Now, given other information we have, we both believe Vince Manchester and Vivian Shortfield *are the same person.* They are not sister and brother.

There is only one person, a young woman who was diagnosed in early childhood with dissociative identity disorder."

"Well, you know when we talked I took what you said as a small warning to me, as Vince's lawyer. Was I representing him, Vince, or someone else? I decided to test your psychological theories by calling that psychiatrist, Dr. Ahmed Estancia. And we've talked. I'm not going to tell you everything I learned from him; I strongly suggest you call him back. Right away. But what he said to me is not a privileged communication, so I will tell you this. Based on what I learned from him, I agree with you. I'm not qualified to diagnose anyone with a psychological or psychiatric disorder. But let's say Vince is an alter identity and Vivian is the host identity. Then just because Vince has a motive to kill Julia, that would not mean Vivian has that motive—she would likely know nothing about what Vince is doing."

"Travis, all of this is a little terrifying because we do not have that damn ATF report. But assuming that Julia is alive—that someone else's body was blown up with Mr. Pipps—which our investigation strongly indicates, we need to find Vince whether or not he really is Vivian's alter. We hope to locate Julia first. We think we know where she might be."

"Where?" Travis asked.

"Possibly in Monterrey, Mexico."

"Why?" Travis pressed.

"We can't share much with you on that because it's an ongoing investigation. You know our rule. But I can say that we're investigating the possibility that the other person whose body was disintegrated in the Brownsville explosion was Julia's twin sister. That won't be known with certainty until we get ATF identity conclusions. That could be weeks from now, maybe months."

"Well, good luck, Nancy Lee. Here's something else you need to know. My office manager, who handles our IT set up, thinks Vince might have hacked into our system. If that's so, he knows some of what we've just talked about. As you know I'm a compulsive note taker; I prepared file memos summarizing my first meetings with both of you. Hell, he probably knows more than I ever did because he's already interacted with both of you. Probably hacked into your systems, too."

"We doubt that; the FBI and all DOJ installations, like the US Attorney's Office, use IT systems that are as hack-free as humanly possible, but I'll still put out a possible intrusion alert about your client, whoever he or she may be."

"Nancy Lee, I hope you're right, but Edward Snowden might prove you wrong. And Sony and Facebook thought they were as hack-free as humanly possible, too."

Sally Lin interrupted, "Travis, let's get back to why we asked you to come here so urgently. We've told you what might be happening in our investigation. We would like you to speculate on a related issue."

"Which is?" Travis asked.

"Is it possible that Vince only retained you as a way to communicate with us? Let me explain why we might think that. First, you've made clear to us that Vince wanted you to give us that note—the one where Julia says she wants to kill Vince. Second, you told Grant Lumberson, that, without Julia's testimony, the state case against Vince cannot be won by the government. Third, and we didn't know this until just now, Vince has hacked into your computer system. That could mean he learns information about us and our investigations from *you*, not by hacking into *our* systems. To us, that could mean that Vince is our primary suspect in the Brownsville bombing, or it could mean that he is just the opposite."

"The opposite? Opposite of what?"

"Well, up until the bombing, we thought Vince, if he's a person, or even if he's an alter personality of Vivian, is not a killer; he's not after Julia. He had a perfect chance to kill her when he duct-taped her to her office desk. But he didn't. He left the scene, drove out of town, and then reported the crime to us. So, has he changed? Does he now want to kill her? If so, why?"

"I think both of you fine lawyers have forgotten the three hallmarks of a murder investigation. Sally, I don't know where you went to law school, but Nancy Lee and I took crim law and crim procedure from the same professor, at the same time. On the investigative side, he told us, prosecutors examine the evidence by looking for three things: motive, means, and opportunity. Where's your evidence that establishes that any of those three tests apply to Vince for the Brownsville bombing?"

Nancy Lee said, "Maybe the note ramped him up? It says Julia wants to kill him, and if his sister doesn't help, she'll kill the sister, Vivian. Motive? Maybe so. Maybe he thinks the only way to protect Vivian is to kill Julia?"

Travis countered, "But Julia does not know what we know, or at least what we think we know. She is not aware of the DID diagnosis or that Vince is back in town. She's not a hacker, just an assassin. I'm sure you are right about the note ramping Vince up. But not to kill her—he wanted to make sure she gets prosecuted in the federal case and put away somewhere. That's clear from what he did both in the robbery in her office and in getting her to confess. He wanted the FBI to arrest her and the DOJ to prosecute her. He worried about Julia showing up for the state court trial and help convict him, at least *in absentia*. That's why he emerged."

"So," Nancy Lee asked, "you talked to him about trial *in absentia*?"

"Attorney-client privilege, Nancy Lee. It lasts until both of us are dead, you know that."

Sally tried to save Nancy Lee. "It only lasts till the client dies. Then the lawyer can write a book about it."

"No, the communications privilege outlives both, now that I think about it. Connor, my law partner says so. But you asked for my speculation, and that's what I'm giving you. Vince, or Vivian for that matter, has no motive to kill Julia. And if the bomb is as sophisticated as I'm guessing it was, then neither of them could be involved. This explosion is either gang related—I mean cartel related—or terrorist related. It doesn't fit what an ordinary Joe, or Jane, would be able to carry off."

"Travis, suppose you're right. Then what? It was a sophisticated bomb electronically triggered by someone who was at least fifty feet from the RV."

"Who says? I thought you didn't have the ATF report yet?"

"We don't, but there is no indication this was triggered by someone inside the RV—no suicide—no jihadist looking for heaven. Pipps had no history of troubles of any kind. We've ruled out suicide on his part. And there is absolutely no reason to think that Julia, if she was in the RV when it went boom-boom, was suicidal."

"Boom-boom? Two separate explosions? I don't remember the press speculating about that."

"No, Travis," Sally said. "The media speculated about a lot of things, but they have no interest in the technical aspects of a powerful bomb that is ignited—boom number one—and a fuel tank with thirty-plus gallons that ruptured and spewed gas all over—that was boom number two. A split second between them, but still two booms. Anyhow, both from the FBI side and from the DOJ side, we're not treating this as a suicide. It's a homicide. And we're confident it was a bomb, not an accident. So, if your client didn't have a motive to blow up either Julia or Pipps, he had nothing to gain. And since he didn't have either the expertise or any access to that level of expertise, we don't think he had the means. Opportunity? Yeah, he had that. He'd wasn't with you that morning, was he?"

Travis didn't answer. But he asked for a bathroom break. Walking back to the conference room, he kept telling himself that what he was doing was in his client's best interest. It's rare to talk to prosecutors and investigators about a client's motive to do anything. But he defended Vince's conduct without being sure it was Vince who needed protection. If he was right, Vince was an alter. He was not Vivian but was indistinguishable from her. Wasn't Vivian his real client?

And if that's the case, shouldn't he be trying to get the FBI and the US Attorney's Office to see the Brownsville bombing investigation from her defense perspective?

When he got back, Nancy Lee was alone in the conference room.

"Sally's on a conference line with her office in Phoenix. They seem to think she needs to keep in close contact with them about the other cases, not the Brownsville bombing case."

"Just as well. As the prosecutor in the bombing case, can I ask you an off-base question?"

"You often ask me off-base questions. Fire away."

"Have you read the 302 that Sally wrote about her interview with Vivian Manchester in Phoenix?"

"Well, that is off base, but harmless, I guess. Yes, I've read it."

"And you've read all the 302s about Vince Manchester, I presume, right?"

"Yep. Those and more."

"So, based on anything you've read about them—Vivian and Vince—do you consider Vivian, whom we know is real, elusive as hell, but real—to be a person of interest in the Brownsville bombing case?"

Nancy Lee inhaled deeply and tapped the table with the end of her ballpoint pen before speaking.

"No, not a person of interest. But you know we had a video conference with Dr. Ahmed Estancia about the DID diagnosis and some legal issues related to that diagnosis. He said something that turned out to be helpful to me as I tried to decipher either Vince's or Vivian's role in the federal money laundering case. Instead of thinking of them as two people, I've been thinking of them as just that—*them*. One person with two identities, at least in their mind. One identity loses time. That happens when the other identity emerges. What makes the alter personality emerge is a threat to the host. The alter is there to manage the threats the host cannot handle. My point is that I don't consider Vivian or Vince to be a person of interest, but I am thinking about *them* in a different way. What if they are targets of the bomber? If Julia is the bomber, did she blow up Pipps as a way to make *them* a person of interest, or suspect in the bombing? Is she so livid about Vince that she'd do that to make his life miserable?"

"So, Nancy Lee, take it one step further. If they aren't suspect, are they a victim? Not two victims, but a victim of the actual bombing—along with Pipps? And if that's the case, do the federal victim's rights laws apply?"

CHAPTER 41

Dish Joandiz had presented his passport and law enforcement credentials to the US Marine guard on the street side of the US consulate's offices in Monterrey, Mexico. The massive, multistory stone and concrete compound at Avenida Alfonso Reyes No. 150 was home to almost a hundred staff and contract employees. The official street address, 66196 Santa Catarina, Nuevo León, was well known to anyone seeking a visa to the US or a US citizen in Mexico on business or pleasure. To his surprise, Dish learned that the consulate general in Monterrey is one of the largest and busiest consulates in the world. Its consular district included Nuevo Leon, Durango, Zacatecas, San Luis Potosí, and most of Coahuila. It was almost as big as Texas and had just over thirteen million inhabitants.

He was escorted into the building and given local papers confirming his "official" presence in the district as an *agent* of the US Federal Bureau of Investigation. His explanation that he was not a sworn agent but an investigator working with FBI agents fell on deaf ears. Better to be in the FBI than just to be an investigator, he was told. He was also assigned a local police officer should he need help on his investigation. The department of state foreign service officer must have been required to make a report and asked questions "for the record."

"So, Mr. Joandiz, you're here to investigate a crime against both an American and a Mexican national, but it was committed entirely on US soil in Brownsville, Texas. Do I have that right?"

"Almost right, I'd say. Call me Dish. It's not my real name, but that's what my . . ."

Looking slightly alarmed, the foreign service officer said, "Not your real name? It's on your passport. What do you mean it's not real?"

"Oh, it's right on my passport, but it doesn't match my birth certificate because Dish is my nickname. I've had it since I was a baby. Wanna know why?"

The consulate staffer was not given to humor or side stories but nodded his head.

"I was the first of two children in our family. My dad had a little speech impediment. He went around the neighborhood telling everyone 'dishes my son.' So the story goes, everyone thought he was serious and Dish was my name. It just stuck. Then eleven months later, my brother was born. His head was a little bowl shaped. My dad took him around the neighborhood saying my brother had a bowl-shaped head. Everyone called him bowl. By the time we could waddle around the neighborhood together, people said here comes 'Dish Bowl,' thinking it was cute, I guess. So, my whole life my name has been Dish and my brother's was Bowl. Funny, eh?"

The staffer was not amused but changed nothing on the entrance and work forms. He asked whether the FBI case Dish was working on involved Mexican or US citizens.

"Yes, sir, it does. I'm following up on the death of a Monterrey woman named Isabel Santerra Reyes. Does that name mean anything to you?" Dish asked.

"I have access to recent visas granted to Mexican citizens. And I have several US citizens who are here in Mexico for various reasons. Is Senora Santerra Mexican or American?"

"We're not sure—we have a Julia Santerra in this investigation, but the name Isabel Santerra is new to us. I can tell you that the person named Isabel Santerra Reyes died here in Monterrey week before last. I have copies of her death certificate and the Mexican documents necessary to remove her remains from here to the US."

"So, she was a Mexican citizen who was buried in the US?"

"Not sure. We have no burial record in the US, because there is no national database for buried citizens. We don't think she was buried. We think she was just taken across the border, for other reasons. They are part of an ongoing investigation, which I cannot discuss with you. I can show them to the consulate, if you wish."

"Yes, that would be wise."

Dish was taken upstairs to the consulate's office. He waited forty-five minutes before he was summoned into a large ornate office festooned with flags and portraits of American secretaries of state in the nineteenth century. The consulate, obviously a busy man, told Dish he did not wish to intrude into an FBI case, but he couldn't understand why someone would take the body of a Mexican citizen across the border with all the necessary paperwork to remove the body into the US but with no intent to bury the body. His only question was whether cremation was the choice of the family. Dish told the consulate that the working theory was that they wanted to blow up the body to throw the FBI off the track of a murderer. The consulate, obviously alarmed, said he'd heard enough. He'd instruct staff to assist the FBI in every way possible. Then he showed Dish how to take the stairs back down to the first-floor exit.

Back at his hotel, Dish called Sally Lin over his SecureNet satellite phone. She summarized her earlier conversation that morning with one of the pathologists at the ATF lab in Atlanta. They had mortuary teams, primarily pathologists, with other kinds of scientists, DNA experts, and odonatologists. As she explained it to him, the ATF plan on cases like this one was to collect every body part. They documented everything, sketched it, photographed it, and categorized every single piece of human remains. If a body was more or less intact, the team would identify it by height, weight, gender, hair color, eye color, dental records, and fingerprints. They created a DNA database of close relatives. Presumably, the next of kin would want to bury a loved one. She said he needed to get DNA samples in Monterrey from other relatives of the Santerra twins—Julia and Isabel.

"But," Dish protested, "we don't know they had relatives here. Do we?"

"No, we don't. That's why Slate wanted you to hustle down there. Knock on doors. Do your investigative thing in Español."

"My gringo Spanish is passable, but I don't look the part. I'm gonna need someone local to knock down doors with me."

"No Dish, don't knock any doors down. Not yet. Is there a US military presence there, at the consulate's office?"

"There was a US Marine guard at the front entrance this morning."

"Well, go back there and talk to him. See if he can give you his commanding officer and start there. Meanwhile, I'll check with Slate and see if there are other law enforcement possibilities down there to help us out. Oh, and here's something else I followed up on. Remember the issue of whether DNA is different or identical with twins?"

"I remember it coming up. But nobody knew, right?"

"Yeah, but we have an answer now. If the Santerra twins are identical twins, then they have identical DNA. Here's the biology. If there is only one egg, and it is fertilized by only one sperm, there is only one baby. But sometimes, after the egg is fertilized and starts to divide, it can split apart. After it splits apart, each half can continue to divide and grow into a baby. They are identical twins because they came from the same fertilized egg."

"So, I have to find out down here whether they were identical or fraternal, is that it?"

"Yes, if you can. If they are from there, maybe there's a local doctor who took care of them. But my working assumption is they were identical. Twins always know whether they are identical or fraternal. It's important to them. So Julia would know if she was Isabel's identical twin. And if they weren't identical, I doubt we'd have this body in the hearse coming across the border the same morning as the explosion. I mean, why would Julia even try this if they were *only* fraternal twins. Fraternal twins do not share the same DNA."

"OK," Dish said, "I have the home address for Isabel off her death certificate. And I have the name of a law firm here. They worked with us two years ago, but it was a financial crimes case, not a murder case. The name of the firm is Sánchez Mejorada, Velasco y Ribé, S.C. As I remember, it's a very old firm with offices in Mexico City and Monterrey. Maybe they have a young *abogado* who could make some calls. As I recall, they were what we'd call a silk-stocking law firm in Houston—doing mostly business stuff. I'll let you know about that."

"Sounds good, Dish. And by the way, did you know that just 60 percent of those who died in the World Trade Center on 9/11 were ever officially identified? More than a decade after Hurricane Katrina hit, the city of New Orleans still has thirty-one unidentified remains. I got this from the ATF guy in Atlanta. So, if you mostly strike out down in Monterrey, it won't be a surprise. Matching body parts to DNA and then finding who the DNA identifies is a huge problem."

CHAPTER 42

Nancy Lee was still in her office at seven p.m. when her cell rang. She was surprised to see Grant Lumberson's face and cell number on her screen. Grant wasn't known as a work-at-night kind of guy. He usually left the district attorney's office at five and headed for one of the many lawyer watering holes in downtown Houston. She clicked "talk."

"Grant Lumberson, my favorite state prosecutor," she exclaimed with a tang in her voice. "To what do I owe the honor of a seven p.m. call from you? I thought you didn't work this late?"

"We all work at mysterious times and in strange places. Some of my best work is done here in my favorite booth at the Cut and Shoot Saloon. It's on the southwest corner of McKinney and Louisiana, less than a block from your office. You know it?"

"Across the street from the Houston Club? Yeah, I know it. Is it on your way home?"

"Don't crack wise with me, Nancy Lee. I'm sitting here with a geezer named Jesus Cantron. You ever heard of him?"

"No, can't say I have. Should I know him?"

"Hell yes. He's a constable for the justice of the peace in Baytown. Knows Julia Santerra-Evans like from the old days. He's been telling me a tale or two about her. I'm buying. But maybe you ought to stroll on over here. Bring your wallet—he's a thirsty man—and likes to talk to high-powered prosecutors like you. You got time for him, and me?"

"Do they have food there? I'm starving."

"The house specialty is a twenty-five-dollar flat-iron steak that tastes like a two-dollar steak from Costco."

"OK, Grant. See you in ten."

Nancy Lee, Grant, and the slack-jawed man with double chin, Jesus Cantron, spent the next hour, eating steaks well-done, beer with whiskey back for the men, and a decent Chardonnay for her. Grant obviously knew this man well enough to recall old cases where he worked for the Baytown JP who presided over low-level criminal activity that somehow made their way to big dog cases in state district court. She learned both had served arrest warrants on dangerous men carrying guns. That apparently was their personal connection. Grant was an occasional answer to Jesus Cantron's relentless thirst for whisky, neat, with beer chasers, and overcooked steaks. It took a half-hour but eventually Grant maneuvered Cantron back into his connection to Julia.

"Yeah, sure, I did some stuff for her. Nothing illegal, but stuff she needed."

Nancy Lee tried to slide into the conversation.

"Well, Jesus, if I buy the next round, will you give me some stories about what you did over the years for Julia?"

"Yeah, but you gotta protect me, ya know. She would get me fired and flayed if she knew I was talking to you guys. I'm already pretty beat up—you can see it in my face, right?"

Grant smiled. "Jesus, I've been meaning to ask you about that mule that stomped on your face. Were you plowing and the mule jumped her traces, flatting your jaw? Don't think you ever told me the story."

"It wasn't a mule. It was a soldado from the Sinaloa Cartel. That's how I first met Julia, ya know. She was also a soldado, but she quit when they let her into law school. Sometimes she'd brag that she's the only soldado from Sinaloa that's a permanent resident of the US with a license to fuck the law. That's what she tole me."

"She hit you? In the face?"

"No, man. It was her ex-husband. He's why she became a soldado, you know that already, right?"

Nancy Lee tried to restrain herself. "She's a former soldier for a Mexican drug cartel? That's what you're saying?"

"I ain't saying nothing. She says that. I thought you guys knew who she was! She's been a lawyer here for what, five, six years?"

"Oh, we knew who she was, but not until two years ago when she got beat up in her own office. Then we knew her. In fact, I interviewed her myself, along with the FBI, and the US Marshal's Office."

"Yeah, that's what I'm saying too. It was that guy she fuckin' hates, name's Vince something. Manster, or something like that."

"Did you talk to her about that case, Jesus?" Grant asked.

"No, not when it happened. But later, about three or four months ago, maybe longer I don't know. Can we order another round? My throats getting dried up."

The waiter brought another beer for Grant, a beer and a shot for Jesus, and a cup of black coffee for Nancy Lee. The professionals from the office buildings around them had mostly gone home. The Cut and Shoot was half empty, even though the soccer game on the seventy-two-inch screen over the bar was still going strong. Jesus wove in and out of his story about Julia. He told Grant and Nancy Lee that Julia had lots of money from banks and gangsters in Mexico and South America. She did legal work, but also arranged packages and people coming in and out of Texas. Some of it was legitimate work, he said.

Nancy Lee had listened patiently for an hour and a half. But she was losing her patience with all the ducking and bobbing Jesus was throwing at her.

"So, Jesus, what you've told me so far is peanuts. You want to become a confidential informant for the US Attorney's Office, you better start coming up with real evidence, real things that happened. Or you won't make it to our payroll. That's what you really want, right? Money for information? As I hear you tell it, Julia's been dropping a Ben Franklin on you here and there, but nothing regular. We can do better than that, but we want current, provable information. You want that, or not?"

Jesus threw back his shot glass, took a sip of beer, and became a CI. "Yeah, hell yes I want that. I been doing shit work for her, but I'm afraid of her. So before I step in the government pond, who is gonna know I'm in, besides you and Grant?"

"Me, my boss, the US Attorney for the Southern District of Texas, and the chief investigator in our office. We work with the FBI and other federal agencies, and we will share your information with them but not your name. We won't share anything that would identify you as a county employee."

"And nothing to the JP I work for as a constable, right? I don't wanna lose that job; it pays benefits and I don't have to do very much."

Nancy Lee shook hands with Jesus. Then both men headed for the men's room. When they got back, Jesus gave them a look at Julia that surprised Nancy Lee and stunned Grant. Julia was a contract killer, Jesus thought. She was rich, he was sure. She kept her soldado status in Sinaloa, but not in Nuevo Leon. She had family in Monterrey. Jesus thought she lived there but wasn't sure. He gave Nancy Lee the cell number Julia had given him to reach him. It was untraceable, she said. Julia had paid him a few hundred dollars in the last few weeks to get information on Vince. All he knew was the state case was back up again. Julia never asked him about the federal case.

Nancy Lee had been taking notes on a little four-by-six-inch pad. Holding up her hand at Jesus, she took two minutes to read over what she'd jotted down.

"OK, Jesus, we have a deal. Don't come to our office. We'll meet when one of us needs to. Me to ask questions. You to answer. We will pay in cash. I'll call you on your cell to make those arrangements. But we have two more important questions you need to answer tonight. Did Julia have anything to do with the Brownsville bombing where her lawyer Amherst Pipps was killed? And also, where is Julia now?"

Jesus paled a little, leaned away from Nancy Lee's side of the booth, and looked down at the table top. He chewed on his upper lip and then asked. "The bombing on the Matamoros border—the one by the zoo? Oh shit, you saying she did that? I never heard that."

"I'm asking what you know about it now. Was she involved?"

"You mean was she blown up? Hell, I dunno know that. If she was, how come you're now asking me stuff about her?"

"The bodies in that explosion have not yet been positively identified by the ATF. But if she was involved, how would she carry that off and who would help her?"

"I don't want to be your confidential informant on something like that. Shit, Prosecutor Lady, that's cartel stuff. I know she knows Lil Loco in Monterrey. She made a slip once, talking to me on that burner phone of hers. She was riding in his car somewhere and talking to me. He must have gone off the road or something, because she screamed at him like 'Lil Loco, you fuck.' I dunno know what he did, but if he's working for her, then you know she's back with the Sinaloa Cartel. You want to know where she is now? Find him. He'll know."

CHAPTER 43

Back in his hotel, The Sheraton Ambassador, Dish made three phone calls. He called a cab. He called for room service in two hours, and he called the concierge downstairs and asked about driver's services in the city. Then he walked down to the lobby and found his cab waiting. The address for Isabel Santerra Reyes was on her death certificate. He gave it to the cab driver, whose English was good.

"Know where this is?" Dish asked.

"It's about thirty minutes from here, up there," he said, pointing to the foothills behind the city center.

"Ok," Dish answered. He gave the overweight cab driver three US twenty-dollar bills. "Will this get me there and back?"

"Yes, with a small tip left over. Unless you want to spend some time up there and keep me waiting on the curb. You know it's all houses up there? Rich people's houses. Most of them have guard gates."

"Well, let's go see."

The ride took more than thirty minutes. The Santerra house at 499 Valle Alto turned out to be a modern looking house built in 2013. It was big, over six-thousand square feet, according to a Zillow listing over a year old. Apparently, the property had been on and off the market. It was listed as a "beautiful luxury residence in a gated community." Dish told the driver to wait for him at the main gate and walked to the guard gate at the front entrance. He tried a half dozen four-digit numbers but nothing worked. His driver whistled for him to come back to the car. For another twenty-dollar bill, the driver said he'd give him the fire department code for all these gates. Dish paid him. The driver said zero, zero, zero, one. It worked. Dish walked through the gate and found the Santerra house—or at least he found the house owned by Isabel Santerra Reyes.

It was a two-story stucco house, painted white with dark-brown accents and a deep-red tiled roof over the front garage and also over the second floor. A double palm tree stood on one side of the short flight of stairs at the entrance, left of the garage doors. All the windows were shuttered. The grass looked dry. There was no sign of life. Dish walked to the main door, knocked, and waited. Nothing stirred inside. He went to the garage, which had a key pad and hit the same pattern as the main gate. Nothing happened. He reversed the pattern. One, zero, zero, zero. That worked. Inside the garage he found a black, nearly new Chevrolet Suburban, freshly washed, with Mexican plates. The hood was hot, and the smell of exhaust was strong. He found a metal door at the rear of the garage with a security key pad on the wall beside the door. There was also what Dish assumed was a high-quality optical lens security camera with a 220-degree visual angle facing him. Whoever was inside could see him from head to toe if he stood a few feet away from the door.

Dish slid his Glock 23 from the holster strapped to his back. Holding the gun behind him, out of peephole view, he held up his FBI identification wallet with the badge and photo flap open. Then he knocked hard on the door and took three steps backward. Two minutes passed. Dish heard something brushing up against the door from the inside.

"I'm an American FBI agent. I'm here to see Isabel Santerra Reyes. Please open the door."

He heard a click, then a man's distant voice.

"Watch you want, FBI?"

"Just to talk to Miss Santerra."

"Watch you holding behind your back, FBI?"

Dish realized his mistake and spun to his left past the front of the SUV. But as he turned to face the door it flew out toward him. A man crouching down low came fish-walking through the door carrying what looked like a tactical assault shotgun. It had a muzzle device on accessory rails. The gun world said these assault shotguns "give new meaning to the term 'doorknocker.'" In the two seconds Dish took to drop his badge, and swing his gun arm around to form a two-handed grip on his Glock, the shotgun man got off five rounds, at chest height, blowing Dish up and against the garage wall. As he slid lifelessly down to the garage floor, he painted the wall black with blood and tissue. The point-blank shotgun rounds blew a lemon-sized hole in his chest. He never knew what hit him.

The cab driver knew well the sound of a shotgun, the ultimate weapon of terror, and dropped his cell phone. As he twisted the starter key, he saw the bulky gunman, holding the shotgun stride confidently out onto the pavement of the driveway. He looked at the cab, parked sixty feet away. Dropping the shotgun, which he knew would be useless at this range, he pulled a long-barreled pistol from his waistband. As the cab sped away, the driver felt the glass shards from the back window, and heard both shots. One hit his rear window, the other the mirror on the outside of the passenger door. He careened the car around the curve and drove as fast as he could down the hill. After a five-minute run, his racing pulse rate seemed to drop and felt safe enough. No one was following him. He pulled over and dialed 911.

CHAPTER 44

Dish's murder in Monterrey, Mexico, rippled quickly through both the US State Department and the US Justice Department. They were, as is often the case, at odds. Dish had followed protocol; he'd reported his official FBI presence in Mexico to the US consulate. They called a cab for him to the murder scene. If State had its way, protocol would be maintained. Mexican law enforcement would investigate the murder. American investigative authorities would be sidelined. When a US citizen, whether with the FBI on business or as a tourist on vacation, is the victim of a crime in Mexico, diplomatic protocols and treaties preside. Consular staff knew which Mexican authorities would scramble at the crime scene, which police force would investigate Dish's murder, and how wide the range of possible outcomes would be. Protocol made it a State Department responsibility, not DOJ or FBI. But the consulate in Monterrey did not investigate crimes, provide legal advice, or represent crime victims in court.

The FBI has a well-defined role in foreign countries. It stations special agents and other personnel in foreign countries to help Americans by maintaining relationships with foreign law enforcement, intelligence, and security services. These FBI offices on foreign soil are legal attaché offices, commonly known as *legats*. Each office is established through mutual agreement with the host country and is situated in the US embassy or consulate. Management comes from the International Operations Division at FBI Headquarters in Washington, DC. The FBI legal attaché works with law enforcement and security agencies in the host country to coordinate investigations of interest to both countries—the FBI doesn't investigate in Mexico, it coordinates. At least that's what protocol dictates. But when an FBI agent is murdered and the murder is committed by a criminal drug cartel hostile to both nations, protocol is pure cover. There is no legat in Monterrey, but there is one in the US embassy in Mexico City—a ninety-minute flight due south.

Slate Blakey in Houston made his case persuasively to the SAIC in the International Offices Division at FBI HQ. His man, Dish Joandiz, was shot down in cold blood, presumably by a soldado of the Sinaloa Cartel. The FBI should not just participate in the investigation and arrest of the bastard who gunned down Dish, it should be out front—damn the protocol. An hour after Slate's call, he got the green light. Coordinate with the FBI legat in Mexico City but take the lead. The Mexico City legat would clear it with Monterrey authorities and the US Consulate's Office there. Get your man. Bring him back to Houston in a jump suit with manacles. If that doesn't work, take photos of the body bag.

That night, Sally Lin and Fred Widnor boarded a MATS flight out of Kelly Field for the two-hour-and-ten-minute flight to Mexico City. Ten minutes after they were airborne, FBI Houston's main switchboard got a call from a man who refused to identify himself but insisted he could help "with that murder down in Monterrey. The one involving Julia Baby."

The operator transferred the call to SAIC Slate Blakey's office. Slate took the call himself.

"This is Slate Blakey," he said. "Do you have information about the murder of one of our agents in Monterrey, Mexico? Our agent was Dish Joandiz. Is that the murder you're calling about?"

Slate could hear what he thought was a door being closed, and what sounded like a TV broadcast being turned off.

"I'm calling 'bout the case you guys are investigating—the big fuckin' explosion of a big-ass mobile home in Brownsville. The papers said a lawyer was killed. I dunno know about that. But Julia the whore was not blown up with him, she was the one that did it. You F Bee Eye dicks figured that out yet? It was Julia that punched the button and she was in Lil Loco's car when she watched the boom, both booms. And I'm pretty fuckin' sure the same dick, Lil Loco, is the one that shot-gunned your man down in Old Mexico, just a few hours ago."

"To whom am I speaking?" Slate asked.

"To me, the man who knows his shit. You're stalling, trying to trace this phone. Waste of time, F Bee Eye Man. I'm calling on a burner, and I'm not connecting by cell. I'm Wi-Fi from a coded phone. I want the name of one of your agents down there in Old Mexico, so I can give 'em a tip or two 'bout this slob killer—name of Lil Loco."

Slate asked, "We appreciate citizen help and tips from people who know what they are talking about. How can we be sure you know something that can aid our investigation?"

"'Cause I just tole you it was Julia fuckin' whore that done the Brownsville bombing. That ain't in the newspapers. I just tole you Lil Loco's name. That ain't public knowledge either. I know my shit and there's a guy in Monterrey who will tell me what the *Federales* are doing down there, long as I pay him enough dinero. If you guys fuck up and don't get Lil Loco and Julia Baby, then I have to go down there and kill her myself. I hate fuckin' Mexico. So, when I get a call from Old Mexico from my man down there, I'll call back. This is a good number, right?"

Slate said it was. Then he heard the telltale click. It would be hours before the man called back.

When they landed in Mexico City, an embassy staffer met them with an armored vehicle. They'd spend the night at the embassy, meet the quickly assembled team, and depart by another military flight the next morning for Monterrey. They desperately wanted to capture Julia alive. They were ambivalent about Lil Loco. There wasn't a customs check at the USAF base in San Antonio, but there was one in Mexico

City. Their papers were in order, and the US embassy staff in Mexico City was waiting at the gate when they landed. No one opened the two metal crates loaded with assault weapons, ammo, and flak jackets as they slid down the ramp onto the conveyor belt at the terminal.

The next morning at breakfast in the US embassy cafeteria, Sally got the good news phone call from Slate. He told her about the mysterious tipster. Just a heads up, he said. The ATF in Atlanta had confirmed by DNA testing that the female explosion victim was *either* Julia Santerra-Evans *or* her sister Isabel Santerra Reyes. The match came from DNA samples at two hospitals in Houston where blood had been taken from Julia for minor procedures. It was confirmed by a second match in Monterrey from bone marrow at a hospital there. The lab tech in Monterrey asked an innocent question of the lab tech in Atlanta, after running the test.

"Could I ask about Ms. Santerra Reyes? I met her once here at our hospital here in Monterrey when she was in the final stage of her uterine cancer. Has she passed? Is that what this DNA match is about?"

This innocently asked question confirmed the last piece of information essential to issuing search and arrest warrants under both US and Mexican law. Julia's sister Isabel had a terminal disease. She died, according to her death certificate, seven days *before* the explosion in Brownsville. Julia was the survivor twin sister and came with Lil Loco across the border twice in the lead-up to the bombing. Lil Loco was at the Santerra residence when Dish was murdered. The cab driver identified him from prior booking photos as the man who shot out the rear window of his cab. Whether Lil Loco would be charged as an accessory to the bombing in Brownsville was irrelevant. His murder of Dish was the focus of Sally Lin's five-member team. But he worked for Julia. Sally hoped they'd get her when they got him. Slate reminded her that the only people who knew that Julia Santerra-Evans was not killed in Brownsville and that Julia Santerra-Evans had not died in the explosion were ATF personnel and the mysterious unnamed tipster. Sally said she'd remember that, but she had the sense that Mexico City was full of tipsters who'd help if the tipster got paid enough.

The hastily assembled five-person team met for the first time in the embassy CIA station's office after breakfast. They turned out to be as tough as they were diverse. Sally Lin, an Asian-American female, was team leader. Fred Widnor, an Anglo-Saxon man, had her back. Gunnery Sargent Chance Otou, an African-American male, was deployed by the US Marine Corps Forces Special Operations Command from his Marine squadron on duty at the US embassy in Mexico City. He was a highly experienced operator with Middle-East credentials. Nacho Contreras, a Mexican citizen, was a six-year veteran of the federal police, formerly known as the *Policía Federal Preventiva*. It is the elite Mexican police force under the authority of the Department for Home Affairs. Nacho looked the part. Agents of the Federal Police are always heavily armed and wear dark blue, black, or gray combat fatigues. The team was selected by Glorieta Villanueva, the number-two ranking CIA officer at the embassy. The CIA station chief would accompany the team as liaison, but would not engage in arrest or search operations. They left the embassy at 12:30 p.m. in a camo-colored Humvee. All were heavily armed.

Before they left Mexico City for their flight to Monterrey, Nacho spent twenty-five minutes briefing by telephone both local and federal police in Monterrey. Glorieta briefed the ambassador, who called and gave instructions to the duly appointed counselor at his office in the US consulate in Monterrey. Gunny Otou checked out two duffel bags with flak jackets, machine pistols, two assault rifles, one assault shot gun, dozens of flash bangs, radios, and first-aid gear from the Marine armory on the grounds of the embassy. Glorieta took a briefing call from CIA headquarters in Langley, Virginia. On the plane, Sally Lin led the discussion about the Monterrey plan.

"By the time we land, we'll have arrest and search warrants for Julia Santerra and Lil Loco. But since we have no intel on their location, we'll spend the rest of today at the consulate working the phones, the Internet, and your local sources on the fugitives. I know you all know the drill, but since we are not an international unit, maybe we ought to talk about decision makers. I'm supposed to be lead operator, but this not my country, and I don't know the rules or protocols down here. So, here's what I suggest. Gunny, will you take the lead on weapons, assaults if necessary, and team defensive positions?"

"Yes, ma'am, you pick the targets, I'll flash bang 'em."

"Thanks, gunnery sergeant. Nacho, you're in charge of liaison with and talking to local police in Monterrey, or any other town we go to. And you're our official communicator with the federal judiciary and prosecutors. Do you have any time table yet for when charges might be filed, if we can find Lil Loco and Julia?"

"Si. I know the prosecutor's office very well in Monterrey. I've already talked to one old friend there. And I can tell you from experience that no charges will be filed until our work is done. I mean until after we arrest and interrogate the fugitives from the Santerra home."

"But won't the prosecutor's office want to know about, and maybe participate in, any interrogations? I mean at least the lawyers, the abogados, will weigh in, right?"

"No, that's not how we do it in Mexico. Many of the *Federales*, like me, are *abogados*. I was first trained in the law, found it dull, and joined the federal police as an agent. But I do lots of interrogations before charges are filed. Then the prosecutor's office in Monterrey, where I used to work, writes up the charges based on admissions secured in the interrogation room. We don't have grand juries down here. So, it's police first, lawyers next, and then trials. No jury trials. So sometimes it's interrogate, confess, and get sentenced. We're more efficient than Norte Americanos in that way."

"Wow, Nacho, that's way too efficient for the US."

Nacho smiled, held his arms out wide, and said, "Sally, am I right that most FBI agents are lawyers before they go through the FBI academy?"

"You're right. But maybe not most. We have lots of accountants, engineers, statisticians, and data experts these days. I'm a lawyer, but I never practiced. I went to the FBI Academy right out of law school."

"OK, let me give you a quick summary. Mexican criminal law does not look at all like American criminal law. Down here, a suspect or a fugitive like the ones we're chasing have no rights. In Mexico, one is deemed guilty until proven innocent. But before you think we're barbaric, I should tell you we don't have a death penalty. No Latin American countries do. In Mexico, there is no parole or bail. But sometimes, if the suspect is rich, or has a good *abogado*, he can get a judge to let him post a bond to be released on bail. But that does not happen if his potential sentence in years surpasses a certain limit under a formula set forth in Mexico's constitution. In murder cases, no one gets bail or parole. They get prison. But our prisons differ from yours. Down here prisoners are allowed regular conjugal visits. They have greater freedoms within the confines of the prisons than in most US penitentiaries. Of course, you have to buy your freedoms. Our prisons are good marketplaces. Being rich won't keep you out of prison, but it will make prison life almost enjoyable."

"Well, thanks Nacho. Let's talk about extradition, particularly for Julia. Glorieta, I think you are in the best position to help us with that."

Glorieta Villanueva was both diplomatic and secretive. Her posting in Mexico City was through the CIA, in cooperation with the State Department. A sensitive matter, like a bombing in America by a Mexican national—even one with permanent resident status in the US, like Julia had—was tricky.

"Well," Glorieta said in her whispery voice, "maybe I should talk first about why I'm here. The Brownsville bombing is complicated because it happened in the US. A US citizen died, and the bombers may include both a Mexican national, Lil Loco, and a person with permanent residency status, Julia Santerra-Evans. My job at the US embassy includes communications between American diplomatic entities, Department of Justice entities, and the interaction that might come about if both suspects are caught here in Mexico. I don't want to bore you, but international extradition is not just about the criminals, or the victims. It's a formal diplomatic process. It's defined by treaty and conducted between the federal government of the US and the government of Mexico. You have to remember that it is definitely not a *judicial* function. It is an *executive* function under the US president's power to conduct foreign affairs. International extradition can only be based on international comity or extradition treaties between nations. If this team makes an arrest of both, the extradition question is delicate. If only Lil Loco is arrested, there will be no extradition. And if . . ."

Fred Widnor jumped in. "No extradition? But that bastard killed Dish Joandiz, an American citizen and an FBI investigator. Don't we have a say in the decision?"

"Yes," Glorieta said. "But he killed your friend in Mexico. My sense is Mexico will put him in prison for it. They won't want to extradite him. They have no death penalty here, remember?"

"Yeah, I remember. That's exactly why he should be extradited. We do. He should be tried in Texas, where Dish's family live. And Texas is big on the death penalty."

"Mexico knows about Texas's frequent application of the death penalty. That's precisely why I think Lil Loco won't be extradited."

Sally, seeing the anguish on Fred's face, took over.

"Glorieta, let me ask the other question. If we capture Julia, she has permanent resident status in the US. That will entitle the US to extradite her, won't it?"

"Maybe. Maybe not," Glorieta said. "Julia is also a Mexican national—she was born here, lived her as a young person, and was living here at the time Mr. Joandiz was killed. I think the evidence suggests that the only shooter was Lil Loco. Julia didn't kill, but she may have assisted or even directed Lil Loco. We don't know that yet. There may be reasons why Mexico would want to try her here and imprison her here. She was, we think, a *soldado* in the Sinaloa Cartel. Lil Loco may be a *soldado* in the Los Zetas Cartel, but I doubt that."

Sally kept at it.

"But Glorieta, while extradition is a question, the more pressing issue is what do we do with either Lil Loco or Julia if we make an arrest? Where do we take them? Not to the consulate or the embassy, right?"

"I won't be on the search and arrest team. My job is to communicate with both State and DOJ in Washington, and maintain close contact with our embassy in Mexico City. But if past experience means anything, I don't think you will arrest Lil Loco. He'll charge at you no matter how many guns he's facing. Julia, I don't know about her. Fifteen years ago, when she was a soldier, she might have died before giving up. Now, maybe she's Americanized. She might prefer prison to cremation."

The announcement from the pilot broke up the conversation. "We're on final approach. Landing at Monterrey in about ten minutes."

CHAPTER 45

Sally, Gunny, Fred, and Nacho piled into the Ford Explorer with consular plates for the thirty-minute drive to the crime scene—at 499 Valle Alto. Sally sat in the front passenger seat, with Gunny and Fred in back. Nacho drove like he owned the streets, which in some ways he did. His uniform gave him a wide berth in Monterrey. The consular plates on the SUV also made other drivers give way. On the way, Sally read the folder faxed from Houston, containing four stapled documents. The first described the 2013 purchase by Isabel Santerra Reyes of her house on Valle Alto. It was solely owned—apparently she was unmarried and had no children. The second was a medical report confirming that Isabel's uterine cancer was first diagnosed in 2017. She underwent surgery, radiation, and chemotherapy before she was accepted into the Mexican version of hospice four months ago. The third was a copy of a power of attorney granted by Isabel to Julia

Santerra-Evans. It was in March of 2018. The fourth was a report by the mortician who prepared Isabel's body for removal from Monterrey, Mexico, into the United States a week before the bombing. It had been sent to Julia Santerra at her sister's address. The bill was paid by a joint account held by both sisters.

When they pulled into the driveway at 499 Valle Alto, they saw two other vehicles out front. One was a black Dodge Charger with the five-star logo of the *Policía Federal*. The other, a white Ford van with Monterrey *Policía* markings. Nacho got out and went to the *Federales* car while Sgt. Otou talked to two men leaning on the front fenders smoking. They learned two technical teams were still inside, gathering evidence. Nacho got permission to go through the front but got a warning not to go inside the garage. "Mucha sangre allí," the man in the white coveralls said. Gunny translated for Fred: "There's too much blood in there. I think they are not cleaning yet, pending lab sign-off. He said we could go into the rest of the house, just nada the garage. He said they would have pictures within the hour."

The white double door at the front was taped off but Nacho lifted it aside and motioned them in. The small foyer had a table with dried flowers, a statue of Jesus Christ, two pictures of small dogs, and a book stand. The living room was large, paved with tiles and featured a fireplace on one wall and a gallery of fretted architecture on the other. Moldings with inset portals held small carved stones and brass pieces of Spanish art. Curiously, there were also escutcheons and ciphers—Arabic characters in high relief. It was probably once well taken care of, but now there were long streaks of dust, dirt, and strewn paper, used dishes, and ash trays everywhere.

They discovered a master bedroom suite on the second floor, with a large bath and clothes closet. It had an expansive balcony facing the three-thousand-foot-high granite mountain shouldering the north side of the city. It was a spectacular view. The walls of the twenty-by-twenty carpeted bedroom displayed a dozen drawings and handwoven tapestries, but no photos or personal mementos. It would turn out this was Julia Santerra-Evans's room. Her sister, the owner of the house, used the downstairs bedroom, which was smaller but featured a handicap bath and an electric movable hospital bed. It had lots of photos of Isabel in various poses but no pictures of Julia. There was a third bedroom just behind the garage, filled with medical supplies and presumably occupied by a live-in nurse for some time. It had clothes and toiletries in the connecting bathroom that suggested a large woman who took good care of her skin and feet. The last room was a small office with built-in filing cabinets, a metal desk, and lots of technology. Everything here spoke of Julia, not her sister Isabel.

Nacho learned from the officers on site that the Monterrey police had canvassed all the houses in the gated community. Everyone seemed to know the owner of the house was sick—none had seen her for more than a year. All talked about a woman they assumed was Isabel's sister go in and out of the house often. She always identified herself as Isabel, even to neighbors who knew better. Isabel, they said, was a prim, very private woman who went to mass daily before she got sick. She never smoked or smelled of alcohol. And she never had men in the house. The other one, they thought her name was Julia, was loud, walked fast, never stopped to talk, and smoked small black cigaros. Large men, most with tattoos and smelling of stale beer, were always there, they said. They missed Isabel and hoped the other one—maybe she's a sister, they said—would be leaving soon now that Isabel, a saintly woman, had gone home to God. "Alabado sea el Señor," they told the *Policía*. "Praise the Lord," Sgt. Otou translated.

Working with local officers, it only took an hour and twenty minutes to fingerprint the upstairs bedroom and the small office. They only found one recent picture of both women. It was taken at a small circus tent and showed Julia, taller and expressionless, standing next to Isabel, shorter and smiling. It had a drugstore marking on the back. Sally Lin asked permission to take an iPhone shot. It arrived at the FBI office in Brownsville seconds later with a request to show the photo around town. Maybe the sisters had been seen together in Brownsville. The local officers did the same in different parts of Monterrey. Eventually they would decide that Julia had pretended to be Isabel for the last year. It didn't fool the neighbors, but others in the large city thought Julia *was* Isabel.

The border-crossing photos all identified Isabel as a Mexican citizen, with her Mexican passport crossing the border into the US, when in fact it was Julia sitting in the passenger seat. There were multiple crossings at McAllen, Juarez, and Brownsville. Border crossing records on the American side indicated Isabel had many crossings. But her close neighbors insisted she had not left the gated community for more than a year. Being an identical twin had many advantages for Julia. She disappeared by becoming her sister, on paper and visually, once she was out of the neighborhood.

There was no evidence inside the house that Lil Loco had ever been there. But they knew he had. The boot prints in the blood in the garage were a size thirteen. Sally expressed concern they might never find Lil Loco.

"No matter," Nacho said. "This man has many enemies. They will turn on him."

At 7:30 that night, Slate Blakely called and told the team he'd just received a call from the strange man who'd called two days ago and offered to help them find Lil Loco. The man told SAIC Blakey that "the motherfucker they call Lil Loco is actually named Admondo Rosales Torres. Go arrest his fat ass and give him a kick in the balls for me while you're at it. He's in a cheap hotel called Posada de Moro, probably fucking Julia Baby." He didn't know the name of the town, only the name of the hotel.

Nacho knew about the Posada de Moro. It was about two kilometers from the Monterrey National Park, in Montemorelos. Nacho called a man in the local police department there and they said they knew Lil Loco. He'd been drinking heavily and hit one of the maids with a wooden stool. They didn't want to confront him. Apparently they were concerned he had friends staying in other rooms at the hotel. The desk clerk had run from the building when one police car stopped in front of the Posada de Moro.

Sally ordered her team to gear up. Nacho called in an SUV-load of three additional fully armed *Federales*. Their two-vehicle convoy took just under an hour to drive the eighty-kilometer narrow road south to Montemorelos. The hotel was on the second floor of a gray concrete slab. The third floor consisted of dozens of seven-foot-tall, rusty wrought-iron rebar sticking up like a metal forest on top of the building. An OXO gas station, a small bar without a name, and a *pequeño café* called "Conchas" were on the ground floor. There were no lights from the ground floor, but three of the small windows on the second floor showed light through slats on two windows and an old sheet hanging on the inside of the third room. The street was dark, but several stray dogs combed the boarded door steps and alleys.

Nacho gave orders to the other *Federales* to set a perimeter around the gaudy building festooned with graffiti and some decent mural painting. The street was paved but had more potholes than paving. Stretching out of sight on either side of the street were identical poured concrete houses interspersed with adobe stuccoes. Most were one-story buildings; none were new. Many had gates and railings bounded with low brick walls. From a distance, Sally thought the street was a long vista of ramparted respectability. Hollow walls, vacant lots, and debris everywhere.

Nacho's persona changed from handsome cop to battlefield soldier. His jet-black hair was invisible beneath his helmet, with the headlight and body camera on top. His flop-down optical goggles projected through a red night vision field of view. He breathed quietly through his nose as he checked two weapons, one of which had been supplied by Gunnery Sgt. Otou. Everyone wore flak jackets with lapel mikes clipped to ammo vests. They all bent down and double tied boot laces. No one talked. Finally, Agent Widnor broke the silence of preparation.

"OK, Sally, are you in the lead position, or is Nacho? I mean, who's giving signals on this?"

Nacho answered. "I'm in charge now. This is Mexico. We're going upstairs, quietly if possible. When I see him, I'll give him a two-second warning. Then I'll kill him. All of you, *attention*, he's not gonna be up there alone! Don't hesitate to shoot anything that is aimed at us. We kill in seconds, or we die in seconds. This guy is *un bastardo asesino, que no?*"

Gunny translated, "Yeah he's a murdering bastard, but he has rights, even here in Mexico."

"He has the right to surrender when I tell him to. That's the two-second warning I told you about."

Nacho had a Star machine pistol with knurled knobs and levers. He'd explained it to Fred in one sentence. "You point, squeeze, and the target has huge holes in a flash. Hellava invention, don't you think?" He also had an M4 assault rifle strapped to his chest.

Fred and Sally, like most FBI agents, were well-trained in small arms and had crime-scene training and weapons qualifications testing annually. And like most agents, they had never fired their FBI issued Glock semi-automatics except on a firing range. As they sat in the car outside what would soon be a hostile arrest scene, they wondered whether the *Federales* saw them as national police officers from the US. It had not occurred to either of them to explain to Nacho that the FBI was a national security organization. It investigated crime but did not work out of patrol cars or carry guns into arrest scenes regularly.

Nacho spoke Spanish to the perimeter *Federales*. While the FBI agents didn't understand the words, they got the message. They were in place, outside, in front and back of the building. Nacho pointed at Sally, "You're right behind me." He pointed at Fred, "You watch her back." He pointed at Chance Otou, "Gunny, you're our backstop. Don't look where we look. Look behind you." Then, as if he was about to catch a moving train, he slow-jogged from the car on the side street to the corner and then catty-corner across the street to the single-door entrance to the stairs.

He pushed open the street-level door. It squeaked. Since it was a humid summer night, they caught a whiff of perfume and heard the buzz of insects. Nacho, with a flash bang in one hand and his machine pistol in the other, climbed the wooden stairs halfway up. Apparently hearing something, he signaled backward for the rest of the team to stop. He crouched in place. So did they. Nacho motioned them to stay low with a downward palm signal. Fred and Sally knelt down and leaned forward. Chance Otou backed away from the lower step and turned backward toward the dark street.

The door at the top of the stairs opened and the ceiling light flicked on. The sound of the flick disappeared into the roar of the shotgun as it sprayed pellets against both sides of the narrow stairway above them. The deafening roar, the sound of metal slashing, and the savaging of the wood panels on either side terrorized the three figures as they flattened themselves on the rough stairs. Total panic seemed a second away.

While the three in front hunched down as low as they could stomach, Gunnery Sargent Otou, now standing at his full six foot four inches on the outside of the street door, stuck his M1014 around the door frame and upward at the light at the top of the stairway. It was a Benelli M4 Super 90, in twelve-gauge. The Marine Corps had a long history of fielding shotguns during World War I and II to breach and clear trenches. The most current version, the M1014, was even more deafening than the upstairs shooter's first round. It gave Otou devastating firepower in a close-quarter battle. That's how he saw their position. The M1014 did its job. As ears rang both at the bottom and top of the stairway, the top went silent.

The upper half of the stairway walls had erupted as if by a volcano's frenzy. Wood disintegrated. The light fixture at the top danced in the smoke. The door hanging ajar from one hinge looked vaporized. As Sargent Otou dropped to one knee to reload, Nacho unleashed himself from the crouch like an offensive guard on a pro-football field. Scrambling upward taking the steps two at a time, he charged and slammed through the doorway, curling his body into a ball as he summersaulted into the second-floor hallway. His ears were barely recovering from the two shotgun blasts over his head, but he heard the faint sound of a running man, maybe two. He jack-knifed down in a bent-over crouch posture. As he moved forward, he sprayed the M4 assault rifle, on full-auto, from right to left. It was suppressive fire. This spray of high-impact bullets was a loudspeaker saying, "Drop your weapons or die." It almost worked.

A woman screamed in Spanish from the furthest door on his left; her words were indecipherable. Nacho said nothing.

The door closest to him on his left was ajar. It seemed as if smoke was coming out of the door into the hallway. Nacho unhitched a flash bang from his vest, crawled forward, and flipped it into the room with a hooked right arm. The bang thundered, but softer than the twelve-gauge shotgun blasts. The bright flash would temporality blind whoever was looking directly at it inside the room. Within seconds, a naked man flew out of the room. His eyes bugged out as he saw Nacho. Then, he stopped, and raised his arms high above his shriveled shoulder blades. His junk swung listlessly between his legs, and salvia dribbled out of both his nose and mouth. Since he was no more than five-feet-five, he was obviously not Lil Loco.

"Parar donde estás!" Nacho said calmly.

The man, looking more bewildered than dangerous, understood and stopped where he was.

In Spanish, Nacho asked if he was alone. The man said no, a girl was inside. Nacho asked if the other rooms were occupied. "Si," the man said. "All of them."

"Go back inside," Nacho instructed. The man turned and slowly walked back inside, almost tiptoeing his way; he left his door open. The rest of the team emerged from the stairway door and huddled beside Nacho in the semi-darkened hallway. They could see three closed doors. Whoever fired the first shotgun blast must be in one of the three. Nacho motioned Sargent Otou to slide around the FBI agents and take a knee beside him.

In a low growl, Nacho told Otou, "There's an alley behind us, on my right. Lil Loco will be in one of those two rooms on our right."

Otou whispered back, "How do you know he's not in that other one, on the street side?"

"*Soldados* on the run like rooms on the second floor with a back alley behind them. Drop a rope and they are gone. Let's check the first room on our right together. If he's not there. Then we'll double up on the other room—the one on the end. OK with you?"

"Roger that," Otou said reflexively.

Nacho told Sally and Fred to hold fast. Then he and Otou started frog-walking slowly down the hall. No one was in the first room on their left. No lights shined under the door of either room on the alley-side of the hallway. Nacho signaled to the nearest room. Otou took a knee on the far side of the door. Nacho laid flat on his left side away from the door frame. Slowly he used his right arm to slide up the frame to the door handle. Turning slowly, he realized the door was unlocked. Lil Loco's in there, he thought. Waiting to ambush us. Motioning Otou to stay down low and pumping his right hand toward the floor, Otou crouched on haunches out of sight from inside the room. Then, as he watched Nacho ease up, the rapid fire of a semi-automatic rifle sent .30 caliber pills through the door frame on his side, knocking him flat down onto the hallway. He took four shots in the upper half of his vest. The concussion almost knocked him out.

Nacho responded by using his M4 on full automatic. He held the trigger down and sent a thirty-round mag blast into the room swinging the barrel from left to right. Someone yelled from the other side of the door. Then Nacho kicked open what was left of the door and lobbed a hand grenade inside, hollering "Grenade down! Grenade down!" to his teammates in the hallway. Sally and Fred dove to the floor facing away from the last room. In three seconds the grenade went off. When the dust cleared, and nothing moved and there were no sounds in the room, Nacho shined his flashlight into the room. Lil Loco was plastered up against a sink, on the side wall. His face was recognizable, but the rest of him only vaguely resembled a human body. He had taken the full force of the grenade standing upright in the center of the room. Everything from his shin bone to his neck was destroyed. His bloody head looked like a watermelon sitting ajar on top of muddy laced-up combat boots.

Nacho whirled to check on Otou, who had sat up, massaging his upper chest.

"Semper Fi for flak jackets," he said with a grin and a wink. He would have chest pain for days, but he was alive.

Sally and Nacho moved to the end room. Fred stayed close to guard them and Otou from the rear side of the hallway. Sally slid along the wall and was almost to the room when they heard gun fire from the alley out back. Kicking open the unlocked door, she rushed in just ahead of Nacho, who was cursing her.

"I told you to stay back."

She said nothing as they cleared the room. Like the other room, this one had a sink but no toilet. Communal toilets were down the hall, they assumed. Bed sheets had been hastily tied to the bedstead, which was now up against the wall below the open window.

"One of 'em escaped!" he shouted at Sally. Spinning out the door, he ran toward the downstairs. Sally jumped on the bed and stuck her head out the window. She saw a *Federale* face down in the alley. The other two on perimeter duty were nowhere to be seen. She holstered her Glock, grabbed the bed sheet, slid down six feet, and dropped down another six to the alley below. She knelt beside the uniformed officer and felt for a pulse at the carotid on the right side of his neck. Nothing. Then she saw the blood pooling behind his head. Turning his head, the other way, she saw a small hole through his right ear. A twenty-two long barrel, she thought. An assassin's gun, she thought.

Just as Nacho appeared around the corner, someone opened fire at him from no more than ten feet from her, behind two old fifty-five-gallon drums. It was Julia. She was taking dead aim with a two-handed grip on her second shot.

"Julia!" Sally screamed as she wrenched her Glock out of its holster.

Julia didn't seem to understand there was another woman in the alley with her. She froze for an instant then panned the gun toward Sally. Too late. Sally had just lined her out. She emptied her nine-shot mag. Four of the shots hit Julia center-mass. The other five splintered past her. She was likely dead before her body hit the cement-strewn alley onto a garbage pile.

CHAPTER 46

Dr. Estancia had just closed the door to his Rice University faculty office when he heard his desk phone ring. He was on his way home and thought about ignoring the ring. It'd been a long day grading graduate papers. But he turned back, unlocked his door, and answered the phone.

"Dr. Estancia here, who's this?"

"Oh, Professor Estancia, it's good I got you. This is Toni, at the front desk downstairs. I just talked to a woman who said to give you a message. She didn't want to talk to you this late in the day, but she'd like a call back some time tomorrow. There's a time gap. She called from New Zealand."

"New Zealand, that's strange. Not sure I have any faculty contacts down there, or students."

"I don't think, Professor, that she's a student, or on faculty. She sounded tense. I think she's English, what with her accent and all. But she has an Italian name, Vinessa DiAmonte."

"Did she leave a number?"

"Yes, its 011, that's the US exit code, then 64, that's the New Zealand country code, then 9, then 481,1972. I looked it up for you. She's in Auckland, New Zealand. And I looked up the time gap too. It's seventeen hours' difference. And, of course, it's tomorrow down there."

"So, Toni, if I called her back now, quarter to six p.m. in Houston, it is a quarter to eleven a.m., in Auckland. Is my math correct?"

"Close enough, for a professor of medicine. Would you like me to place the call for you?"

"Splendid, thank you so much."

Ahmed listened as the call was placed and heard a voice with a brogue answer, "I'm returning a call from Ms. DiAmonte, my name is . . ."

"Yes, Professor Estancia, right? I placed the call to you just a bit ago. I think Ms. DiAmonte is still in her suite. Let me ring her up."

"Professor Estancia, so good of you to call back. I trust you've forgiven me for such a sudden departure from the clinic. I'm afraid I was about to lose time. Have you got a little time to talk now?"

"Yes, of course, Vinessa. I'm talking to Vinessa right?"

"Of course it's me. What I'm asking is could you recommend someone here in Auckland that I could see? I won't be coming back to America very soon and Texas was not good to me anyhow. I lost time there, you know that, right?"

"I suspected that, when you left the clinic. Perhaps we could talk about that. And I'll talk to one of my colleagues, here, who did a post-doc in Australia. He will know who might be available to see you down in New Zealand. Do you have a minute for a couple questions about our last meeting?"

"Maybe, but I don't think psychotherapy works over the phone, do you?"

"No, I don't. But my question is whether you lost time after you left my clinic office three weeks ago."

"I did. And thanks to you and some detailed reading I've been doing, I know why. Well, I probably don't *know* why, but I have a good guess. It was because of that terrible bombing thing in that border town, something brown, I forget. Anyhow I saw it on TV and it scared me. They said one victim was a lawyer. They said his name on TV, but I didn't know him. They said it was thought by the police that his client was also killed—a woman named Julia. That's when I lost time—the second I heard the name Julia."

"Was the name familiar to you? Is that why you lost time?"

"Not familiar. No, I wouldn't say that. But the name made me ill because I thought it was her."

"Her?"

"Yes, her. You know, one of the other women that help me when I lose time. There are several. You know that because you upset me when you asked about them. I could see it on your face, doctor. But now, I'm enjoying the day. I had a lovely flight to the South Pacific and some time on a yacht sailing from Papeete to Auckland. We had glorious weather. But let's not go into that, doctor. I never knew anyone named Julia, but I think maybe someone else did, when I was losing time. Do you have someone you can suggest I talk to down here near the bottom of the earth?"

It took a day but Dr. Estancia got the name of a psychiatrist with some experience in treating dissociative identity patients. He sent a full CV to his former patient in care of the Swiss-Belsuites Victoria Park Hotel. Then he called Travis Danders.

After two games of telephone tag, they made contact.

"Dr. Estancia, sorry about our calling one another at odd times. But I'm anxious to hear whether you've heard from your former patient."

"Ah, Mr. Danders, we're both too busy I think. But yes, I did hear from my client. I think you'll be happy to know she's well and is several thousand miles from here, down at the bottom of the planet. That means your client is not here in Texas and is not at risk from our robust prosecutors in Houston."

"Good to hear that, doctor. I gotta run, but let's keep in touch."

They never did.

EPILOGUE

It took three weeks for the US attorneys and the state of Texas prosecutors to submit their reports and file court motions dismissing all pending cases related to Julia's original crimes. No new charges were filed out of the Brownsville bombing. Travis Danders returned to a law practice that now seemed dull. He and Nancy Lee went on one last date. The Mexican authorities took possession of the bodies of Lil Loco and Julia. No one claimed their remains at the medical examiner's office in Monterrey. The body of the dead *Federale* was claimed by his large family; they buried him with full military-style honors in his hometown. Five weeks after the bombing, the ATF report was sent to FBI HQ. But since there was no case to prosecute given Julia's death, no one bothered to read the report.

No one knew where Vince, Vivian, or Vinessa were. Dr. Ahmed Estancia got a handwritten note, postmarked Auckland, New Zealand, three months after the dismissal of all cases and after the lives of Amherst Pipps and Dish Joandiz had been memorialized by their families.

The handwritten note read:

Dear Dr. Estancia,

We heard the news from Houston about Julia Baby. We know calling her that must sound unkind, given her violent death. But if there ever was a person who deserved a violent death, it was her. I'm using the royal "we" in this note. You'll understand why. We could not find a psychiatrist in either New Zealand or Australia who knew much about multiplicity, but it is of no consequence. A young counselor, who trained in the UK, has a master's degree. He knows us, and our issues. In fact, he's one

of us. We will always think of you kindly.
Our business is flourishing. Did we mention
to you it is called Emergence, Inc.? We're
happy to report that it finds favor in Europe,
the UK, and in Australia. We help
others in the multiplicity community deal with
financial issues, identity issues, and ways to
make up for lost time.

Warmest best wishes,

V's

The End

www.ingramcontent.com/pod-product-compliance
Lightning Source LLC
Chambersburg PA
CBHW021401110726
47901CB00008B/2012